Kalki's
PONNIYIN SELVAN

Dr M. Rajaram is an exceptional IAS Officer with balanced views on administration. His efficiency in administration has brought him many prestigious awards, notably the Best Collector Award, Malcolm Award, Anna Award, etc., from the government. He has authored more than 40 books: *Quality Educational Administration: Who Will Bell the Cat?*, *Thirukkural: Pearls of Inspiration*, *The Elemental Warriors*, *Food for Thought*, *Passport for Success*, *Blossoms in English*, *The Yellow Line*, *Glory of Thirukkural*, *Higher Education for Better Tomorrow*, *Better English*, *Glory of Tamil*, *The Success Mantra in Bhagavad Gita*, *Tic-Toc-Tic*, *Bosses: The Good, the Bad and the Ugly*, *Corporate Wisdom in Thirukkural*, *Oriental Wisdom*, etc. His English translation of *Thirukkural* earned him a well-deserved tribute from Dr Abdul Kalam, the late President of India. His book is so popular that it has been added to the White House Library.

Praise for the book

'*Ponniyin Selvan*, a popular Tamil novel unfolds an epic story based on historical facts and characters with lot of twists and turns keeping the readers spellbound reflecting the glory of Indian literature.'

—**Sri M. Venkaiah Naidu**
Hon'ble Vice President of India

'*Ponniyin Selvan* is an outstanding historical Tamil novel rendered in simple and elegant style by Dr M. Rajaram.'

—**Ki Rajanarayanan**
Sahitya Akademi Award Winning Tamil Writer

'*Ponniyin Selvan* is a story of plots within plots highlighting the greatness of the Chola Empire rendered in elegant style without losing its original flavour.'

—**Dr Avvai Natarajan**
Former Vice Chancellor, Tamil University, Tanjore

Kalki's
PONNIYIN SELVAN
Volume 2

Translated by M. Rajaram

Published by
Rupa Publications India Pvt. Ltd. 2022
7/16, Ansari Road, Daryaganj
New Delhi 110002

Sales centres:
Allahabad Bengaluru Chennai
Hyderabad Jaipur Kathmandu
Kolkata Mumbai

Translation and Abridgment Copyright © M. Rajaram 2022
Cover Illustration Copyright © Maniam Selven

All rights reserved.
No part of this publication may be reproduced, transmitted,
or stored in a retrieval system, in any form or by any means,
electronic, mechanical, photocopying, recording or otherwise,
without the prior permission of the publisher.

This is a work of fiction. Names, characters, places and incidents are either the product of the author's imagination or are used fictitiously and any resemblance to any actual person, living or dead, events or locales is entirely coincidental.

ISBN: 978-93-91256-16-6

Tenth impression 2022

15 14 13 12 11 10

The moral right of the author has been asserted.

Printed in India

This book is sold subject to the condition that it shall not,
by way of trade or otherwise, be lent, resold, hired out, or otherwise
circulated, without the publisher's prior consent, in any form of
binding or cover other than that in which it is published.

Contents

1. Distressed Soul — 1
2. Dutiful Captain — 6
3. True Friendship — 8
4. Raging Storm — 11
5. Whirlwind — 16
6. Smashed Boat — 20
7. At Kodikkarai — 23
8. Net of Passion — 26
9. Call of a Hooting Owl — 30
10. Delirious Fever — 33
11. The Greedy Woman — 36
12. Poonkulali's Anxious Moments — 39
13. Divine Nymph — 41
14. Ghost! Ghost! — 46
15. Commotion Near the Monastery — 49
16. The Blacksmith — 53
17. Royal Sword — 59
18. A Flying Horse — 63
19. Vandiyathevan's Tricks — 66
20. Puppet Prince Madurandakan — 68
21. Soothsayer — 71
22. Timely Help — 75
23. Mother and Son — 78

24. Angry Mob	82
25. An Angel with Joy and Grief	83
26. Nandini, My Stepsister	85
27. The Prime Minister Arrives	87
28. Prime Minister's Appeal	89
29. Spying on the Spy	93
30. Change in Vanathi's Attitude	96
31. Two Prisons	98
32. Mother Nature	102
33. Kidnapping of Vanathi	104
34. Opportune Time	110
35. Cunning Foxes	113
36. Canvassing for Madurandakan	117
37. Vanathi's Shock	120
38. Madurandakan's Gratitude	125
39. Where Am I?	129
40. Let Us Save Our Country	133
41. Love Has No Reason	138
42. Aditya Karikalan at Kedilam River	141
43. The Falcon and the Dove	146
44. The Ayyanar Temple	149
45. Hunters' Hall	151
46. Princess Manimekalai	153
47. A Tailless Monkey	155
48. Horror in the Hunters' Hall	157
49. A Ferocious Dog	160
50. Manhunt	165
51. A Friend or Foe?	168

52.	The Broken Spear	170
53.	Her Heart's Secret	174
54.	Manimekalai's Dream	177
55.	Royal Reception	180
56.	Poonkulali's Desire	185
57.	The Arrow	187
58.	Raakammal the Crook	191
59.	Golden Opportunity	196
60.	Disappointed Prime Minister	199
61.	Flood Relief	205
62.	The Prime Minister's Blunder	208
63.	Mute Queen Disappeared	213
64.	Mute Queen's Hot Pursuit	215
65.	Secret Underground Chamber	217
66.	Touching Moments	221
67.	Grievances Against the Prime Minister	223
68.	Emperor in Dream World	227
69.	Why Torment Me?	230
70.	Ravana in Danger	234
71.	The Emperor's Anger	238
72.	Mysterious Night	242
73.	Karikalan's Peace Formula	244
74.	Nandini's Anger	248
75.	Water Sports	252
76.	She Is Not a Woman	256

I

Distressed Soul

'I won't mistake it, Poonkulali. There is no reason for you to trick me. Where were the ships when you saw them?'

'There, at that turning. I vividly remember.'

'Perhaps they have moved a little away. Let us go down and find out.'

'Good, if those ships have gone away…' said Poonkulali cheerfully.

'You may think so, but I will be very disappointed.'

Soon they found a ship deeply buried in the mud. But there was no one around. Poonkulali recognized it as one of the ships which she had seen two days earlier.

Prince Arulmoli and Poonkulali reached Tondai river and saw the ship broken and strewn about here and there. They looked around to see whether anyone was nearby. The prince clapped his hands and Poonkulali cupped her hands and called out but there was no response from anywhere. They climbed onto the sides of the ship, the bottom planks of the ship had split; sand and water had run into the hull. Prince Arulmoli was anguished to see the mutilated tiger-flag lying amidst the ruined deck.

'Poonkulali, is this one of the ships you had seen?'

'Yes, the other ship must have completely sunk to the bottom!'

'Chola soldiers have been known for their sailing skills for several generations. I cannot believe that they could have made a mistake to accidentally sail this ship into the sandbank. The men onboard must have somehow escaped from here. Come, let us look for them.'

'Where can we look for them, Prince? The sun is setting and it's soon going to be dark all around.'

'Poonkulali, that's alright. Let us walk further to find the soldiers. Perhaps, they might have anchored the other ship behind the trees hidden from the sea.'

But there was no sign of any ship or boat except a few sea birds. They returned to the place where they had started.

Suddenly they saw a spire of smoke rising up behind the deck of the wrecked ship. The sweet smell of yam cooking floated in the air.

A woman was cooking food; she was not surprised to see them. She welcomed them silently and soon served them delicious food, tastier than the food served at royal banquets. After eating, all three climbed up to the deck in the bright moonlight.

'I wonder how she got here so quickly!'

'Nothing surprises me about my aunt. She is capable of more astonishing deeds. There is no limit to the love she has for you. The power of love can do anything,' said Poonkulali.

Her aunt understood what they were speaking about and turned Poonkulali's face around and pointed to the far bank. Their elephant was tied to a tree over there and by its side stood a beautiful, well-bred stallion. It appeared to be one of the best of the exquisite breeds of Arab horses. How did it come here? How did this woman get it?

Arulmoli and Poonkulali were immensely surprised.

'I didn't know that your aunt could ride a horse!'

'There is nothing that my aunt does not know. She can ride not only a horse but an elephant too. She also knows how to row. She could glide over the winds and swiftly reach any place.'

Poonkulali was talking in sign language to her aunt, the mute queen. She replied that she found the horse ashore near Elephant Crossing. She tamed it till it calmed down and later brought it here.

Arulmoli was all the more surprised by this. Poonkulali was drowsy and went to sleep.

Prince Arulmoli felt sad about the mute queen. How many wishes and emotions—joy and sorrow, anger and frustration must be in her mind.

As though she read his mind, the mute queen came near Arulmoli, brushed his curly hair and fondly caressed his cheeks. Arulmoli bowed and touched her feet. She took his hands and held them to her face. Soon, his palms were wet with the tears from her eyes. She signed that he too should sleep. He was not sleepy. He lay down and closed his eyes to satisfy her. After some time, a cool breeze lulled him to sleep.

Day was breaking and Poonkulali woke up to the sound of hoofbeats; the mute queen was riding away like the wind.

Arulmoli awoke to see the blooming face of Poonkulali.

'Where is Elder Mother?'

Poonkulali told him how she had ridden away early in the morning.

'Ocean Princess, you may leave now. I will wait here till my men arrive. Meanwhile, I will examine this wrecked ship more carefully.'

Suddenly they saw a large sailing ship and a rowboat with five men in the sea.

Commander Bhoothi Vikrama and Alvarkkadiyan arrived along with two soldiers and a boatman. The prince was concerned about Vandiyathevan who seemed to be missing. That messenger sent by his beloved sister Kundavai had become his close friend in just a few days. His character and nature enchanted the prince.

The commander posed a series of questions.

'Prince, when did you come here? Did you meet those ships sent by the Paluvettarayars? Where are they now?'

'Commander, I will tell you our story later. Where is Vandiyathevan? Tell me!' demanded Prince Arulmoli.

'Oh. That imprudent youth is on that ship which is sailing away.' The commander was pointing at a ship near the horizon.

'Whose ship is that? Why is Vandiyathevan going away in that?'

'Sir, I am totally confused now. Ask this Nambi who knows and understands your affairs and the affairs of that young man.'

Prince Arulmoli turned towards Alvarkkadiyan.

'Nambi why is Vandiyathevan going on that ship?'

Chaos had prevailed after Poonkulali and Prince Arulmoli had left on the speeding elephant.

The commander was worried about the safety of the prince. 'Now we have to save the prince? Tell me how to go about it.'

Alvarkkadiyan responded.

'The elephant has not really gone mad, the prince suspected that you are deliberately delaying his journey. Therefore, he incited the elephant to escape from us. Our prince is an expert in handling elephants.'

The commander realised the truth behind his statement.

'Let us go to river Thondai and find out what is happening over there.'

Soon they reached Elephant Crossing and using a small rowboat reached the mouth of the river Thondai at dusk. Beyond that, the coast was rough. They had to wait till daybreak.

Meanwhile, Vandiyathevan had picked an argument with Alvarkkadiyan, blaming him for losing the prince.

'No, my dear man. I won't hinder your efforts. I will leave in the morning and go my own way,' finally said Alvarkkadiyan.

'Nambi, the prince has been delivered to the enemy. So, your task is over and you are leaving!' exclaimed Vandiyathevan. After that they went to sleep.

At daybreak, they were shocked to see a ship ready to leave the shore followed by a boat carrying three men. Probably the ship had been hiding behind the tall trees on the channel last night.

Whose ship, was it? Where was it going now? Why was the boat hurrying towards it? Who are the men in the boat? All these questions flashed in Alvarkkadiyan's mind.

Commander Bhoothi Vikrama, Vandiyathevan and the others noticed the sailing ship first. 'Perhaps that is a Chola ship sent by the Paluvettarayars! I wonder if the prince is there on that ship? Let us try to catch the ship!'

It was the boat that they had come by the previous night that was going towards the ship. They called the boatman, and the boat stopped and Vandiyathevan climbed into the boat.

Among the three men in the boat, one was an Arab, the other two were Tamils who had hidden their faces with their turbans.

One of them was Ravidasa the sorcerer. The other one was Thevaralan who performed the folk dance at Kadamboor. They were the conspirators who had come to kill Prince Arulmoli.

The boat was fast approaching the ship. The men remained silent.

On reaching the ship, they all jumped on to the deck. Vandiyathevan looked around quickly, shouting, 'Where is the prince?'

Several Arabs surrounded him like demons.

Vandiyathevan realized his folly of having boarded the wrong ship and he decided to escape. When he was about to jump down, an iron fist grabbed his throat and Vandiythevan fell back onto the deck.

Vandiyathevan put up a stiff fight, punching the face of the man who had beaten him. Soon all the Arab men surrounded him and bound his hands with a rope and threw him on a stack of logs in the lower deck.

Ravidasa came before him and removed his headband, 'Dear boy! I came in search of that Chola tiger. But I have found the Vaanar cub!' laughed the sorcerer.

By then the boatman had returned to the shore. The commander and his men boarded the rowboat. Knowing that they could not catch up with the sailing ship, they started their search for the other ship to find the prince.

Alvarkkadiyan narrated all this to the prince.

A while later, they were surprised to see an old woman riding towards them on a great stallion without using any saddle, stirrups or reins.

2

Dutiful Captain

Recognizing the woman on the stallion, Prince Arulmoli and Poonkulali hurried towards her. The mute queen had seen something in the jungle and took them to an inland lagoon in the midst of the jungle. They were shocked to see dried blood and piles of dead bodies scattered all around. This kind of carnage was no new to any of these warriors who had seen many battlefields; yet it shook them.

'Quick, quick! See if anyone is still alive!' ordered the prince. They examined all the dead bodies to find they were all sailors from Chola lands. The mute queen took the prince further away to show a man on the verge of dying, badly wounded and bleeding. On seeing the prince his lips uttered a few words.

'But for this woman, I wouldn't be alive. I suffer now on account of having commited a sin against you.'

Prince Arulmoli recognised him as a captain of the Chola Naval Force, 'Captain! What sin? I don't understand!'

'I came here on the orders of the Paluvettarayars to arrest you.'

'You just obeyed the orders of the emperor. Knowing that, I came hurrying to meet you. But, how did this misfortune occur?'

The captain narrated the incidents holding his fading breath.

'On receiving the orders from the emperor, I left with two ships from Nagapattinam port with much reluctance and sadness. When I was leaving, the Paluvettarayars gave me certain strict instructions. On reaching the shores of Lanka, I had to anchor the ships in an isolated place and proceed after ascertaining your whereabouts. Later, I had to personally meet you and give the emperor's orders without the knowledge of Commander Bhoothi. After the orders were delivered, I was ordered to arrest you by force if you resisted. The Paluvettarayars had also sent some of their confidential retainers to accompany me.

My men were not aware of the mission. I anchored the ships near the mouth of river Thondai and left with a small company of sailors to find you.

On knowing the truth all the sailors began questioning me. "We cannot be a party to arrest our beloved Prince Ponniyin Selvan." My efforts to convince them failed.

"We want to join the prince's army," they said.

Only ten men, including the four from Paluvoor were ready to stand by my side to carry out my duty.

The others left the ship without anchoring it. The ship moved away with the incoming tide and hit the sandbar in the night. Suddenly several men with horrifying statures attacked us with thundering cries. We fought a valiant battle; yet we lost all our men. I escaped into the forest with these death wounds. I am happy to meet my beloved prince and narrate this disgraceful tale. God has punished me for my treacherous deeds. My most beloved Prince Ponniyin Selva! Please forgive me!' said the captain of Chola ships.

'My most dutiful Captain! Why should I forgive you? After all you have done your duty.' The prince comforted the dying man. Tears flowing from the captain's eyes mixed with the drying blood on his face. With much effort he greeted the prince with folded hands. Tears trickled down the prince's face. Soon the dutiful captain's soul left his body.

3

True Friendship

They laid the bodies of the dutiful captain and his men on a pile of wood from the jungle and lit it. Seeing the tears of the prince, Commander Bhoothi Vikrama asked, 'Prince! Why shed tears for these traitors?'

'Commander, they are not traitors. They have done their duty. Can there be a greater disaster to the Chola Kingdom than the sailors refusing to obey their captain? There is a small crack now. I wonder what other bigger cracks will undermine this Chola Empire. The very foundation of this great empire will be shaken by such cracks. I should not be a party for such catastrophe.'

'Beloved Prince, nothing like that will happen as long as you are there...'

'Stop it! I am tired of hearing such words. Anyway, the time has come for us to part. I have a request to ask of you. If those defiant sailors and soldiers come to you asking to join your command, don't take them back. Arrest them all and dispatch them to Tanjore.'

'Prince, we shall make proper enquiries and then decide...'

'You do what is appropriate. I cannot be here any longer. I must take leave immediately. Where is that boatman?'

'Where do you want to go, beloved Prince? Why do you want that boatman?'

'I have to save Vandiyathevan who has boarded that ship under the control of Arab pirates. How can I forsake my dear friend?'

'Vandiyathevan is a hasty and imprudent youth. How can you be responsible for the dangers he invites on himself?'

'Commander, Vandiyathevan is rendering all possible help to me. Even our renowned sage Thiruvalluvar says,
"A timely help tho' tiny in worth
Is greater than the earth"
I have to leave now and find that ship.'

'How will you go?'

'I'll go by that boat you came in...'

'How can you hunt a lion with a rabbit? This tiny boat won't be useful to find that fast-moving sailing ship.'

'That boat is enough for me. If I am unable to save my friend, I will give up my own life. Where is that boatman?'

The prince hurried towards the boatman standing near Poonkulali and the mute queen.

He noticed Poonkulali arguing with the boatman. 'Oh dear! What is this?' asked Prince Arulmoli.

The boatman fell at the prince's feet, 'My Lord, I was greedy and committed this sin unknowingly! Please forgive me!' he said.

'Prince, this fellow is my brother Murugaiyyan! He brought those two sinners, the assassins from Kodikkarai, to Lanka in his boat for the lure of gold coins. This morning he took them in his boat to that Arab ship sailing with your friend Vandiyathevan.'

'My Prince! Please chop off my head with your sword. I never knew that those men were traitors,' wailed the boatman prostrating before the prince.

'Dear man! At this moment your life is priceless to me! Take me immediately to that ship to atone for your misdeeds.'

The boatman took his boat into the water.

'There, the ship is there. We can catch up,' said the prince examining the horizon.

'Prince, a ripe fruit had fallen into the milk!' Commander Bhoothi Vikrama said with joy. 'That ship which we see is not the ship that carries Vandiyathevan. It is the ship of Parthiban Pallava. It is coming towards us,' said the commander.

'Maybe... I am not going to wait till that ship comes here. I will use this boat and reach it. None of you need to come with me.'

The prince approached the mute queen and was about to touch her feet. She stopped him and kissed his forehead in blessing. Then the prince jumped into the boat.

All on the shore were watching the boat go away with the prince. He too was gazing at them, focussing on the tear-laden face of Poonkulali.

What a surprising phenomenon! The figures of the people on the shore was becoming smaller and smaller. But, Poonkulali's face alone was growing bigger and bigger and came closer and closer to the prince. Soon a scene from the previous night's dream flashed in his mind: his sister, Kundavai called out to him, 'Brother! Don't forget Vanathi who is waiting here for you!'

4

Raging Storm

Parthiban was filled with joy to see Prince Arulmoli on the rowboat approaching his ship. He was perplexed though, wondering why he was coming alone in a small boat.

What happened to the ships sent by the Paluvettarayars? Perhaps he is not aware that this is my ship.

After the prince boarded the ship, all his doubts were cleared. The prince updated Parthiban on all the new developments.

'Vandiyathevan is on board a ship seized by Arab pirates. We have to free him immediately.'

'We can catch up with that ship and free Vandiyathevan,' said Parthiban

'If the wind blows steadily like this, we can catch that ship before nightfall,' declared the experienced captain.

Suddenly the winds died down and the sea was very calm. The sun was blazing down and the sea water was too hot to touch; the ship slowed down.

'The ship is standing still. When will the wind rise again? How long will this last? Won't that ship move away from us?' asked the prince with deep concern.

The sea captain said, 'The wind cannot be still like this for much longer. A whirlwind is rising up somewhere nearby. The sea is going to rise up boiling and mountain-sized waves will rock this ship. We will fly sky high and fall down in stormy waves. Only god can save us if that happens.'

'Is it still possible for us to find that ship?' enquired a concerned prince.

'At present that vessel too would be standing still without winds, what if it has reached some shore?' asked the prince.

'The men in it could escape,' declared the sea captain.

The face of gallant Vandiyathevan flashed in the mind of the prince repeatedly. Where could he be now? What must he be doing?

Meanwhile, Vandiyathevan was struggling for his life in the Arab ship.

He was chained to a log in the lower deck of the ship. He had been thrown amidst logs and bales of provisions. For a long time, he was in a daze; his hasty decision was tormenting him,

What ship is this? Where is this ship going? How did these rough Arabs, sorcerer Ravidasa and Thevaralan get into this ship? What will they do with me? I must not lose hope as long as my mind is alert.

He started to look around and spotted several weapons piled in one corner of the deck.

As time passed, it became very hot and humid; the ship had stopped moving. He was very thirsty now and his tongue stuck to the roof of his mouth. He noticed a mound of coconuts in a corner; this could relieve his thirst and hunger! He loosened the knots around his wrists and tried reaching out to a knife...

Just at that moment Ravidasa and Thevaralan entered.

'How is the sailing trip my friend? Is it enjoyable?' asked Ravidasa.

'Thirst is killing me; give me some water?' spoke Vandiyathevan with difficulty.

'Ah! We are also thirsty. No water here.'

'Aren't you a sorcerer?'

'Yes! My spells have made this ship stand still. By night, a whirlwind will rise up with a swirling storm and thundering rain. You can also quench your thirst in the rain if you do as we say.'

'What?'

'Those Arab pirates have captured this Chola ship and killed the soldiers. We bought horses from them earlier in Lanka and followed the prince. They want to take this ship to Kalinga. Help us kill them

and take this ship to Kodikkarai or Nagapattinam,' said Ravidasa.
Vandiyathevan didn't reply.

'We will loosen your knots if you agree.'

'I cannot kill sleeping men.'

'Fool! These pirates killed Chola men when they were sleeping.'

'Just because others do atrocious deeds, why should I...?'

'Fine, do as you wish.' Ravidasa left with his companion without closing the door. Immediately, Vandiyathevan freed himself using the knife. He jumped up and picked up a coconut from the corner, broke it open and quenched his thirst. He was ready to step out any minute.

Thud. Thud. He heard the noise twice. Two bodies were thrown into the sea. A big shout and the sound of clashing swords came from the upper deck.

Vandiyathevan ran up with his sword. Four Arabs were attacking Ravidasa and Thevaralan. They were in a perilous position. Vandiyathevan jumped forward with a roar.

He attacked the Arabs and threw them into the sea. Ravidasa and Thevaralan were saved.

The three victors sat down to catch their breath on the deck.

'Young man, you came at the right moment. How did you free yourself?'

'The rope loosened by itself and this sword appeared in my hands by your spell!'

'What about your thirst?'

'A coconut appeared before me and it broke by itself, pouring sweet water into my mouth.'

'You are a clever fellow!' they laughed.

'Brother, do you want to stay alive? Do you like wealth and comfort? Rank and power? Join us, all that will be yours!' roared Ravidasa.

Ravidasa spoke to Thevaralan, 'He must either join our group or let us sacrifice him to the ocean.'

'Fine. Tell him everything,' agreed Thevaralan.

'We are the bodyguards of King Veerapandiya of Madurai. We have sworn blood oaths to guard his life with our own...' began Ravidasa.

'You didn't succeed in that! Prince Aditya Karikalan won!' said Vandiyathevan.

'How did he win? Because of the folly of that woman Nandini! She had promised to guard our wounded king, but could not keep up her promise. We were about to burn her; she swore an oath with us seeking blood revenge. But for her help, we could not have progressed much. Our beloved king's head rolled down in the dust. They took it to Tanjore in a procession in an open palanquin. Wait and see what will happen to that city,'

Ravidasa's eyes reddened, spitting fire.

'What is done, is done! What can be done about it now? You cannot bring Veerapandiya back to life,' said Vandiyathevan.

'True, but we will avenge the killers of the Pandiyas. Will you join us?'

'After destroying the Chola clan, what would you do?'

'We will crown whoever is selected by our great queen.'

'Who is your great queen?'

'Paluvoor's young queen.'

'Then, what about Prince Madurandakan?'

'He too is a Chola snake.'

'What about Paluvettarayar?'

'We will make use of the power and wealth of that old fool.'

'That's why your queen dwells in his house!'

'Correct!'

'You know our secret now, join us, luck will smile upon you. You may ascend the great throne of Madurai,' said Ravidasa.

'I have accepted allegiance to serve the Cholas. I can never join you.'

'Are you one of the sworn bodyguards of the Cholas, the Velakkaras?'

'Nothing like that.'

'Then why hesitate? You are a soldier of fortune. You are better off joining the forces that have more opportunities.'

'I cannot join you conspirators.'

'Then be ready to sacrifice your life to the Ocean King,' said Ravidasa.

5

Whirlwind

In a flash, Vandiyathevan picked up the broad sword and said, 'No brother! The Ocean King wants a sacrifice of a sorcerer and a dancer. Both of you bend your heads.'

Ravidasa was taken aback and said, 'Sure, but give us some time to finish our prayers.'

'Come quickly, don't try any of your tricks,' replied Vandiyathevan allowing them to move to the other side of the ship.

Suddenly the ship began dancing amidst the splashing of the waves. Vandiyathevan heard something falling into the sea and walked towards the mast poles. Ravidasa and Thevaralan were rowing away in the rescue boat!

He was alone in that large wooden ship amidst strong waves. He knew nothing about sailing or ship navigation.

The logs and boards on the deck started to roll and crash in the sudden whirlwind.

Suddenly, pebble-sized hailstones started showering over him followed by a heavy downpour with loud thunder and blinding lightning.

The wind and the rain grew louder and stronger. Sails and masts howled like ghouls and danced with the ship. Darkness grew even darker. A sudden streak of lightning flashed from one end of the sea to the other instantly followed by rolling thunder. Lightning and thunder danced quicker and quicker.

The whole deck was drenched by the downpour of rain. In the lightning, the mast caught fire and the ship was in flames.

Vandiyathevan began roaring with laughter keeping in tune with the thunder reverberating all around him. The ship was surely going to sink and he couldn't possibly escape. He wanted to experience all the nuances of this cosmic phenomenon. He bound himself tightly to the main mast of the ship and watched.

The sky completely broke open drowning everything in a deluge. Waves danced in violent rage. Lightning flashed like swaying mountains. How long could the ship bear this attack from all the five elements of the universe?

Wind and water were not so powerful to destroy that mighty Chola ship. He was astounded by the mastery of Chola carpenters and shipbuilders. Even in such a ferocious whirlwind nothing happened to the ship. The wind could not tear it down. Water could not drown it. Finally, the god of fire—Agni—succeeded. Vandiyathevan remained bold to embrace a glorious death. His only regret was that the job assigned by Princess Kundavai was only half done.

The ship rose high upon the crest of massive waves. The light from the burning mast revealed everything all around.

He was delighted to see another ship at a distance with the tiger-flag. No limit to the marvels of nature! His conscience told him that Prince Arulmoli would be on that ship looking for him.

Parthiban's ship was also caught in the same whirlwind. Fortunately, it had more experienced navigators.

The captain of Parthiban's ship said, 'Darkness in the mid sea is more dangerous than the raging storm. I have seen whirlwinds and monsoon storms worse than this. I have sailed my ship through worse waters than this. No need to worry.'

However, he was concerned about the dark clouds gathering all around as it meant that they would not be able to spot Vandiyathevan's ship even if it passed by their side. That ship would also be turning and tossing just like this one. If both ships were to collide accidentally in the dark, it would be a disaster. Unmindful of all these concerns, Prince Arulmoli's bright eyes were searching for his dearest sister's messenger who was in the grip of those Arabs.

In a brilliant flash of lightning, he saw another ship, its mast on fire, dancing in a ghostly frenzy.

In the light of the fire the prince saw Vandiyathevan. Could anything be more miraculous? Prince Arulmoli made up his mind in an instant and ran up to the rescue boat in the ship asking, 'Who volunteers to come with me?'

'Prince! What is this? How can we save anyone from that burning ship? Please do not go. I will send some men and try,' protested Parthiban.

'Nobody should obstruct me; two men will suffice!' ordered the prince in a royal voice.

The rescue boat was lowered. Prince Arulmoli and two others selected by him jumped into it. Slowly, the boat went near the burning ship dancing madly over the ferocious waves. By now, the fire had spread to adjacent poles.

Vandiyathevan saw the other ship and also the boat coming towards him. Soon the fire would engulf the whole ship. It would be impossible to save him after that.

The prince called out to Vandiyathevan. 'Jump into the sea!' But Vandiyathevan could not hear him.

The prince quickly picked up the rope from the rescue boat and tied one end firmly to his waist, the other to a hook in the boat. He jumped into the sea cautioning the two seamen not to follow him. The waves lifted him to the sky for a moment and tossed him down the next. Without losing sense of direction, he swam against the strong waves and towards the burning ship. A huge swell tossed him onto the deck of the burning ship.

Vandiyathevan ran forward with a cry to help the man tossed onto the deck. Arulmoli immediately threw his arms around him and shouted, 'Hold me tight! Don't let go.'

The next moment, Arulmoli and Vandiyathevan jumped into the water. Arulmoli tried to swim to the rowboat carrying Vandiyathevan on his shoulders. One moment they were within reach, next minute it moved far away. After what seemed like an endless struggle, another great wave helped them into the boat.

'Pull on the oars! Quick! Hurry up!' roared Arulmoli as the burning ship was about to collapse into the sea. The mighty sinking ship could easily topple the small boat. If the ship sank and the fire were to go out, they may not be able to find the other ship in the darkness.

The burning ship started sinking. The tiny boat somehow moved away staying afloat. Now the prince lost all sense of direction.

They stopped pulling at the oars as they had no idea of the direction that they were supposed to go in. The wind died; the rain stopped; the lightning and thunder also stopped. But, the rage of the waves continued. Another unexpected danger awaited them.

One of the ship's huge masts that was not completely burnt came floating closer and closer to the rescue boat. Nobody in the boat noticed it till it came very close, because of the darkness. Before the boat moved away, the huge log hit the bottom of the boat. The tiny boat split into pieces.

'My friend, don't be afraid. That mast pole is safer than this tiny boat. Grab it,' Prince Arulmoli advised his friend Vandiyathevan.

6

Smashed Boat

Those waiting on the shores were curiously watched Prince Arulmoli till he reached Parthiban's ship. The boat that had carried the prince to Parthiban's ship returned to the shore.

'God is on our side. Parthiban will safely carry our prince to Kanchi. Let us move to Tanjore,' said Commander Bhoothi Vikrama Kesari.

Looking at Alvarkkadiyan he asked, 'What are your plans? Are you coming with us to Mathotam?'

'No, Sir. There is another task assigned by the prime minister.'

'What is that?'

Alvarkkadiyan looked towards Poonkulali and the mute queen standing nearby.

'Is it something to do with these women?'

'Yes. The prime minister has asked me to bring that mute woman to Tanjore.'

'Who is she? She has a lot of affection for our prince.'

'This boatgirl seems to be attached to the mute lady. I must warn her about something. Ask her to come here.'

Alvarkkadiyan brought Poonkulali to the commander.

'You are an intelligent girl. You have been of great help to us. I will never forget it. I will reward you appropriately at the right time,' said the commander.

'Thank you, My Lord! No need for any reward,' replied Poonkulali courteously.

'After all this confusion is over. I will find a suitable groom from the Chola army for you.'

Poonkulali was enraged. However, she restrained herself. She calmed herself.

What is the point of quarrelling with this foolish old man?

'Don't imagine that you can take liberties with the prince because you helped him. You can cast your nets in the sea for fish but not for the prince. I am warning you,' the commander spat venom.

His words dropped like molten lead into Poonkulali's ears.

She was so enraged that she could not speak. Her tongue stuck to her choking throat. Her eyes were bloodshot. She quickly left the place.

I don't want to hear any human voice. Men are cruel. How blessed it would be if all men were mute!

Soon she reached the river Thondai looking for her boat.

'I must get away far into the open ocean where no human voice can be heard. My heart, wounded by the commander's poisonous words, will be healed. How could that old man say such a thing? Am I casting my net over the prince?'

She found her boat—her dearest friend and sanctuary.

Let the commander hang that Kodumbalur girl around the prince's neck! Why should I care? I have my boat and my oars, strength in my arms and the wide ocean before me. My Ocean King will never forsake me.

Poonkulali got into her boat and reached the sea soon. Noticing the signs of approaching storm, she found shelter in Ghost Island and watched nature's fury uproot thousands of coconut trees and tall palms. But she was concerned about the prince's safety.

After the storm blows over and the sea begins to calm down, I can row my boat towards Kodikkarai.

Soon the storm was over and day broke. She went to the beach to examine the devastation. She saw a log floating on the waves, drifting towards the shore. A man was bound to that log. She helped him ashore. The half dead man was a Lankan fisherman caught in the storm last night.

He told her about the fate of two great ships in the ocean caught in the whirlwind. 'One ship caught fire and was sinking. No one was on it. The other ship with some men in it vanished in the darkness.'

'The men from the burning ship may still be in the sea. They might be floating on some log. I should help them. Otherwise, what is the use of this life?'

Poonkulali pulled at the oars. And her boat flew over the waves.

Vandiyathevan and Prince Arulmoli were floating on the water by hanging on to the drifting mast pole. Vandiyathevan's throat was parched with thirst. He felt like dying. One night seemed like an era. Arulmoli comforted him, 'Friend, I see some palm trees at a distance. Don't lose hope. Be patient.' Suddenly, they heard the familiar song of Poonkulali which sounded like a song of hope for them.

'When the sea is still and so is the sea
Why should the inner sea rant and rave?
When the earth maid is asleep
Why should the heart be restless and weep?'

Vandiyathevan's spirits revived. He came back to life, 'Prince, it is Poonkulali's song. She must be nearby. We are saved!'

Soon the boat was visible to their eyes. It came closer and closer. Poonkulali was surprised, 'Can this be real?' she wondered as she extended her hand to the prince.

Arulmoli climbed into her boat and then helped his friend get in. Poonkulali stood motionless, holding her oar.

7

At Kodikkarai

The previous day's whirlwind had played havoc in Kodikkarai when it crossed the coast, uprooting numerous ancient trees and houses.

Two days after the storm, Senior Paluvettarayar and his retinue arrived at Kodikkarai followed by the ivory palanquin, with the young queen, Nandini herself.

The old man readily accepted Nandini's suggestion with joy when she expressed her desire to accompany him, caught in the grip of passion to travel in the company of that young beauty. Who needs incentive to chew sweet sugarcane?

Three days before coming to Kodikkarai he had been in Nagapattinam, a very important sea-port collecting levies and duties. As the finance minister of the Chola Empire, Paluvettarayar was inspecting such activities.

Some weeks ago, two monks from the Nagapattinam Choodamani Buddhist Monastery had visited Tanjore and conveyed the following message to the emperor:

'My Lord, we want to give you a happy news! A large congregation of Buddhists in Lanka are eager to offer the ancient Lankan throne to Prince Arulmoli selecting him as their monarch. We are very happy about such honours being conferred on your son!'

A strange idea struck Senior Paluvettarayar who was present during this audience. After the monks had left, he expressed his thoughts to Emperor Sundara Chola.

'My Lord! There is none in our land to dare disobey your orders. But your two beloved sons are exceptions. Some high officials in our empire are giving them ill advice.

Let us declare that Prince Arulmoli conspired to capture the throne of Lanka. Therefore, let us order for his arrest to bring him here. He will surely come here willingly after receiving your orders!'

Smiling upon hearing this peculiar idea, the emperor said, 'Unusual! Let us try it. I am eager to see my sons and disclose my mind to them. Arulmoli would readily accept to give away the Chola Empire to Madurandakan. He would also help to convince Karikalan.' Sundara Chola approved of Senior Paluvettarayar's plan.

Two ships sailed to Lanka to arrest and bring back the prince. Senior Paluvettarayar wanted to reach Nagapattinam and await the arrival of the arrested prince to personally escort him to Tanjore. There were some other reasons too: neither the Queen Mother nor Princess Kundavai must be allowed to meet Prince Arulmoli before he met his father. They would turn the prince against the Paluvettarayars. Till the appropriate time, nothing should go amiss.

Nandini was very eager to meet Vandiyathevan again to know the content of the letters given by Kundavai and the news from Ravidasa the sorcerer. That's why she accompanied her husband to Nagapattinam.

Senior Paluvettarayar's dream of pleasure cruises with Nandini were drowned by the devilish storm that lashed the coast! He spent most of the time in trying to find out the status of the ships that had gone to arrest Prince Arulmoli. Some fisherman who had returned to the shore after the storm reported that they saw two ships caught in the storm; one had caught fire and capsized. The other one was lost in the darkness.

Senior Paluvettarayar was deeply worried about Prince Arulmoli.

He is the darling of the Chola nation. The public will blame me if anything happens to him. How will I convince the people and the emperor?

He decided to visit Kodikkarai to get more details.

When informed about his visit to Kodikkarai, Nandini readily approved, showing an interest in visiting the beautiful island.

There were two ways to reach Kodikkarai from Nagapattinam. One was a canal, another a coastal road. Nandini preferred the road route as she need not suffer the privacy of being with her husband and his love games while traveling in a boat.

Upon reaching Kodikkarai, the lighthouse keeper welcomed them. Tents were pitched for Nandini and her Lord and the others.

They saw a huge ship with torn sails and broken masts without the tiger-flag, approaching the shore. It anchored as close as possible to that shallow coast.

Senior Paluvettarayar was excited.

Who was in that ship?

A boat was sent to bring the men from that ship. One of them was Parthiban Pallava.

Prince Arulmoli had jumped into the sea to save his friend Vandiyathevan and had never returned to Parthiban's ship. Parthiban was upset beyond description. He sailed here and there, searching the sea for Prince Arulmoli. One of the seamen who had gone with the prince in the boat was rescued in a weary condition. He informed them about the fate of Prince Arulmoli and his friend Vandiyathevan who were hit by the floating mast.

He had hope that the prince might have been washed ashore at Kodikkarai.

Parthiban was taken to Senior Paluvettarayar who was like a ferocious lion. At that very moment a shimmering beauty arrived like a lightning flash. Parthiban was completely dazzled. Nandini asked her husband, 'Who is this brave warrior? I have not seen him before.' Her cooing words intoxicated Parthiban.

8

Net of Passion

Old men who marry young maids always dwell in the world of suspicion. They have a natural dislike for any stranger or newcomer or youth. Senior Paluvettarayar didn't like Nandini coming out and starting a conversation with young Prince Parthiban. But he couldn't reveal his displeasure.

Parthiban introduced himself, 'Let me introduce myself, My Queen! I am Parthibendra Pallavan.'

Senior Paluvettarayar added in a mocking tone, 'Parthiban, why have you forgotten all the titles and ranks? When did you turn so humble and modest? Nandini, he is not merely a Pallava prince. He is the one who beheaded the Pandiya king, Veerapandiya!'

'My Queen, I have no claim to that title. The only person who can own that title is Prince Aditya Karikalan.'

'Why do you say that Parthiba? Don't you want to share the credit of killing a dead snake?' asked Paluvettarayar with a thundering laugh.

'No, My Lord, Aditya Karikalan did not kill a dead snake. When he raised his sword, Veerapandiya was a fully live serpent. A maiden more divine than a heavenly nymph stood before him with folded hands, begging for his life. If it were me, I would have immediately thrown the sword away at the wink of that nymph and Veerapandiya would be alive now.'

Though Parthiban was answering Paluvettarayar, his eyes were fixed on Nandini.

Nandini felt that the talk was turning towards dangerous grounds. Turning around she asked,

'My Lord! Let us find out why this young man is here.'

Upon that, Paluvettarayar asked with some urgency, 'Yes, Parthiban. Forget that old story. What is your mission here?'

Parthiban, still under Nandini's spell, replied, 'My Lord, Prince Arulmoli who left Lanka along with me in my ship jumped into the sea in the whirlwind storm. I don't know his fate. I came here with the hope of finding him here on this shore.'

On hearing this Paluvettarayar swooned and fell down like a palm tree uprooted by the storm.

Parthiban ran forward to hold him, Nandini knelt down lifting her husband's head on to her lap and cried, 'Fetch water!'

Sprinkling some water on his face, she softly called, 'My dear! My dear!'

Soon, the old man opened his eyes.

'Nandini, has the ocean taken away Ponniyin Selvan? Oh! When that brave man was a child, I carried him with these hands of mine! And now these same hands signed the orders of his arrest! Oh! What will the countrymen think of me?'

He started wailing, hitting his head with his palms. Nandini had never seen him in such a state!

'My Lord, he has not given us all the news. Let us listen to him fully.'

'Parthiba, you said that Arulmoli drowned at sea? Are you cooking up stories? Don't play with a hungry tiger!' growled the old man, his eyes blazing with fire.

'My Lord, forgive me. I did not say that the prince died. All that I said was that he jumped into the stormy sea from my ship. He must be alive with God's grace. I came here only to look for him.'

'Why did he jump into the sea during the storm? Why was he in your ship? What were you doing when he jumped?' asked Paluvettarayar in some agitation.

'My Lord, please listen to me! News reached Kanchi that you and other chieftains are conspiring against the Chola Empire. Upon that, Prince Aditya Karikalan and King Malayaman sent me to Lanka asking me to bring back Prince Arulmoli to Kanchi.'

Paluvettarayar lamented, 'Oh God! Disaster has befallen the Cholas.'

Nandini tried to calm him down, 'My Lord, it is not your fault. Even if you had not given the arrest orders, the prince would have set sail for Kanchi in this man's ship. Don't be distressed unnecessarily. Moreover…' At this point, Nandini whispered something into her husband's ears.

His face brightened a little,

'Yes, yes. That didn't strike me!'

He turned towards Parthiban saying, 'Parthiba, I want to examine your ship. Till I finish my inspection, you stay right here and don't try to escape.'

'My Lord, don't worry about this man. I shall watch him.'

'My darling! Our men will watch this fellow, you take rest.'

'My Lord, I will be rooted to this spot watching out for you till you come back.'

She whispered something again in Paluvettarayar's ears and he left. Nandini stood with her eyes fixed on that boat for some time. She sensed that Parthiban was staring at her without a wink. Will a honeybee that has spotted a fragrant flower turn away?

'Don't try to escape!' warned Nandini.

'Why frighten me? How can I escape from you? Can a fish that is caught in the nets escape? I have heard of the enchanting powers of women only in poetry and mythological stories. I am experiencing it now.'

'Oh, stop it, Sir! Why do you speak of such things? I sent away my husband intentionally. I need to ask you something.'

'I understood. That's why I stayed back.'

'Did Prince Aditya Karikalan speak to you about the Pandiya war?'

'Yes, he spoke to me about beheading Veerapandiya. Though Aditya Karikalan did not give in to your wish on that day, he has been feeling tormented with all those memories for the past three years. He feels sorry for not heeding to your prayers.'

Their conversation about the Pandiya war lasted long. Parthiban fell into the net of passion cast by Nandini.

Finally, Nandini asked Parthiban.

'I will ask you for a favour that will bring happiness to both. When my husband returns you should explain the truth to him.'

'What truth?'

'That boastful princess who lives in Palayarai influences every segment of this Chola Empire—she has fallen in love with that insignificant, impudent youth Vandiyathevan,' said Nandini.

'What are you saying?'

'Yes, she fell in love with that youth. That is why she helped him escape the wrath of the Paluvettarayar brothers by sending him away to Lanka with letters. Poor man, my husband thinks he is responsible for the misfortune of the prince. In truth that arrogant Kundavai is the real culprit. If she had not sent that letter…'

'Yes, it is true! This calamity could have been avoided…'

'When my husband returns, tell this truth to him. I will be very grateful to you.'

'Queen, is that the only way to earn your thanks? I am prepared for any other orders. Tell me now… Aditya Karikalan had an opportunity, but he failed. And now he suffers for that folly day and night. I shall never make that mistake. Tell me! I will forgive my worst enemy and make my dearest friend a foe upon your orders!' Parthiban spoke as if possessed.

9
Call of a Hooting Owl

Nandini was looking at the sea till Paluvettarayar's boat reached the ship. Parthiban was wondering why Nandini was so concerned about that old man.

Why did she marry that old devil?

Nandini turned her face away from the ship to look at Parthiban and said, 'See his love and regard for the Cholas? How disturbed he feels to hear the fate of Prince Arulmoli! Prince, is there any chance that he might be alive?'

'No, it is most unlikely…Who can be blamed for the whims of fate?' replied Parthiban.

'Fate is not to be blamed in this matter. The greed of that devil at Palayarai is the cause. She studied her brother's horoscope and strongly believed that her brother would one day rule the entire world as an emperor. Now she will suffer to hear his fate. I wish to remain by her side to see her mourning. The darling daughter of the emperor! A world-renowned beauty!'

'Kundavai's beauty can never equal to the grace of your little toe! Order me! What should I do? I will carry it out this very minute,' said Parthiban.

'I have no authority to give you orders I can only request you. People blame me for the discord in the Chola Empire after I married Senior Paluvettarayar. They also say that I tutored Madurandakan to claim the throne. I want to disprove it. I need your help for that,' said Nandini with a sudden change of mood.

Parthiban expected a difficult assignment. But she spoke of politics.

'Tell me Queen, what should I do?'

'Sir, it is Kundavai who destroyed peace in this Chola country. She was dreaming to seat her younger brother Arulmoli on the Chola throne and rule the country through him. But the ministers, nobles and even the emperor want to crown Prince Madurandakan.'

'Is that so?' asked Parthiban with some surprise.

'Yes, sir. Otherwise, why these orders of arrest? There is scope to amicably settle this matter. They can divide the kingdom: north for Aditya Karikalan and south for Madurandakan. Help me save the Chola Empire and avoid the civil strife between cousins. Bring your friend Aditya Karikalan to Kadamboor Sambuvarayar's palace. He has a daughter. If Aditya Karikalan agrees to marry her, my mission will be fulfilled. The blame on me will be gone. Later, I will go by destiny... Perhaps drown in the deep seas...'

Suddenly Nandini asked an unconnected question.

'Prince Parthiba, do you believe in palmistry?'

Instead of giving a direct reply he asked for her palms and started examining her right palm.

'Amazing lines! Has anyone read your palm before and said anything to you?' asked the youth.

'Yes. Once Kundavai read my hands and said I will face an early death...'

'Of course, she is only half right. There is another life of glory where you are likely to travel to distant shores and enjoy a life of greatness brought to you by the genuine love of a youth you meet on a seashore.'

Parthiban suddenly took hold of both her palms and brought them to his face. Pulling away her hands she said, 'My husband is returning. We shall talk later.'

'When, My Queen?'

'Come with us to Tanjore.'

Senior Paluvettarayar arrived with eyes full of anger to see them engaged in intimate conversation for such a long time.

'Yes, my dear. I examined his ship and spoke to the seamen there. This man speaks the truth. The darling prince of the Cholas, Prince Arulmoli is gone! And this murdering devil—Parthiban is the cause for it!'

'My Lord, let us hear what he has to say,' Nandini's voice calmed Paluvettarayar's rage.

'Oh, My Lord! Blame me not. I am in no way responsible for that. A she-devil who keeps the entire Chola nation under her sway is responsible for this calamity. That devil at Palayarai sent secret letters for the prince in Lanka through that adamant youth Vandiyathevan. The prince jumped into the sea to save him. That is why I said that Kundavai is squarely responsible for the death of the prince,' said Parthiban.

'You are also responsible for the prince's untimely death. Why did you let him climb off the ship in the middle of a whirlwind? Get lost!' he told Parthiban.

Nandini spoke again, 'My Lord, let us take him to Tanjore. Better if he explains the facts personally to the emperor. Or else they may even accuse us, saying we drowned the prince.'

'Yes. I must meet the emperor personally and explain things...' said Parthiban

'Then let us go,' declared Paluvettarayar.

At that moment they heard the call of a hooting owl from the nearby forest. Nandini looked in the direction of the sound which was not noticed by the others.

'The Kodikkarai jungle is very strange. Owls hoot even in daylight!' said Prince Parthiban.

The owl called twice, again.

Nandini asked, 'Do we have to leave immediately? Let us wait here for one more day? Prince Arulmoli may come ashore by holding on to a log.'

'Look at the intelligence of my young wife. It did not occur to us! Let us wait for one more day. I will post my men all along the coast and look out for the prince,' said Paluvettarayar.

10

Delirious Fever

The boat was swinging like a cradle, in the middle of the sea. It was difficult to believe that two days ago these waves had been violent and grew as tall as the coconut trees. Poonkulali was listening to the discussion between the prince and Vandiyathevan.

They were talking about things they had to do after the boat reached Kodikkarai. Vandiyathevan was insisting he should go to Palayarai and not to Tanjore.

'Your sister has something serious to discuss with you. I promised to bring you back to her. I must keep my promise,' said Vandiyathevan.

'Do you want me to disobey my father because you have to keep your promise?' asked the prince.

'They were not the orders of your father but the Paluvettarayars,' Vandiyathevan continued, 'Better meet your father as a free man rather than a prisoner. If people come to know that the Paluvettarayars have arrested Ponniyin Selvan, the whole nation will rise in revolt. Your beloved motherland will be in unrest. God prevented such disaster by sending that whirlwind. Do you want to cause trouble in the nation against God's wishes?' said Vandiyathevan.

The prince was aware of the adoration people had for him. 'How can we avoid them, when Paluvettarayar's men are waiting for me at Kodikkarai?' said prince Arulmoli.

'This girl will help us again by secretly taking us into the jungles behind the Kodikkarai beach. Poonkulali, can you do that?' said Vandiyathevan.

'We can take the boat into a canal surrounded by thick cactus bushes. Nobody can take that route from land. I will leave you there and go to Kodikkarai to gather news,' said Poonkulali.

'Dear friend, I have to enter my motherland like a thief,' said the prince sadly.

Suddenly the prince started to shiver and his body became hot.

'Do you remember that the mute queen alerted me about the poison delirious fever rampant in Lanka? It is rare that a man gripped by this fever survives,' said the prince

His eyes were staring and his lips mumbled incoherent words. Soon he was tossing in delirium. The undaunting Vandiyathevan and Poonkulali were shattered.

'Sir! What can I do? Where shall I take you?' asked Poonkulali

'Poonkulali, is there a doctor at Kodikkarai?' asked Vandiyathevan anxiously.

Poonkulali had gone mute! Suddenly the prince jumped up. His shivering body was staggering dangerously.

'Take me to my sister Kundavai!' said the prince

Vandiyathevan held the prince with two strong arms. The prince tried to struggle free. Vandiyathevan called for help, 'Poonkulali.'

Poonkulali and Vandiyathevan carefully lowered the Prince, to the bottom of that small boat. The prince lay down quietly.

Vandiyathevan realized that it was his responsibility to save Ponniyin Selvan.

'Poonkulali, can you row quickly?'

The boat skimmed forward swiftly; Vandiyathevan's mind considered different alternative courses of action.

'Poonkulali, will your family help to safeguard the prince?'

'Sir, I have a sister-in-law who is very greedy. My father is paid by the Paluvettarayars. And those men who followed you in Lanka might also be there.'

'So Kodikkarai is not a safe place? Then we will go to the canal.'

'We can reach there by dusk. Sir, do you remember that leopard's pavilion where you were hiding before? The canal goes very near that place. If you can stay there with the prince, I can go into the village and find out about things and come back quickly. There is no other option but to reach the jungle by canal.'

'Poonkulali, does the canal stop there?'

'No, it goes up to Nagapattinam.'

At dusk, the small boat entered the mouth of the canal surrounded by marshy jungle. Tall trees covered the sandy banks.

For fear of Paluvoor men Poonkulali avoided Kodikkarai. She went to the temple in the forest to get medical help and some food. Luckily there was no one there except the priest who told her that Senior Paluvettarayar, his young queen and Prince Parthiban were camping in Kodikkarai looking for Prince Arulmoli who had gone missing at sea.

The priest gave her the few bananas, coconuts and milk which had been offered to the Gods in the evening pooja. Suddenly an owl hooted somewhere in the distance.

Poonkulali walked silently towards the direction from which the owl had called. Unmindful of the thorny bushes that scratched her bare arms and legs, she walked noiselessly, her ears pricked for any unusual sounds. There she heard soft whispering voices: one a man's and the other a woman's. Poonkulali hid herself carefully and started listening.

'Sorcerer, everyone like you believes that the prince drowned in the sea. Paluvettarayar is deeply disturbed. But I do not believe it,' said the woman's voice.

11

The Greedy Woman

After Paluvettarayar and Parthiban left to search for the prince on the shore, Nandini kept watching the waves. She turned around when a voice called softly,

'My Queen!'

The daughter-in-law of the lighthouse keeper stood there.

'Who are you?' asked Nandini.

'I am Raakammal.'

'Why are you here?'

Instead of replying, the woman stared at Nandini's face. 'What are you looking at, you dimwit? What is there on my face?' asked Nandini.

Raakammal said, 'Forgive me, Queen, when I saw you, I remembered another face.'

'Who is that?'

'She is my father-in-law's uncle's daughter in Lanka. She is mute and looks like you. Sometimes she comes here.'

'Any children for the Lankan mute?'

'She gave birth to twins long ago but no one knows what happened to them. I have been dying to know that well-guarded family secret without any success.'

'Bring her to me when she comes again. I will reward you.'

'Queen, she never remains in the same place for long. Are you not from the Pandiya country?'

'Yes, you?'

'I am also from the Pandiya country.'

'Why have you come here?'

'Queen, some days ago, two men came here mentioning your name.'

'My name?'

'They said that they had to visit Lanka on your business. I sent my husband to row the boat for them,' said Raakammal.

'Has he returned?'

'Not yet. But the men he took to Lanka have returned. I am worried.'

'How do you know the men who went to Lanka with your husband are back?'

'Just now, I heard the owl hoot!'

'Are you one of them?'

'Yes, Queen!'

After that, Raakammal made the sign for fish with her fingers. Nandini was surprised.

'The sorcerer wants to meet you alone. He doesn't want to see that Pallava nobleman and your husband. He wants to meet you on the banks of the stream near the temple in the jungle,' said Raakammal.

'Queen, one more piece of information. The day after the sorcerer left with my husband, two other men came here. Paluvoor soldiers followed in search of them. My sister-in-law, Poonkulali, took one of these men to Lanka in her boat the same night.'

'Does she know how to row?'

'That is her only pastime. Everyone is worried about someone having been drowned in the sea. Only after Poonkulali returns, we can confirm that news.'

'She too might have been drowned.'

'Impossible! The sea is her cradle and also… I saw a boat in the far distance some time ago and it did not come to this shore.'

'Where else can they go?'

'They might have gone into the marsh canal behind the cactus bushes.'

'Is that possible?'
'Nothing is impossible for Poonkulali...'
'Okay! Let us go now to the temple,' said Nandini
They soon reached the temple.

After offering prayers, Young Queen Nandini and Raakammal took leave of the priest and walked towards the stream in the middle of the cactus grove in the starlit night.

12

Poonkulali's Anxious Moments

Poonkulali was hiding behind the fragrant cactus grove. Nandini and the sorcerer were whispering softly; yet their voices were audible to her in that still night. When Nandini said that she didn't believe the rumour about the prince drowning in the stormy sea, the sorcerer replied, 'Queen, believe me!'

'Did you see him drown in the sea?'

'I saw the ship catch fire.'

'Whatever you say, I don't believe it. My mind tells me that both of them are alive. Do you know Poonkulali?'

'Very well. She gave us much trouble in Lanka. She too must have drowned in the stormy whirlwind.'

'No. Sometime ago, a boat was seen in the distance. Raakammal saw it from the top of the lighthouse. It disappeared with three men in it,' said Nandini

'Raakammal, if Poonkulali saved them, where would she keep the prince?'

'There is a ruined leopard pavilion in the forest behind the cactus grove which is her favourite hiding place. She kept that Kanchi spy for one full day in that place,' replied Raakammal.

'Good. I know that place. I'll go there and find out,' said Ravidasa the sorcerer.

'What is that idiot Parthiban going to do?'

'Sorcerer, we are taking him with us to Tanjore.'

'Be careful of him.'

'Don't worry about him! A wink is enough to make him fall at my feet!' laughed Nandini.

'Even then, be careful. Earlier you were outwitted by that Kanchi spy.'

'Yes! That's why I want to see him alive once again.'

After that, they left that spot. Poonkulali started shivering at the thought of all the dangers surrounding her beloved prince. She felt faint and her throat felt dry. She was confused. She wanted to go back to her boat as quickly as possible...

The prince is in the grip of a delirious fever. Paluvettarayar's men are ready to arrest him. The assassins are hiding all over the jungle to kill him. This devil in female form, Nandini, is helping all of them! Even Prince Parthiban has fallen prey to her witchery. My secret hiding place, the leopard pavilion, is no longer safe.

Poonkulali realized the responsibility of safeguarding the prince. Suddenly something happened to her, she became totally disoriented and giddy. The world swirled around her. She had lost her way. Finally, after great difficulty she was able to reach the canal bank where she had left her boat with the prince. Her heart skipped a beat and almost stopped because the boat was not where she had left it!

'Where has it gone? Where is the prince? Have they arrested the Prince and his friend? Or has the sorcerer Ravidasa found them?' mumbled Poonkulali. She started running towards the leopard pavilion. Suddenly she felt she had lost her way again. She also heard some footsteps following her.

Who is it? Could it be that sorcerer? Why should I be frightened of him? Let me take out the dagger. This is not the time to pick a quarrel with anyone. I must run and escape. I must keep myself alive to save the feverish prince.

She ran deeper into the dense forest. But the footsteps came closer and closer. She kept on running as fast as a deer. She was exhausted and her tiredness turned into anger.

She drew out her dagger and turned around to see who was following her.

13

Divine Nymph

Suddenly Poonkulali heard a melodious song in the jungle. She recognized the singer. Yes, it was her cousin Chendan Amudan. She laughed, forgetting everything for a moment

'Amuda, is that you?' she asked.

'Yes, Poonkulali.'

'Where are you?'

Chendan Amudan stepped out in front of her.

'You frightened me! Why did you chase me like that?'

'Poonkulali, I traveled several days and nights and came here from Tanjore to listen to your songs. I waited for several days to see you. When I saw you accidentally, I ran behind you. Let me hear your songs!' said Chendan Amudan.

'Ridiculous! Is this the time for rejoicing?'

'Won't you sing?' asked Chendan Amudan loudly and then whispered, 'There is another fellow following you. I began singing to warn you. He and your brother's wife were sharing secrets this evening. Who is he?'

He then continued loudly, 'Are you ready to sing or shall I sing?'

She started singing only to mislead the other unknown person following them. She again whispered, 'Amuda, how did you know that I was here?'

'I saw the boat from the top of the lighthouse. I thought it might be you and came here in search of you. When I came here, I saw my friend Vandiyathevan and the prince in the boat. I told them about Paluvettarayar's soldiers, we shifted the feverish prince to the safety of the leopard pavilion,' he whispered.

'Oh dear! What a blunder! What happened to the boat?'

'We drowned the boat in the canal to avoid suspicion.'

Poonkulali sang a song about an owl. In between her song, she whispered, 'Amuda, the fellow who followed me, is he hiding here?'

'I didn't hear any footsteps after we stopped. He must be hiding. Who could it be?' Amudan whispered.

In a louder voice she said, 'In olden days, poets wrote about owls hooting, these days even men hoot like owls! I know a sorcerer who hoots like an owl. Let me see if I can imitate that evil night-owl.'

She then hooted three times like an owl.

Before she finished, Ravidasa, the sorcerer came out from hiding with a devilish laugh.

'Oh! You devil! It is you! You tried to kill the prince in Lanka. You were not successful there; so, you created a storm in the calm sea and drowned the prince and his friend.'

'Do you know they drowned? Did you see them?'

'Their bodies were found on the shore of Ghost Island and I buried them there. May you be cursed!'

'Don't lie like this to this Ravidasa. I have an inner eye to study everything. My magic is very powerful. I can see something happening even a thousand miles away through my magical powers.'

'Then why did you ask me?'

'I was just testing you. Where are they now? Tell me or else I'll burn you both. Speak the truth!' His eyes became hot embers and he started chanting something.

Poonkulali feigned fear and called out to Ravidasa loudly,

'Spare me! I will take you to where they are hiding. Don't do anything to us! Follow me.' She started running in the opposite direction from the leopard pavilion.

She ran like a deer and Ravidasa followed her like a hunter. She ran faster than him. Poonkulali stood over a hillock. The sorcerer running behind was gasping for breath.

'You dragged me here promising to show the hiding place of the prince and Vandiyathevan.'

'They are dead; you didn't believe me. What can I do?'

'Is it true? Can you swear on it?'

'Why should I swear? Look at the sky.'

Ravidasa looked up to see a bright comet.

'Don't you know what the appearance of a comet signals?'

'Give me water, I'm thirsty. Running after you like this...'

Poonkulali began to run again. Ravidasa lost all his sense in fury and chased her.

'I will choke you to death, wring your head and throw it to the wolves.'

Suddenly Ravidasa could not move. His legs were caught in a deep mudhole and his efforts to pull himself out were futile. His legs were sinking. Soon the mud rose inch by inch up to his thighs. He felt as if a vampire hiding under the marsh was pulling him down.

Poonkulali laughed, 'Caught in the mouth of the vampire! Try your magical spells now?'

Fright and anger danced on Ravidasa's face. Grinding his teeth, he said, 'You she-devil! What have you done?'

'You wanted to wring my neck; now crack your knuckles and pray for help!'

Reining in his anger Ravidasa said, 'Dear girl! I promise you... Give me a hand and save me.'

Poonkulali continued to laugh, 'I cannot give you a hand. Call all the ghosts that obey your sorcery.'

Ravidasa was now buried up to his waist; his face became terrible with fright and his eyes were bloodshot.

Amudan had caught up now. Poonkulali took his hand and said, 'Come let us go.'

'How can we leave him here like this and go away?' asked Chendan Amudan.

'Why? Do you want to wait till he is completely buried?' asked Poonkulali.

'No! If I leave him to this fate, this sight will haunt me as long as I live. Come, let us pull him out.'

'Amudan, he was going to kill me!'

'God will punish him for his evil intentions. Let us save him now.'

'If you feel so, give me your head scarf,' said Poonkulali. She took the long scarf and tied one end of it to a sturdy bush on the bank and threw the other end to Ravidasa.

'Sorcerer! Hold this scarf-end tightly. Don't pull too hard and uproot this bush. Be careful. Don't try to climb out by yourself. By daybreak, someone will come this way and help you out,' she said.

Poonkulali walked away with Amudan listening to the distress-filled calls of the sorcerer.

Finally, she asked, 'Amuda, you arrived at the right time and helped me. How did you come here? Why?'

'After my experience in the dungeons of Tanjore's prisons, I didn't like to remain in the capital. Paluvoor soldiers often entered my garden and troubled me. So, I went to Palayarai and met Princess Kundavai, she sent me here. She was very concerned about the dangers threatening her brothers. She wanted Vandiyathevan to take Prince Arulmoli to the Buddhist Monastery at Nagapattinam. That's why I am here. I was also very eager to see you.'

'You found the appropriate time to listen to my songs! All sorts of dangers surround the prince; the worst is that he has the delirious fever in addition to all his other troubles.'

'Yes, I could see that when we carried him to the leopard's pavilion. Anyway, let us move him to the Buddhist Monastery; the monks there are trained doctors. They will cure the prince.'

'How do we reach Nagapattinam?' she asked.

'By the canal, of course.'

'How can we go by the canal? You have drowned the boat!'

'The boat is just hidden under the water. We can pull it out and use it!'

'Then, let us leave immediately. But, all of us cannot go in that small boat!'

'Don't worry Poonkulali. Vandiyathevan can take my horse and reach Palayarai directly from here. You and I can take the prince in your boat and reach Nagapattinam.'

They reached the leopard pavilion. Vandiyathevan came out from hiding and said,

'The prince is sleeping. Someone came here some minutes ago. It looked like the sorcerer, Ravidasa. That's when you started singing. He must have heard and turned away. Did you see him?'

Amudan replied, 'We did. She buried him in the mudhole and came away.'

'We have to spend the night here, somehow, and leave at daybreak,' said Vandiyathevan

'No. If we stay here till daybreak, we will never be able to escape. We have to leave now,' said Poonkulali

Vandiyathevan and Amudan carried the sleeping prince on their shoulders. Poonkulali walked ahead to the canal in the moonlight. They laid the prince down beside a tree with Poonkulali by his side and waded into the water and began to pull out the boat.

Prince Arulmoli opened his eyes and said, 'Poonkulali, is that you? I thought it was a divine nymph.'

Poonkulali was excited with the thought that she was going to spend a few more days with the prince.

14

Ghost! Ghost!

The pleasing words of Ponniyin Selvan calling Poonkulali a nymph mesmerized her.

'Prince, I am not a heavenly nymph, merely a boatgirl,' she said.

'Surely you are the divine darling daughter of the Ocean King. Ocean Princess, you have saved my life! How can I ever repay you?'

'Poonkulali, who is the other man with Vandiyathevan near the boat?'

'My cousin, Chendan Amudan. Princess Kundavai has sent orders through him to take you to the Buddhist Monastery at Nagapattinam.'

The prince heard a piteous cry from afar and asked, 'What is that?'

'It is an owl hooting.'

'No! It sounds like a human being in the grip of some terrible danger! Let us help him before we leave.'

The prince took a few staggering steps. Poonkulali prevented him from falling.

The prince became unconscious again. They carried him to the boat.

'I take leave of you. You are both responsible for his safety!' said Vandiyathevan in a voice choked with emotion.

The owl hooted again and again. Prince Arulmoli woke up asking, 'What is that?'

Poonkulali stood up.

'The prince won't forgive me if he comes to know about it. Wait here for some more time. That place is not far away, let me rescue that sorcerer Ravidasa and come back.'

Vandiyathevan jumped up.

'I'll go with her. I have some unfinished business with that sorcerer.'

Poonkulali and Vandiyathevan reached the mudhole where she had left the sorcerer. But he was not there.

They turned back towards the canal with heavy steps. On the high canal bank, they saw two figures parting a tree branch and peering at the water. One was a man and the other a woman. They were watching the boat.

'Yes, do you recognize them?' asked Vandiyathevan.

'The sorcerer and my sister-in-law. She must have rescued him.'

'All for good.'

'It is not good! They have seen my boat. They have seen us too!'

'Then follow me; I will play a trick on them,' said Vandiyathevan.

They went to the water's edge near the bush where those two were hiding. Vandiyathevan knew that whatever they spoke about would be overheard by those hiding in the bush.

'Poonkulali, why worry? It is good that the sorcerer is dead, why do you worry after killing him?' said Vandiyathevan.

'Me, a killer?' asked Poonkulali.

'Then who trapped him in the mudhole? You are a ruthless killer.'

'No, I am not. I am no murderer, like you.'

'Yes, of course. I drowned the prince at sea. You drowned the sorcerer in the mudhole. We are now equals. If you don't reveal my secret, I won't reveal yours.'

'I will not utter any more lies. Do you agree to our pact?'

'What if I refuse?'

'I will complain to Queen Nandini about you murdering the sorcerer. There are no witnesses to my crime. Your cousin was a witness to what you did, you will surely be punished.'

'Oh! How terrible! What shall I do?' Poonkulali covered her ears with her palms.

'There, your cousin is coming in that boat. Get into it and go to Lanka with him. Don't come back here.'

'Why should I go to Lanka?'

'If you remain here, you might give my secret away to Paluvettarayar. He loves the prince. He will surely kill me. I have to stay alive and do some more work in this evil world.'

'Why did you kill the prince?'

'The prince and his sister conspired to snatch the crown from my master Aditya Karikalan.'

'You will surely pay for your evil deed.'

'It is no worse than yours; go, get into that boat! Turn the boat towards Lanka, don't try to go back to Kodikkarai,' ordered Vandiyathevan.

'I agree, may a thousand hyenas eat you!'

She cursed him and moved towards the boat. Amudan rowed the boat away quickly from that spot while Poonkulali covered the prince with her saree. Vandiyathevan continued watching till the boat vanished.

'Ha ha ha!' Laughter came from behind the bush. Vandiyathevan jumped around in pretended surprise. The sorcerer was standing behind the bush.

'Ghost!' shouted Vandiyathevan and he ran towards the temple in the jungle.

15

Commotion near the Monastery

The dark beauty called night parted reluctantly, bidding farewell to her beloved earth. A thousand songbirds sang melodies; buds on bushes and trees opened their petals. Bees hummed near the fragrant flowers. Multicoloured butterflies danced a ballet. The crescent moon disappeared with reluctance.

The boat was floating gently down the canal. Poonkulali woke up to see the prince asleep; a charming look on his face even in delirious fever.

Amudan requested Poonkulali to sing a song.

'I would like to… but it might disturb the prince.'

Meanwhile the prince woke up.

'I won't be disturbed. Both of you sing together.'

Poonkulali felt shy and cast her head down.

'Where are we going?' asked the prince.

'To the Buddhist Monastery in Nagapattinam.'

'Where is Vandiyathevan?' asked the prince. At the same moment Vandiyathevan turned up on a horse. The boat stopped and he dismounted. 'I have come to see if you were all safe. No danger from hereafter.'

'What about the sorcerer?' asked Poonkulali.

'He has no suspicions about the prince being on this boat. He believed everything I said.'

'How is the Prince now?'

'He wakes up now and then, and speaks a few words and again, becomes unconscious.'

'That is the nature of this fever.'

'For how many days will this last?'

'Maybe for months. Take him safely to the monastery. The monks will be able to cure him in a couple of weeks. Poonkulali, take care of the prince. When the prince wakes up, tell him that I am going to Palayarai and that I will send word from there as soon as possible.'

Vandiyathevan turned and rode away.

The canal meandered through the beautiful flower bushes intoxicating the air with fragrance. It was like the path leading to heaven. Every now and then, they came across a village. Amudan went into those villages and brought back milk and food for the prince and Poonkulali.

In the company of the prince, Poonkulali felt as if a million birds flew with noisy wing beats in her heart. Poonkulali and Chendan Amudan took turns to sleep and row the boat.

On the second day, they reached Nagapattinam. The canal led to the backyard of the monastery where they could get down unnoticed. Amudan rowed the boat there.

They noticed some commotion going on in the front yard of that renowned monastery. Monks were running here and there in panic. The backyard near the canal was empty. Amudan decided to go to the front yard to find the cause of the confusion.

Nagapattinam was an important port city on the coast of Tamil Nadu. Many foreigners were trading with the Cholas in the fertile Cauvery delta. Goods were being brought by large sailing ships. In addition to the pearls, jewels, coins, perfumes and iron-work, Arab horses were also imported.

The Cholas were tolerant to all faiths in the countries they ruled. Sundara Chola gave special privileges to Buddhist monasteries in his kingdom. There were even more as Prince Arulmoli had rebuilt the Buddhist temples and Viharas in Lanka.

When Amudan entered the front yard of the monastery, he saw that many people had come with platters full of flowers and fruits to offer worship. But all of them appeared to have forgotten their purpose and stood there with tear-laden eyes.

Amudan understood the situation. They must all have surrounded the seaman from Prince Parthiban's ship who had accompanied Prince Arulmoli on the rescue boat to save Vandiyathevan and he was breaking the news about the prince getting lost in the sea.

The seaman said, 'The prince jumped into the sea when the whirlwind was very strong. After that, he never returned!'

On hearing this, wails, moans and sobbing cries were heard. Tears streamed down the faces of all present, including the monks.

The chief monk was lamenting,

'When I met the emperor in Tanjore recently, I spoke to him of the wondrous deeds of the young prince in Lanka. Later, when I met Princess Kundavai, she promised to provide funds for our monastery and said, "Sire, there are all kinds of rumours in the nation. Perhaps, the young prince may seek asylum in your monastery. You have to safeguard him for a while." I promised to guard him as my own eyelids. What is the use now? The prince has drowned. Why is the Ocean King so cruel?'

Amudan approached the chief monk and introduced himself requesting for private audience.

'There are no secrets among monks. Speak!' ordered the chief monk.

'Sire, I have brought a patient with delirious fever,'

'Oh God, the delirious fever is contagious!'

The chief monk continued, 'All of you wait here. I will go with this young man and see the sick person.'

When the chief monk saw the youth standing in the middle of the backyard, he was shocked. He recognized the youth. Surprise, amazement and happiness mingled on his serene face.

'It is our beloved Prince Arulmoli, is it not?'

The prince was blabbering due to high fever...

'No, I am just a boatman...'

Chendan Amudan whispered to the chief monk that the prince was in a feverish delirium.

He informed the other monks who had gathered there now, 'This youth has delirious fever. I will take this man to my private chambers to nurse him.'

The prince was taken inside. Once inside, the doors were closed with a bang which echoed in Poonkulali's heart as she waited near the gate.

Will I ever see him again on this earth?

With such remorseful thoughts, she gazed at the door of the monastery through which the prince had gone away.

16

The Blacksmith

Vandiyathevan led his horse towards Palayarai. The horse was finding it difficult to walk in the rough terrain of the jungle. It was exhausted, like its master. It had been several days since he had slept well.

He was rejoicing over his forthcoming meeting with Princess Kundavai to give her the good news of the successful mission assigned by her.

His attitude to life had completely changed ever since he and Prince Arulmoli had become friends. He had always been under the presumption that those in politics must be full of trickery and falsehood. But now, his mind had been completely changed, thanks to Prince Arulmoli's principles, law and justice, love and truth. He made a vow to himself to never lie.

Suddenly, his horse stumbled. A small, sharp stone had pierced the hoof of one leg. He plucked it out and patted the horse before mounting it again.

Soldiers in the battlefield wear armour. Similarly, I should armour this horse with some comfort before it falls down. Soon he reached a wayside village and located a blacksmith.

There appeared to be some confusion in that small village. The villagers had gathered in small groups, talking in an agitated way about something.

What is worrying these people?

The smith was at work assisted by his son, working on a beautiful sword.

What a beautiful and marvelous sword! Vandiyathevan was lost in admiration.

The busy blacksmith turned to Vandiyathevan

'Who are you, sir? What do you want? A spear or a sword? Nowadays no one needs spears and swords!'

'Sir, you say so yet you hold a beautiful sword in your hands!'

'Oh, this is an old rare sword brought here for polishing. Tell me why have you come here now?'

'I need a cladding for my horse. Can you do that?'

'Yes, but I will take it up after finishing the job on hand.'

Vandiyathevan decided to stay and leave after the cladding got done. He sat watching the blacksmith working on the sword for a while.

'What excellent workmanship; I am sure this sword belongs to some royal family. Whose sword is it?'

'Ask me no questions about this sword and I won't speak untruths.'

'Oh, that's fine. Please finish my work as quickly as possible.'

The blacksmith continued his work.

Vandiyathevan was staring at the sword. He was bewildered to see a fish engraved on the handle of the sword.

Why a fish symbol?

While thinking about this new mystery, sleep engulfed Vandiyathevan. He dreamt of various things. One dream was about the royal sword. A man came back asking for the sword. The smith gave it to him and refused to accept the fee money and said,

'Let this work be my gift to the Queen of Paluvoor.'

'Be careful, no one should know about this. Never quote the Young Queen's name.'

'Why should I mention her name? I won't open my mouth to anyone.'

'There is a young man asleep here and you are speaking loudly.'

'He is in deep sleep. He cannot hear even a thunder storm.'

'What if he has heard, throw him into the furnace!'

After this conversation, the blacksmith and the sword owner began to drag him to the furnace. When they were about to throw him into the fire, Vandiyathevan woke up with a scream,

'No! No! Don't do that.'

He woke up sweating.

'Did I sleep for a long time?' Vandiyathevan asked the smith.

'Not too long! Just a couple of *jaamams*—about six hours. How can you sleep like this in broad daylight?'

'Have you finished my work?'

'Not yet. What is the use of doing something for a sleepy head like you? If you sleep like this you are likely to lose the horse or even your own self!'

Vandiyathevan was shocked and ran out to check on his horse.

The horse was not there

He came back shouting. 'Where is my horse?'

'Don't panic. Your horse is safe in the back yard,' assured the blacksmith.

Vandiyathevan ran up to the back yard. His horse was there. A small boy was feeding the horse.

'Who brought my horse here?'

'I did,' said the boy.

'Why?'

'Senior Paluvettarayar and his retainers were passing through our village some time ago. If they had seen the horse, they would have simply taken it away.'

Vandiyathevan expressed his gratitude. He came back to the blacksmith and enquired,

'When did the Paluvettarayars' entourage cross this village?'

'About an hour ago. They were making such a loud noise. Even that did not wake you. I was surprised.'

'I was asleep yes, but you could have started the work after you completed the work of the other customer.'

'Yes, I could have, but the news from Lanka upset me. I was in no mood to work. Our beloved Prince Ponniyin Selvan was drowned in the sea.'

Vandiyathevan feigned a shocking expression on his face. 'Oh God! Who told you?'

'That has been the rumour since yesterday. The news was confirmed by Senior Paluvettarayar today. May a thunderbolt strike that wicked nobleman's head!'

'Why curse that old man?'

'This happened because of him. He conspired some trick and drowned our prince. We cancelled the reception we had planned for him.'

'Do people love the prince so much?'

'The whole village is in tears. No, the whole Chola nation is wailing and cursing the Paluvettarayars.'

'Paluvoor men are very powerful. You are cursing them. What if someone hears of it? Be careful.'

'You have to be more careful than me! At least, I speak when I am awake. You blabber in your sleep!'

'What did I blabber?'

'You called the Paluvettarayars as death's messengers. You called the Paluvoor's young queen a female devil. Of course, you are right. But, what if anyone other than I had overheard you say such things? It was when you were prattling such nonsense Senior Paluvettarayar's retinue was passing through this street. I was frozen.'

'What did you do?'

'I stood outside and closed my smithy. My son had already taken your horse to the backyard.'

'Did I say anything else in my sleep?'

'No dearth of your blabberings!'

'Oh my God!'

'You insisted that some prince should go to Palayarai. But he insisted in surrendering to the Paluvettarayars. You said so many things. You said something about Princess Kundavai. Be careful, brother, be careful.'

Vandiyathevan was embarassed. 'Did I say anything improper about her?'

He vowed that in future he would sleep only in a closed chamber and that too alone or else he would sleep in the forest or desert.

'Sir, I have to rush to Palayarai, preferably without being seen by Paluvoor men. How should I go?'

'Senior Paluvettarayar and his men are taking the royal highway. If you go along the banks of river Mullai, you can soon reach Palayarai.'

'It would be good if you can finish the shoes for my horse as quickly as possible.'

'Sure.' He began beating the red-hot pieces of iron, bending them into shoes, saying, 'This blow is for Paluvettarayar's head, this is for Sambuvarayar's head!' as he struck the metal with his hammer. Vandiyathevan recognized the anger felt by common folk against the powerful noblemen. Soon, shoes were fixed on the horse's hoofs. Vandiyathevan tried to pay the blacksmith but the man refused to accept the money. 'I did the work because you are a good man.'

Vandiyathevan thanked him and left.

The sun was already setting when Vandiyathevan resumed his journey. The ride along the banks of river Mullai was very pleasant and picturesque. And he was elated. When the whole world was mourning the loss of the Prince, he alone knew that it was not true. He was happy because he had outwitted Ravidasa the sorcerer, once again. He was also happy he was going to meet Princess Kundavai again. He started singing.

'The lights in the sky
Are intoxicated
Your voice is sweet
Is it made of honey?'

The moment he finished the song, he heard wolves howling in retaliation. He also heard a man laughing aloud.

Vandiyathevan was shocked. Instinctively his hand reached for his sword.

A figure emerged from the shadows of a tree.

'Brother! Your song was marvelous; the chorus of the jackals was even more wonderful!' said Thevaralan as he began to laugh once again.

17

Royal Sword

Vandiyathevan was shocked to see the folk dancer Thevaralan in that forest. He blamed his fate for leading him to confront this evil man again in this godforsaken place.

He slowed down his horse and asked Thevaralan,

'How did you appear so suddenly over here?'

'I too wanted to ask you the very same question! We had bound you to the ship's mast and abandoned you at mid-sea. How did you escape?' asked Thevaralan.

Why is this monster following me? How to escape him? I wish there was a mudhole here too, like at Kodikkarai. I could have buried him in a mudhole. Or, shall I drown him in this river? That will not work. This river is shallow. Perhaps, I may have to use my sword...

'Brother, I know what you are thinking. It will not work. Don't try it.'

Suddenly Vandiyathevan sighted a covered palanquin at a distance. Thevaralan led Vandiyathevan's horse to it. About seven or eight persons sprang from hiding and attacked Vandiyathevan and immobilized him. His hands were tied, eyes covered and his sword was taken away from him. Vandiyathevan was thrown into the palanquin. Immediately the palanquin started moving. His horse followed them. He could not believe that he had been caught. Gradually, he was able to free his hands and legs and also removed the cloth over his eyes. He wanted to escape but he succumbed to the sweet fragrance lingering in the palanquin and became unconscious. When he regained consciousness, he was not in the palanquin. He was in a large well-lit room with several oil lamps. He sat up and looked around. To his surprise, Nandini, the unearthly beauty, entered the room. The striking resemblance of Nandini to that mute woman in Lanka baffled him.

'Sir! You are a very good man!' said Nandini in a sweet voice.

'Thanks.'

'The sign of a good man is to vanish without even informing. You disappeared from Tanjore Fort without taking leave of me! That is the sign of a good man! I gave you my signet ring and helped you enter the mighty Tanjore Fort. You should have at least returned my signet ring before you left. You could return it at least now.' She extended her hands towards him.

'My lady, Lanka's commander, Bhoothi Vikrama, confiscated that ring. Please forgive me.'

'You gave away my ring to my sworn enemy! Your sense of gratitude is admirable!'

'I didn't give it willingly, it was taken away from me by force.'

'The bravest of warriors, of the noble Vaanar clan, you were forced to do something against your will? I should believe it!'

'My lady, my presence here at this time, is it not by force?'

'Tell me the truth. Look at my face and speak. Were you really forced to come here? Who prevented you from jumping out of the palanquin and running away?' she asked, her words were like poisoned arrows piercing his heart.

'Yes, I came willingly.'

'Why did you come?'

'Why did you want me to come?'

'I wanted my ring back.'

'Just that?'

'There is one other reason. Did you think that I didn't know about your presence in the treasury vault that night when you escaped from my garden gazebo? But for me, you could not have escaped.'

He could not hide the shock from his face.

'I know everything. My husband also knew! He ordered the guards to kill you instantly. I changed the order when he had moved away and that's how you escaped. While your friend Kandamaran became the victim. But for me, your skeleton would be decorating the pearl heaps in that treasury vault.'

Vandiyathevan was lost in a sea of surprise.

But, how did she guess that I was hiding in that vault?

'Do you know why I mentioned saving your life that day? Just to warn you not to use that tunnel once again. It is heavily guarded now.'

'Ok I won't go back that way.'

'You never think of those who help you. Your friend was in danger because of you. I brought him to my own palace and nursed him. Betrayal of friendship is part of your character, just like the betrayal of trust. The doctor's son, Pinakapani, came with you to Kodikkarai? You deserted him to be caught and escaped out of the country? You are least bothered about him.'

'I was about to ask. What happened to him?'

'I'll tell you provided you tell me what happened to the prince who left Lanka with you.'

'Queen, please don't ask me about that matter.'

'Yes, I must not ask you about that! Even if I ask, you will not answer. Let it go. How is your sweetheart?'

Vandiyathevan was embarassed. 'Whom do you mean?'

'I didn't mean that 'empress' of Palayarai! She will not even look at you, I am asking you about that boatgirl, Poonkulali, who took you to Lanka.'

'No. Not possible. She took me to her lovers one night. They were the fiery devils rising from the marshes.'

'She is lucky. Her lovers are bright; formed of light. But my lovers are made of darkness; they are formless. Have you ever slept in a ruined jungle pavilion at midnight? Have you seen bats and owls fly silently, in the darkness of such abandoned buildings?'

She started staring around in a frenzy. Her eyes were crazy and deranged. Nandini spoke as if possessed. Even iron-hearted

Vandiyathevan was shaken. He felt sorry for her on one hand and a meaningless fear filled his mind on the other hand.

'My Queen! Don't! Please, control yourself!'

'Who are you to advise me?'

'I am a poor youth of the Vaanar clan. Who are you, my Queen?' asked Vandiyathevan

'You ask who I am? I do not know! I have been trying to find out. Who am I? A human being? Or a devil?'

'No, perhaps an angel come to earth because of a divine curse.'

'Yes, there is some divine curse upon me. But I do not know what it is. Who am I? Why was I born? But God has given me an indication. Look at this!' Nandini showed a sword to Vandiyathevan.

Vandiyathevan immediately recognised the marvelous sword he had seen in the smithy.

When he saw the sword, his heart became stronger. He had always liked swords and spears since his childhood. He would face it like a true warrior even if it was used against him.

'My Queen, I see a beautiful sword, finely crafted. A jeweled sword meant for the royal family. It should be in the hands of the best of warriors. I wonder how it reached your flowery hands. What does God tell you by this signal?' asked Vandiyathevan.

18

A Flying Horse

Nandini lifted the shining sword and held it fondly, close to her breast. Then she caressed it to her face and kissed it with her rosy lips. Suddenly Nandini transformed into a pagan goddess, a gory deity asking for human sacrifice. Her beautiful face became frightful. Even then it was charming. She placed the sword on the table. After that she became calm.

'Yes, this sword is God's sign to me. I am yet to understand its meaning. I send this sword quite often to the blacksmith for sharpening. I am yet to get God's approval to use this sword. Perhaps it is a divine command that I should use the sword on someone wicked or on my own self. I await that moment. Day and night, anytime, anyplace, I am prepared. The whole world knows that Paluvoor's young queen, who is the most beautiful among women, is very fond of rich, fashionable clothes and jewels. I dress myself in preparation for that moment. My husband, that old man, thinks I present myself with all this glamour to please him. He is not aware of the deadly passion burning in my heart.'

Vandiyathevan who had been engrossed in listening to her long speech came to his senses.

'My Queen, where is your husband?'

'Why? Are you afraid of him?' asked Nandini.

'No, my Queen. When I fear not even you, why fear others?'

'Senior Paluvettarayar, who is such a brave soldier, fears me. My brother-in-law, Junior Paluvettarayar, who scares even the god of death shivers with fright in my presence. Madurandakan who wants to rule this empire approaches me with fearful dread. Sundara Chola who is already at death's portals shivers with paranoia if I go near him; he even faints when he sees me! And that great warrior Pallava Parthiban, Aditya Karikalan's most trusted friend has totally changed within a few minutes in my presence. He remains completely enslaved, forgetting his mission and obeys my every wish and whim. Yet, even he hesitates to be alone with me. The great, Prince Aditya Karikalan was very fond of me. But fate separated us.

Among the men I have met, you are the only one with courage. You speak without hiding your feelings. I like you for your frankness. It is not my habit to meet many people. I don't ride in chariots and go out like that princess of Palayarai. I go by covered palanquin. I meet only those with whom I have some business.'

'No one can hide anything from you. Your keen eyes will unlock all secrets,' said Vandiyathevan.

'But I have not yet found out your secrets. Sir! I ask you again. Do you know the truth about the missing Prince Arulmoli? Can't you share it with me?' asked Nandini in a very charming voice.

'No, Your Highness. I cannot share it with you. I have made a resolve not to speak lies. I can't tell you anything about the prince. In fact, I spoke a lie just now forgetting my resolve. Forgive me!' Vandiyathevan opened his waist-pouch and gave the palm tree signet ring to her.

'Sir, it is not my practice to take back what I have once given. I was just testing you. You may keep this ring in remembrance of me.'

'Please don't be hasty. If I keep it, I may use it again.'

'I don't care. I'll ask my men to bind your eyes and take you back in the palanquin. They will leave you at the river bank.'

'What if I refuse to go with them?'

'You can never get out from this ruined fortress.'

'I will go with your men. Is there anything that I can do for you?'

'Yes, I need a flying horse.'

'What? A flying horse?'

'Yes, a flying horse!'
'Do you mean an Arab horse?'
'No, I want a flying horse like the ones in fairy tales.'
'Some days ago, were you in Lanka?'
'No. I have never been away from Paluvettarayar's men. Why do you ask?'
'I saw you in Lanka some days ago. Perhaps, you already have a flying horse and visited Lanka on it. You were wearing an ordinary dress with no jewellery and your tresses were unkempt.'
'It was not me sir; did that woman open her mouth and speak?'
'No, she spoke in sign language. She is a mute woman. And she looks exactly like you.'

Nandini's eyes were focussed on something in the far distance. She sighed heavily. 'Sir, you promised to help me in some way…'

'Yes.'

'Then, do this for me. If you ever happen to see that woman again, bring her here. If that is not possible, take me to her.'

Soon, Vandiyathevan was back on the banks of river Mullai. His horse was waiting for him. Vandiyathevan rode his horse at a slow trot and travelled all night along the river. Thoughts of Nandini troubled him. He no longer had a negative opinion about her. She must have had a bitter past.

I feel nothing but pity for her. I don't know what her real intentions are. Her real story is full of mysteries. She is stunningly beautiful aided by some mesmerizing power. I shouldn't have any more dealings with her. Why did she refuse to take her ring? Can I throw it away in this river?

But he had no heart to discard something that might be useful later.

Vandiyathevan saw the planet Venus rise; one should not travel with Venus in the sky. He dismounted from the horse and fell asleep under a tree.

19

Vandiyathevan's Tricks

Vandiyathevan woke up at the sight of the golden morning sun. He mounted his horse and passed through several villages where the people were attending to their daily chores, unaware of the news about Ponniyin Selvan.

He finally reached Palayarai Fort just before sunset. He saw Prince Madurandakan arrive in a beautiful gilded chariot in the company of the footmen bearing lances, banners and flags. Immediately his mind had devised a clever way to gain entry into the palace. He goaded his horse to quickly run towards the chariot. Madurandakan's men did not anticipate this. Before anyone could stop him, Vandiyathevan stood up on the stirrups and peered at the prince then shouted, 'Oh! Danger!' The next instant Vandiyathevan fell down from his horse.

All this happened within a few seconds. The footmen drew out their swords sensing the danger to their prince; but they put them back when they saw him fall and laughed at him. Prince Madurandakan also laughed. The chariot stopped. The prince signalled to his guards and Vandiyathevan was brought in front of the prince.

'Who are you?' asked Prince Madurandakan.

'I… me… emperor, don't you know me?' asked Vandiyathevan.

'Have you seen me before?' asked Madurandakan.

'I have seen you twice or someone like you. I am not sure if you are you or the person I had seen. That is why…' Vandiyathevan deliberately created confusion in the mind of Madurandakan.

'I can tell you where I saw you, or the person I think was you. You can decide after that.'

'Speak clearly.'

'A huge fort. Midnight, dim light from oil lamps. Several nobles gathered together there. A handsome man stepped out of the palanquin. On seeing him, all raised cheers. "Live long the Crown Prince!" Sir, the face of the person who came out of that palanquin strongly resembles you. If I'm wrong, please forgive me.'

Madurandakan who was listening keenly, began to sweat.

'Hey, you fellow! Were you present in the midst of the warriors at that time?'

'No sir! I was not there.'

'Then how are you able to describe it so precisely?'

'Listen to one more scenario, it is a dark treasury vault. A winding tunnel underground. Three men came down that way—one with a torch in front, another guard at the back, a handsome man in the middle. The handsome person in the middle strongly resembled you!'

'Are you a soothsayer?' asked the prince.

'No, My Lord, that is not my profession. But I can reveal the past; I can tell what is likely to happen.'

Madurandakan thought about something.

'When you stood up on the horse, just now, you shouted something. What was that?'

'I said, "Danger".'

'Danger for whom?'

'For you!'

'What danger?'

'Many dangers. At the same time, great fortune awaits you. I can narrate all that at leisure. Please take me with you into the palace.'

Madurandakan ordered that Vandiyathevan be brought to the palace along with his retinue. The captain of the group was not happy but he had no choice.

20

Puppet Prince Madurandakan

Prince Madurandakan was the only son of Kandaraditya Chola and Sembian Madevi. His parents were deeply spiritual and highly noble. They spent most of their time building and renovating temples across the empire. Kandaraditya did not believe in expanding his kingdom by waging wars. He was upset by the devastating wars. He was always preaching peace. Therefore, the Chola Empire shrank in size during his reign. In his old age, Kandaraditya married Sembian Madevi who is the Queen Mother. Their only child was Madurandakan. Enemies grew powerful everywhere in the kingdom.

Sundara Chola was a valiant youth who had won many battles. Kandaraditya therefore decided to crown Sundara Chola as the emperor. On his death bed, Kandaraditya requested his wife Sembian Madevi to raise their only son Madurandakan in religious ways. Accordingly, she injected all the spiritual thoughts into her son's veins.

Till Prince Madurandakan was twenty, his mother's word was law to him. Prince Madurandakan obeyed his mother's will and followed a life of religious devotion. He had no interest in politics or governance.

But after he married the daughter of Junior Paluvettarayar, his mind changed. Nandini, the young queen of Paluvoor fuelled his interest in political affairs. Many nobles supported his cause in a conspiracy against Sundara Chola's family for some reasons. They eagerly awaited Sundara Chola's death to place their puppet, Prince Madurandakan, on the throne.

Prince Madurandakan however, wanted to ascend the throne

immediately without waiting for Sundara Chola's death. Now that Sundara was bedridden.

Why not seize power and crown myself immediately?

It became Paluvettarayar's responsibility to keep Madurandakan's ambition in check for some reasons. Sundara Chola's two young sons, like their father, were very popular among the people for their bravery and noble deeds.

There were only two main obstacles. One was Princess Kundavai and the other was Madurandakan's mother—Queen Mother. Managing Princess Kundavai wouldn't be very difficult for the cunning Paluvettarayars. Queen Mother, Sembian Madevi, was revered by all her subjects like a goddess. If she raised objections, it would be difficult to overcome them. Therefore, they decided to wait for her death or change of mind. The Paluvettarayar brothers asked Madurandakan to convince his mother. Queen Mother herself sent word to her son for a meeting. His father-in-law, Junior Paluvettarayar advised him to make use of this golden opportunity and talk to his mother about his rights to the throne.

Prince Madurandakan entered Palayarai with his retinue and Vandiyathevan.

Queen Mother received her son.

'Son, you have come in time! Saint Naraiyur Nambi is arriving; refresh yourself quickly and come to the audience chamber!'

Madurandakan was not eager to go to the audience chamber. After repeated calling by his mother, Madurandakan along with Vandiyathevan reluctantly reached the auditorium to see a poor reception awaiting him.

Queen Mother was attending to the guests accompanied by Princess Kundavai and the other royal women. A young saint was seated on a high pedestal at the centre of the auditorium.

Vandiyathevan's curious eyes rested on Princess Kundavai's moonlike face. Her eyes widened in surprise to see him, but she didn't turn towards him! Queen Mother introduced the young saint.

'Son, this gentleman is from Naraiyur; fully blessed by the grace of the Lord. He has rare religious manuscripts never found by anyone before.'

But Madurandakan disliked the honours given to that wayfaring saint. The saint rendered a spiritual discourse.

Queen Mother's eyes shed tears of joy. But while all were keenly watching the event, Vandiyathevan's ears and eyes and thoughts were fixed only on Princess Kundavai.

After the event, the Queen Mother announced that arrangements were being made for this young saint to visit all the temples in the kingdom and render spiritual discourses and it would be sponsored by her. Loud cheers followed her announcement.

21

Soothsayer

After Naraiyur Nambi's discourse, Queen Mother spoke to Madurandakan,

'My son, I will see off the guests and get back to discuss something very important with you.'

Ire and anger danced on Madurandakan's face to see the royal reception given to the wayfaring saint.

No wonder, Paluvettarayar brothers complain about my mother. She spends lavishly on such beggars and empties the royal treasury quickly! Worst of all, Princess Kundavai also gives away all the wealth to some hospitals and pilgrim shelters! If these people spend like this, what about my dreams? How can I ascend the throne and order vast armies to go and conquer lands to expand my empire?

My mother wants to discuss matters with me! What will she discuss? She will indulge in silly talks of yoga, meditation and pranayama to reach salvation. This is how she made me into a half-crazed fool.

Before my mother returns, I must talk to that soothsayer to know my future. He knew all the secrets not known to anyone. He must surely possess some supernatural powers. He studies the past and foretells the future. Let me ask him...

Meanwhile, Vandiyathevan's eyes were trying to catch the attention of Princess Kundavai hoping to seek an audience with her, but, he could not.

I keep thinking of her day and night but she never even looks at me. The bee looks for honey and buzzes around the flower; why should the flower worry about the bee? How to meet her and tell her about all the developments?

Vandiyathevan entered Madurandakan's private chambers lost in these thoughts.

'Hey soothsayer, lost in thoughts?' asked Madurandakan.

Vandiyathevan was surprised to be called a 'soothsayer' by Madurandakan.

What will the prince ask me? How do I answer, if he asks me to foretell the future? How to escape from him and meet Princess Kundavai?

'What is the future of that young saint who was singing those hymns?'

'A very good future! A spiritual destiny mingled with royal destiny. Kings and queens will honor that youth. His name will remain in fame!' Vandiyathevan spoke this in some sort of a blind guess.

'What about my destiny?'

'Your destiny also is similar to his; a religious fortune mingled with royal fortune! But it is much better than his fortune.'

'Explain a little more clearly!'

Vandiyathevan needed time to cook up something. 'Let me light up the lamp, meditate and look into the incense fumes. You will have to be seated in front of the flame. Then I will look into the future and tell you more clearly.'

Madurandakan was very excited: he ordered his men to bring a lamp and embers for the incense. Two low stools were placed opposite each other with a lamp in the middle. The prince sat eagerly on one seat. Vandiyathevan took his place opposite with eyes closed in meditation for some minutes. His lips mumbled some meaningless incantations. He shook his body in a shiver and pretended to be possessed by some spirit. With wide open eyes, he looked into the flame of the oil lamp. After some minutes he spoke:

'Prince, yours is not an ordinary fortune, what I see in this flame is astonishing!'

'What are you seeing in there? Tell me!' ordered Madurandakan impatiently.

'There... as far as my eyes can see, crowned princes are waiting in line. Ministers and nobles line the opposite side. People are crowding everywhere, cheering loudly about something.'

'Tell me! Tell me what they are cheering about!'

'A tiger-flag flies sky-high in the middle of that crowd. A beautiful golden throne is in the middle of a large hall decorated like a heavenly palace. On the table is a golden platter on which is placed a jeweled crown that shines like a million suns. Heavenly nymphs are standing on both sides of that throne holding white deer tail fans. Prince, the preparations for a coronation are all ready.'

'Whose coronation? Tell it man!'

Vandiyathevan looked at Madurandakan before he looked back into the flame. 'Sir, it looks like your coronation. Ah! What is this? A woman with unkempt, unbraided hair comes between you and the throne. "No!" she stops you. You are pushing her away... and.... Ah! What is this? Why is the smoke growing cloudy? I cannot see anything more.'

'Look! Look carefully. See what happens next.'

'Prince, forgive me! A smoke screen hides everything.'

'Look into it again. Have you seen her before?'

'Prince, the woman is gone; you are gone; so is the throne, the crown and the crowds. There is someone with powerful magic in this palace. They have cast their spells and prevented me from seeing anything. Oh dear! My face is burning and my eyes are stinging!'

Vandiyathevan buried his face in his hands. Only after several minutes did he look up.

Every blood vessel in Madurandakan's face turned red with uncontrollable anger. His eyes were bloodshot.

'Look again! Tell me!' ordered Prince Madurandakan.

'It's no use, Prince. A scene that vanishes won't come back immediately. It will appear only after a few days. Now I can see another scene. People are in some confusion; they are angry. A messenger comes with the news that someone of the royal family was drowned at sea. Poor fellow, the people are about to lynch that messenger.

Prince, if any such thing ever happens, you must not venture amidst the people. Be careful if you have to go out at such times.'

'Who was it that drowned?'

'I cannot hear the name in all the noise. That scene is gone.'

A footman came to announce that the Queen Mother was waiting for her son. Madurandakan decided to shower all his anger on his mother!

'Sir! I have a splitting headache. Please give me permission to go out for a while,' asked Vandiythevan.

22

Timely Help

Pinakapani, the son of the Palayarai doctor was envious of Vandiyathevan. His envy increased when Poonkulali refused his love whereas she was very cordial with Vandiyathevan.

Therefore, he turned a betrayer and told the soldiers who had come in search of him about the whereabouts of Vandiyathevan.

As Paluvoor soldiers were unable to capture Vandiyathevan in Kodikkarai, they took his accomplice Pinakapani to Tanjore. That bitter experience in jail infuriated him all the more. Young Queen Nandini freed him from prison before Princess Kundavai could and thus, earned his loyalty. He was waiting for a chance to take revenge on Vandiyathevan.

He got an opportunity when Nandini engaged Pinakapani to spy on Vandiyathevan on her behalf when he came to Palayarai to meet Princess Kundavai.

'You must keep a careful watch on Vandiyathevan. Find out who he meets and what he says. I will reward you well,' instructed Nandini to Pinakapani.

Junior Paluvettarayar also gave him the same assignment, to spy on Vandiyathevan. 'Help us catch that traitor-spy; I will place you in our secret service.'

Pinakapani was no more interested in medicine. He wandered in the streets of Palayarai to identify Vandiyathevan. Like a mad fool, he would run up to strangers and peer at their faces. 'Not you!' he would say. People construed him to be mad. He ignored such comments expecting the favour from the Paluvettarayars.

Pinakapani saw Vandiyathevan enter Palayarai Palace in Madurandakan's retinue. He followed the retinue and noticed Vandiyathevan in the audience chamber amidst the reception given to the young saint Naraiyur Nambi. Our old friend, Alvarkkadiyan was keeping an eye on both of them.

When Vandiyathevan came out of the palace after donning the role of a soothsayer and predicting Madurandakan's future, Pinakapani, called out to him, 'Brother, who are you?'

Pretending not to hear him, Vandiyathevan said, 'What did you ask?'

'I asked who you are.'

'You ask who I am? Which I? Are you asking about this body of mine made of five elements? Or about the soul in this body?' After saying these words, Vandiyathevan quickly mounted his horse and left.

Pinakapani's suspicion was confirmed. He complained to the officer in charge of the city guards. The chief sent two men with him to look for the spy. Soon they found Vandiyathevan in a market square.

'He is the spy! Arrest him!' shouted Pinakapani.

'Don't trust him. I am the soothsayer of Prince Madurandakan.'

'No, he's lying! Arrest him!'

Alvarkkadiyan appeared in the crowd asking loudly, 'Where is Prince Madurandakan's soothsayer?'

'Here I am!' answered Vandiyathevan.

'No! He is a spy!' shouted Pinakapani.

Alvarkkadiyan said, 'You prove that you are a soothsayer and then come with me.'

'How do I prove that?'

'Two messengers are bringing some urgent news. Tell us what news they bring.'

Vandiyathevan looked at some horsemen approaching and said, 'They bring news about some ocean calamity affecting the royal family.'

The messengers confirmed Vandiyathevan's news.

'Yes, we bring the sad news of Prince Arulmoli who was lost in the whirlwind while trying to save someone in the deep sea.'

On hearing this, the crowd started cursing the Paluvettarayar brothers for deliberately drowning the prince.

Meanwhile, Alvarkkadiyan moved the crowd aside making way for the messengers to get to the palace. The growing mob followed them.

'Sir, that was a timely help! You have saved me. Thank you,' said Vandiyathevan.

'This has become your habit. You get into some problem and someone has to come to your rescue!' Alvarkkadiyan dragged Vandiyathevan towards the boathouse behind the Palayarai Palace.

A beautiful woman could be seen on the boat. Vandiyathevan's heart skipped a beat when he saw her.

23

Mother and Son

Prince Madurandakan went to his mother's chamber cursing her mentally.

Why should I be born to such a mother!

But when he saw his mother's serene face, he became quiet. His mother blessed him and seated him by her side

'Madurandaka! How is my daughter-in-law? How are your in-laws?'

'All are fine, why bother about them?' mumbled the son.

'Did you see the emperor before you left Tanjore? How is his health?'

'Yes, I saw him. But his health deteriorates day by day. The pain in his mind is much more than the pain in his body.'

'What is the cause of his agony?'

'Those who covet other's belongings will naturally suffer mental agony.'

'What do you mean?'

'What else? Is it not a sin to sit on a throne that rightfully belongs to me for all these years?' asked Madurandakan.

'My son, your mind was as white as milk. I don't know how it has become so poisoned,' said his mother.

'No one poisoned me. Am I an idiot to listen to others?'

'Even the most intelligent can be misled by ill advice. Kooni's ill advice changed the mind of Empress Kaikeyi of the epic against her beloved Rama. Are you not aware of that?'

'Yes, a woman's mind can be changed by ill advice. Tell me why did you asked me to come here!'

'Son, before I explain why I called you, I must tell you the story of how I married your father. Please listen to me.'

'When I was young, I was deeply spiritual. My father, that is your grandfather, was an important chieftain of Malapadi. Our clan was very ancient.

Even in my teenage, I was always offering prayers and performing meditation apart from my service to humanity. I was least interested in marriage. But somehow, I got married to your father who was also deeply spiritual.

Your father and I devoted our lives to the service of God. Neither of us wanted any children. There was an important reason for that. I never thought a day would come to explain all this to you. Listen carefully.'

Prince Madurandakan was listening with rapt attention.

Queen Mother continued talking to her son,

'Son, when your father Kandaraditya ascended the Chola throne, there was a crisis in the empire. You know the greatness of your grandfather, Emperor Paranthaka. His empire spread from Lanka in the south to the banks of river Krishna in the north. But, during the last years of his life he faced several setbacks.

Destiny made your father bear the burden of this Chola kingship. Emperor Paranthaka was hurt by several setbacks; the invasions; the deaths of his children. When he was on his deathbed, he called for your father requesting him to accept the burden of ruling this country. Your unwilling father had to accept the throne. Your grandfather was concerned about the succession after your father. Men who had gone in search of your uncle's son, Sundara Chola, brought him back to Tanjore. Emperor Paranthaka had a lot of affection for his grandson Sundara Chola and he had raised him personally. All the nobles felt the Cholas would regain their glory through Sundara. Because of this, the emperor wanted to crown your father as king and Sundara as crown prince simultaneously, giving the right of succession to the descendants of Sundara.

Your father was fully resolved to fulfil the wishes of the dying Emperor Paranthaka and leave no obstructions to Sundara Chola and his descendants ascending the throne. You and I are bound to fulfil the wishes of such a saintly man.'

Madurandakan intervened now.

'How can that be, Mother? My father never spoke about it to me.'

'Son, when your father died you were a mere baby. As promised, I raised you in a spiritual way with no worldly attachments. You have deviated from the path of devotion with the desire to sit on the Chola throne. Our enemies have poisoned your pure heart. I will be at peace if you deny all these rumours.'

Prince Madurandakan jumped up with fury.

'No enemy has poisoned me. How can those who want to crown me be my enemies? Mother you are my real enemy. Are you a mother? Why do you want to take away a kingdom that rightfully belongs to me? You say that it is my father's wish. Where is the proof for all that? I don't believe you! I won't listen even if my father comes back from heaven. I throw away the holy beads I am wearing now, you may pick it up if you want.' Prince Madurandakan spoke as if possessed.

Queen Mother closed her eyes. After he finished his shouting, she opened her serene eyes.

'My son! You spoke about the nature of motherhood; even a monster will not harm its offspring.

I too will protect you in a similar fashion. There are other reasons for you to give up the kingdom. If you covet the kingdom, you will become the enemy of Sundara Chola's children, Aditya Karikalan and Arulmoli, who are very valiant. You are not trained in warfare. All Chola armies will support the sons of Sundara Chola.

The Chola people are extremely fond of the emperor and his sons. Once, the people were fond of you also. Ever since you allied yourself with the Paluvettarayars, you lost popularity.'

'Mother, I am not bothered by issues of popularity and people's approval! People will show devotion to whoever sits on the throne.'

'Son, your advisors have not even taught you the rudiments of politics. No king can rule for long without the people's support...'

Even as they were talking, they heard a huge noise outside the palace. Wails, curses, angry shouts, a thousand questioning voices mingled with each other into a roar that rose like a hurricane.

'My son! A grave calamity awaits the Chola Empire, the first signs of that calamity is visible now. You stay here. I will go out to find out the cause of this stormy commotion.'

24

Angry Mob

As soon as Vandiyathevan neared the boat, he recognized the beautiful maiden to be Princess Kundavai.

'Princess Kundavai has been waiting for long. Break the news of Prince Arulmoli's safety without mincing words. I have to go now,' saying this, Alvarkkadiyan left.

Vandiyathevan was astonished:

How does this man know the prince is safe? He is a born spy unlike me.

With such thoughts, he got into the boat. On seeing the princess's beautiful face, he forgot everything: the world around him, his troubles and his successful mission.

The boat danced on the water and Vandiyathevan's heart also danced.

'Sir, was your mission successful? Where is the prince now? Is he well and safe? Who takes care of him?'

Vandiyathevan answered, 'My mission was successful. I have brought back the prince from Lanka overcoming all barriers. He has the delirious fever. But he is in the safe hands of the boatgirl Poonkulali and her cousin, the garden-keeper, Chendan Amudan.' Vandiyathevan continued to narrate his experiences in Lanka and Kodikkarai.

Suddenly they heard a loud noise. It was a collective wail from a thousand voices. Both Vandiyathevan and Princess Kundavai turned towards that noise. The deaf boatman continued to row the boat.

Kundavai said worriedly, 'It looks like an angry mob has gathered outside the palace.'

25

An Angel with Joy and Grief

Vanathi's beauty is something beyond description. Vanathi's nature, like her beauty, swung from one extreme to another in no time. At one time she would be distressed and at another she would be immersed in joy—singing and dancing all day without any care.

Today, she was distressed. Princess Kundavai was not there and all the other girls in the palace were teasing her. She couldn't bear it.

A few years after Vanathi was born, her mother died. Her father, the younger chieftain of Kodumbalur showered all his love on her but that did not last long. Even his only daughter could not stop him from going to the battlefield. He died a heroic death at the Lankan battlefield. Vanathi became inconsolable. As a parentless girl, she grew up in the luxury of Kodumbalur Palace. Some consoled her saying, 'Don't grieve my child; your father will be born as your son and will make you a proud mother by his great deeds.' Vanathi comforted herself with the thoughts of her unborn son. When she came of age, she realized that she could have a child only through marriage.

After she shifted to the Palayarai Palace, a major change happened in her life and attitude. Kundavai was her source of inspiration.

It was at this time she met Ponniyin Selvan for the first time and her joy became boundless. Princess Kundavai could read Vanathi's mind and showered her love on her. She was with her all the time. She made her understand that marrying Prince Arulmoli was not an impossible dream and encouraged the love she had for the prince.

The astrologer's predictions about Vanathi's son fanned her desires, her dream castle was growing in size.

There is already enmity between the clans of Paluvettarayars and the Kodumbalurs. Will the Paluvettarayars allow me to marry the prince? Nandini hates Kundavai, there is every reason that hatred could be directed to me as well.

She was distressed at the thought of Kundavai's mysterious disappearances.

She went in search of Princess Kundavai. She found the princess holding a secret meeting with Vandiyathevan.

Just then, a girl called Varini came running to Vanathi.

'Ponniyin Selvan was drowned in the sea,' she announced.

Vanathi froze.

All the girls were crying and screaming. Looking at Vanathi they commented, 'Unlucky devil, the prince lost his life because of her ill luck.'

Vanathi could not bear that blame. She ran towards the canal at the backyard of the palace.

She decided to plunge into the canal to meet the prince and she fell into the water. She began to sink in the water.

What followed resembled a dream. They rescued Vanathi and took her to a large hall. Ponniyin Selvan welcomed Vanathi, celestial conches started playing. Flowers were showered on them. The prince and Vanathi exchanged garlands and became man and wife. Unable to bear the happiness, she fainted. Two hands lifted her; it was Ponniyin Selvan. The prince hugged her and kissed her; initially she thought it was Ponniyin Selvan but when she felt bangles on the hands that lifted her, she realized it was Princess Kundavai.

'Sister, why didn't you come to my wedding?'

26

Nandini, My Stepsister

Vanathi was in a semi-conscious state. She mumbled to herself, 'Why should she save me? I can hear her talking to somebody. Who is it? What are they talking about?'

'Thank God she has been saved…' said Kundavai.

'Princess, it would have been better if her life had ended on a good note,' said Vandiyathevan.

'Who is this person who talks with such concern for me? Oh! The young man we met at astrologer's house,' mumbled Vanathi.

'Sir, why are you so heartless? Don't you know how much I have struggled to bring her up?'

'Princess, did you listen to her? She said something about marrying the prince.'

'Yes, she did. Her love has gone deep into her being.'

'That's not good for the girl. She might get disappointed.'

'Why? Marrying the prince is not just a dream in her mind, it is my will too.'

'Even then it may not happen.'

'Why? You said just now that the pPrince is safe in the Buddhist Monastery in Nagapattinam.'

'Thank God! He is safe in Nagapattinam! It's good that I was also saved,' thought Vanathi to herself.

'Yes Princess, the prince is safe. But what is the guarantee that he will accept this girl?'

'My brother will never go against me. My word is divine law for him.'

'Please include me in that list. I know he will never go against your word. He is not interested in the crown. If you insist, he may even agree to be the king. But to marry this girl…'

'Do you think he will reject this beautiful angel?'

'Princess, this girl is a perfect angel but there is a chance that the prince's heart belongs to some other woman.'

'I don't understand.'

'I saw with my own eyes…'

'Go ahead, tell me, I will listen, however painful it may be.'

'Didn't I tell you about the boatgirl Poonkulali? She is the one who took me to Lanka on her boat. She is the one who saved the prince and me in the sea. She is the one who has taken the prince to the monastery. She will lay down a thousand lives…'

'So what? After all she is only a boatgirl.'

'Oh! Is the boatgirl so cheap? The blood that runs in her body is also red and not black. Her heart also beats the same as that of the prince. Her love is pure. The prince also believes that. Now let us take my case. If only I could open up my heart and show who is there in it…'

'No! No! Don't do that. Let it be safe.'

'Why don't you tell me about the dangers you encountered in Lanka?'

'Yes, Princess! In Anuradapura, the front portion of a mansion collapsed suddenly. We would have been crushed to death. An old woman saved the life of the prince.'

'How old?'

'Old enough to be your mother. She is also mute.'

'Please, tell me more about her.'

'She closely resembles the young queen of Paluvoor, Nandini.'

'Oh my God! My suspicion is confirmed! I also suspected Nandini could be my stepsister. Cruel are the ways of destiny.'

Vanathi was fully conscious now; she decided to stay alive at least to prove that her love for the prince was greater than the boatgirl's love.

27

The Prime Minister Arrives

A large crowd consisting of men and women, young and old, were all crying and cursing the Paluvettarayars. The palace guards could not control the crowd. They pushed aside the guards and entered the front yard of the palace. It was like a small leak in the dam, growing in size and flooding the vicinity. The conversation between the Queen Mother and Prince Madurandakan was interrupted by the ruckus at the gates. As the Queen Mother walked towards the balcony, the crowd turned silent to greet the divine-looking Queen Mother with folded hands.

'Queen Mother, where is our Prince Arulmoli?'

'Where is Ponniyin Selvan?'

'Where is our darling Arulmoli?'

The Queen Mother was shocked. She did not know anything. She could only guess that Ponniyin Selvan was in danger.

What danger? Did the Paluvettarayars do something to cause a perennial strain?

Meanwhile, horsemen from Tanjore entered the grounds with great difficulty. With her permission, they broke the news of the prince's drowning in the sea in the process of rescuing the soldiers in the ship. They also announced that the emperor wanted them to come to Tanjore immediately.

The moment the Queen Mother heard these words, tears poured from her eyes and the people also started crying more.

'Queen Mother! Don't go to Tanjore. Let Princess Kundavai remain here. Let us bring the emperor here.'

'Ponniyin Selvan was not drowned in the sea. The Paluvettarayars must have killed him.'

Kundavai also appeared and explained the situation. Kundavai thought about the options before her. She could not tell them that the prince was alive for security reasons. At the same time, the crowd had to be pacified. Otherwise, the consequences would be disastrous. By that time Alvarkkadiyan and Vandiyathevan joined the crowd. The princess signaled to Alvarkkadiyan to come up to the balcony. She whispered something into his ears. He waved his hands requesting the crowd to be silent and announced in a majestic voice,

'Even the princess doesn't believe the news of Ponniyin Selvan drowning. Once Mother Cauvery saved child Arulmoli. She believes that the Ocean Princess would do the same again. She asked the soothsayer who has also confirmed her views. The princess will make arrangements to find the prince. Meanwhile, she requests you to remain calm and leave the palace.'

The whole crowd heaved a sigh of relief.

'Where is the soothsayer? We want to hear what the soothsayer has to say!'

'It is true that there was a major threat to the prince's life. But he is now safe and will return soon,' Vandhiyathevan told the crowd.

'You are not a soothsayer. You are a spy!'

It was the doctor's son, Pinakapani, who had failed in his earlier attempts to get Vandiyathevan arrested.

'Are you calling me a spy? Whose spy am I?'

'You are Paluvettarayar's spy.'

'What did you say?' roared Vandiyathevan and sprang on the doctor's son and a fiery fistfight followed to the delight of the crowd.

At the same moment came the voice of the herald announcing the arrival of the prime minister. The crowd stepped aside in reverence.

28

Prime Minister's Appeal

The prime minister appeared before the crowd waving his hands. He also bowed to the Queen Mother and Princess Kundavai. On seeing Vandiyathevan and the doctor's son engaged in a fistfight, the prime minister ordered their arrest.

Alvarkkadiyan signaled to Vandiyathevan to accept without protest. The prime minster appealed to the people to disperse quietly announcing that search parties had already been set in motion to find the prince and also assured that he would bring the emperor to Palayarai. Pacified by the words of the prime minister, the crowd dispersed. The prime minister then had a chat with the Queen Mother after sending away Princess Kundavai.

'I am upset by the recent events. Any more unpleasant news?' asked Queen Mother.

'I have brought some news, but whether it is good or bad depends on how you look at it,' said the prime minister.

'See how my son Madurandakan has changed in the recent past. You didn't make any efforts to change his mind.'

'Queen Mother! No need to change his mind. I have come here to change yours.'

'What?'

'Queen, Madurandakan feels that the Chola throne belongs to him. He wants to succeed the emperor immediately. Nothing wrong in it. Better to go with him. I came here on the orders of the emperor. The emperor wants to crown Prince Madurandakan as the new emperor and retire. He wants your approval.'

'The emperor may approve it but I won't. I won't go against the wishes of my late husband. Don't you know the deep secrets about the succession rights of the Chola throne?'

'Yes, I know. I also know certain things that you don't know. That is the reason I agreed to be the emperor's messenger. There will be a great war between brothers and cousins, uncles and nephews as in the great Mahabharata war. I now seek your help to prevent this impending war from happening in this Chola Empire.'

Queen Mother was lost in deep thought.

'Prime Minister, you have confused my mind. But I won't go against the wishes of my husband.'

'Then Queen, I have no choice but to reveal the truth; the truth which you are not aware of.'

Presicely at this moment, Prince Madurandakan entered with a big bang. Ignoring the prime minister, he spoke to his mother, 'Mother, is it true that Prince Arulmoli is dead?'

The prime minister left, requesting the mother to console her son. Madurandakan then blurted, 'This man is my first enemy; he has come to you to give you ill advice.'

The prime minister heard the pungent words but did not react.

The prime minister then visited Princess Kundavai and showered his blessings,

'May you be blessed with a valiant husband.'

'Sir, is this the right time for this kind of a blessing?'

'Princess, what kind of blessings were you expecting?'

'We are all deeply concerned about Arulmoli.'

'But I see no trace of grief on your face.'

'Born in a family of great warriors; why should I cry like an ordinary woman during a crisis?'

'No, I only request you to comfort people like me who lack courage.'

'Acharya, who am I to console you? Your heart is made of diamond.'

'See what havoc you have caused by your interference in the nation's governance?'

'Oh! My God! That is a grave charge.'

'I visited Lanka to prevail upon Ponniyin Selavan to continue his stay there. But you sent a message asking him to return immediately. The whole world knows your action has led to this tragedy. The darling of the people is no more. Revolts are happening throughout the country just like the one at the gates of your palace today and you are responsible for all this.'

'How can you say that the prince left Lanka only on receiving my message? The Paluvettarayars also had sent two shiploads of men to arrest him.'

'Yes dear, if that had been the only reason, we could easily blame the Paluvettarayars. Moreover, their ships were destroyed so they can say that you are responsible for the prince's death.'

Princess Kundavai was shocked and then she spoke, 'Acharya, I have a request.'

'A request? Command me, Devi!'

'When you entered, you saw two men fighting at the gates. They were arrested. Please release one of them.'

'Who is that lucky man who has your sympathy?'

'The messenger I sent to Lanka.'

'But he has been charged with a grave offence, Devi. He pushed the prince into the sea. You trusted him but your trust is misplaced. He could be the enemy's spy.'

'Never! He is my elder brother's trustworthy messenger too.'

'Even your elder brother might have been duped or the messenger who started well could have been manipulated on the way by the enemies. The other man in the mob also called him a spy.'

'Acharya, that messenger is Vandiyathevan from the noble Vaanar clan. The other person who called him a spy is the doctor's son—who has now fallen in Nandini's net of passion.'

'Oh, then how did Vandiyathevan get the signet ring of the Paluvoor family?'

'That devil, Nandini, gave the signet ring to him.'

'So, he could also be Nandini's spy.'

'How?'

'Vandiyathevan got the signet ring from Nandini when he entered the Tanjore Fort and her chambers. She hid him in the underground treasury and sent him out. On returning from Lanka, he met her on the way here. Even after the meeting, the signet ring remains with him. Still, you believe him?'

Kundavai appeared perplexed.

29

Spying on the Spy

After hearing the charges leveled against Vandiyathevan, Princess Kundavai was quiet for a while.

'Princess, do you still believe him?' asked the prime minister

'Sir! I've nothing to say.'

'We live in hard times surrounded by foes. We cannot trust anybody easily.'

'How did you gather so many details about my messenger?'

'Oh, my dear! I have a thousand ears and eyes! My men are everywhere. One of the personal bodyguards of the junior queen is my spy. I have spies in the dreaded Paluvoor palace also. I have many men like Alvarkkadiyan who gather news from all directions.'

Kundavai was in deep thought,

Perhaps he knows that the prince is safe in the Buddhist Monastery at Nagapattinam. However, I don't feel like revealing that to the prime minister.

'Acharya, my messenger cannot be Nandini's spy. Please release him.'

'I will think about it, Princess. That girl Nandini has some magical powers. Madurandakan who was deeply spiritual is now thirsting for power after coming in contact with her. Kandamaran and Parthiban have become her slaves. They have even agreed to the proposal to divide the Chola Empire into two—one half for Karikalan and the other for Madurandakan.'

'Oh my God! How can they ever think of dividing the empire? What kind of magical powers does she possess?'

'Ok! Let me know how you are so sure that Vandiyathevan could not have fallen for her charms?'

'Acharya! Something tells me my messenger won't betray me.'

'We have to send a trustworthy messenger to Kanchi immediately. Nandini is several times more dangerous than a venomous snake. She is planning to destroy the entire Chola clan. She has instigated Sambuvarayar to invite your elder brother Prince Karikalan to Kadamboor Palace. She is planning to marry off Sambuvarayar's daughter to Karikalan. She proposes bifurcation of the Chola Empire to arrive at a compromise formula. But these are all her outward moves. No one knows her inner motives. We should prevent Karikalan from going to Kadamboor Palace. Let us send Vandiyathevan as messenger to Karikalan. If Karikalan ignores our warning, Vandiyathevan should accompany the prince to Kadamboor and he should never leave Karikalan.'

'Acharya! Why should we prevent Karikalan from meeting Nandini?'

'Nandini and the personal bodyguards of the deceased Pandiya king, Veerapandiya, have all vowed to eliminate the Chola clan. Nandini is funding them from our treasury under the control of Senior Paluvettarayar.'

'What about Prince Arulmoli?'

'Special prayers are being performed in all the temples in the kingdom for the safe return of Prince Arulmoli especially the Buddhist Monastery in Nagapattinam.'

'Acharya, it appears that Senior Paluvettarayar is not happy with the Buddhist Monastery at Nagapattinam because the monks in Lanka offered the throne to Prince Arulmoli. He might take action against them. So, I request you to give special protection to that monastery.'

'Sure, Princess. Let us use Vandiyathevan as our messenger.'

The princess felt happy about it.

'Yes, we can send him but he is rash and emotional.'

'Then I will send my disciple Alvarkkadiyan also with him. He is known for his composure and poise.'

Kundavai started thinking, *Even God Himself does not know what is in the mind of the prime minister. He is sending a spy to spy on that spy.*

30

Change in Vanathi's Attitude

Kundavai was going to free Vandiyathevan from the prison and send him on the important mission of guarding the crown prince, Aditya Karikalan. She informed Vanathi, 'I am in the middle of an important task. I will be back soon, wait here.'

'Sister! Permit me to go to my home town Kodumbalur.'

'Why leave me Vanathi? Are you angry?'

'Not at all sister! I have to offer a special prayer to our family deity in my hometown.'

'Stay here, Vanathi. I will make arrangements for special prayers there on your behalf.'

'Sister, I have another reason. My father's brother, the elder chieftain of Kodumbalur, is returning home from Lanka. I want to hear directly from him about what happened in Lanka.'

'Now I understand why you want to leave. You want to know about Ponniyin Selvan from your uncle.'

'Is that so wrong, sister?'

'Not at all. But leaving me alone here at this time of… Tell me the truth, Vanathi, how did you fall into the canal? Did you faint or did you deliberately jump into it?'

'Why should I? I fainted and fell down, you saved me.'

'Anyhow, don't worry, Vanathi. I'm sure Prince Arulmoli's life is not in danger.'

'Let us hope so, sister. Let me go now.'

Kundavai was surprised. This girl had become so bold all of a sudden!

'The whole nation is in chaos. I will arrange proper security guards for you.'

'No need, sister. Who will dare to hurt Princess Kundavai's best friend? Let me also visit the Kumbakonam astrologer on the way.'

'I too want to consult him but you are in a hurry.'

'No sister, this time I will meet him alone.'

Kundavai was astonished all the more. *This girl has changed a lot. No point in holding her back*

'Ok, Vanathi! But come back soon.'

31

Two Prisons

After Vanathi left, Kundavai visited the prison where Vandiyathevan was confined in a separate cell. She found him happily singing a song.

'Oh! My dear
The stars above
Forget themselves
And become elated
On seeing you'

Kundavai cleared her throat and only then did Vandiyathevan spring up to receive her.

'Princess, please be seated.'

'Where do I sit?'

'This is your palace. Everything happens at your command. You may choose any seat.'

'Why were you so furious with the doctor's son?'

'Princess, I have my own reasons. In Kodikkarai he tried to brand me as the enemy's spy and hand me over to Paluvettarayar's soldiers. Again, he called me Paluvoor Queen's spy before the mob at the Palayarai palace gates only to turn the people gathered there against me.'

'He spoke the truth. Are you not Nandini's spy?'

'Princess, I have vowed to speak only the truth.'

'Excellent! You have taken that vow after meeting Nandini on the way here.'

'No, I had taken the vow much earlier. When I uttered lies,

everyone believed me. No one believes me now if I say the prince is safe in Nagapattinam.'

'It is better if you don't commit such blunders.'

'I promise I won't commit any more blunders. Let me go away and lead my own life.'

'No release for you. You will be imprisoned here for life.'

Vandiyathevan laughed, 'You think I cannot escape from this prison?'

The princess tossed a pointed glance at him, 'I know you are smart enough to escape from jails. I have the authority to have the gates opened. You can walk out of this prison. But there is another prison from where you can never escape. The prison of my heart...'

'Princess, I have no land of my own. All the glories of my clan are past now. You are the darling daughter of the great emperor.'

'Sir! Nothing can stop true love.'

'Princess, I have already suffered a lot. I had to hide myself, travel in stealth, do many tricks and speak lies. I can't do this anymore. Please let me go.'

'My best friend Vanathi has already let me down. She has gone to her hometown. You too want to go away from me.'

'Princess, kings and princes are waiting in line to hold your golden hands.'

Princess Kundavai extended her hands. Vandiyathevan could not believe it. With reluctance he held her hands and touched his eyes with her beautiful hands. He was in a state of unbound ecstasy.

'After holding your hands, my hands will never hold any other man's hands.'

Vandiyathevan became speechless when he saw the tear-laden eyes of the princess.

'Your life is at risk because of your daring deeds. Just imagine what will happen to me if you land in trouble...'

'Princess, how can I be a coward?'

'Cowardice is different from caution. Even our prime minister has no doubts about your valour. But he suspects you to be a spy of Nandini.'

'Let me meet the prime minister and answer him like I answered the doctor's son.'

'The prime minister does not know how to fight. His weapon is his sharp intellect. In this country, he is second only to the emperor. He is my father's childhood friend. Even the Paluvettarayars won't oppose him openly.'

'That is because they are guilty, whereas I am not. Why should I fear him? Please tell me what I should do to win his confidence?'

'The prime minister wants you to be my messenger to Kanchi.'

'Princess, send me anywhere but not to Kanchi. That is what my inner voice says.'

'Is that the voice of the junior queen of Paluvoor?'

'Not at all! Would I ever listen to that venomous snake?'

'Please don't use derisive words for her.'

'Why this sudden change?'

'Yes, my mind has completely changed after you brought the news from Lanka.'

'Oh God! That means I have to act with utmost reverence in her presence. Even if she gives me that sword that she was worshipping and commands me to behead someone, I should have to obey her.'

'Give her respect but there's no need to listen to ill advice. One more request. Once you return from Kanchi, you have to leave for Lanka again to bring that mute woman here. You alone can do that.'

'It's easier to bring a typhoon than her. But princess, please don't send me to Kanchi.

The crown prince in Kanchi is my boss. If he comes to know that the emperor is in a state of imprisonment and about the conspiracy of the Paluvettarayars, he will be furious. Also, if the news about Ponniyin Selvan has reached him, he will be marching to Tanjore with his army.'

'I am sending you to Kanchi precisely for that reason, to prevent him from leaving Kanchi. Even if he has left Kanchi, please be with him always. You should be the protective shield to my brother. If needed, disclose the true identity of Nandini. It is your responsibility to make him believe.'

'Princess, I promise to do my best. But if I fail in my mission, please don't blame me.'

'Whether you win or lose I will never release you from the prison of my heart!'

32

Mother Nature

Vandiyatheven was riding along the river Arasalar the next day carrying the letter of the prime minister; enjoying the beautiful scenery on the way. Mother Earth dressed in glittering green appeared very young and beautiful. But how many shades of green were there on her dress?

The paddy crops wore a shade of green. The leaves of the banyan tree were of another shade of green while those of the pipal tree yet another. Next came the shade of green chosen by the luscious lotus plants in the ponds. The plantain leaves displayed a catchy shade of green while the coconut trees were of the rare shade of ivory green. There was also the green shade of the tender grass, the green colour of the clear water and the green colour of the hopping frogs.

In contrast to the green silk of Mother Earth were varied dashing colour of the flowers. Vandiyathevan's eyes were drinking in the beauty of nature. The croaking sound of the frogs and the buzzing of the insects filled his mind with a vague sense of grief though there were enough reasons for him to rejoice. He had won the love of Princess Kundavai, the goddess of beauty. At the same time the fear of the uncertainty of life haunted his mind.

What is this world? Full of sorcerers like Ravidasan, devils like Nandini, conspirators like the Paluvettarayars, betrayers like Kandamaran and Parthiban.

Thank god I'm somehow saved from all dangers, but now caught in the mother of all dangers. Yes, the prime minister has assigned me the most dangerous assignment. My mission is to stop the devil Nandini from executing her murderous plan and come out of it successful and unscathed.

He saw a cluster of trees with exposed roots which looked like deadly crocodiles. He dismounted from his horse and walked along the river bank.

This is where I first glimpsed the golden face of Princess Kundavai.

He saw the beautiful face of the princess in the water. Suddenly a deep male voice came from the top of the tree. It was Alvarkkadiyan sitting on the branch of the tall tree.

At the same moment, Vandiyathevan saw a palanquin moving along the river bank.

'Could it be Princess Kundavai?'

'Young man! Why poke your nose in others' matters? Come on, let us continue our journey. You reach river Kollidam and wait for me,' repied Alvarkkadiyan

Vandiyathevan suspected that Alvarkkadiyan was involved in some secret mission. That is why he avoided him. Vandiyathevan saw black clouds gathering in the sky and asked Alvarkkadiyan whether it would rain.

'I don't know astrology. But there is a fair chance of rain.'

Vandiyathevan spurred his horse. Alvarkkadiyan's words, 'I don't know astrology', reminded him of the Kumbakonam astrologer. The astrologer's house was on the way. He decided to visit him and find out the dangers around him and his future.

Vandiyathevan crossed the palanquin which he had seen a little while ago. He noticed the Kodumbalur princess, Vanathi, sitting inside. Though he wanted to stop the horse, he didn't do it.

Why is she traveling only with a lone maid and two palanquin bearers in these troubled times without proper security?

He caught another strange sight—two Kalamukha ascetics keenly looking at the palanquin from a hiding spot.

Why are they looking at the palanquin? What are they going to do?

He was reminded of Alvarkkadiyan's advice:

Why poke your nose in others' matters?

By then he had reached the Kumbakonam astrologer's house.

33

Kidnapping of Vanathi

When Vandiyathevan entered the astrologer's house for the second time, all the sweet memories of his first meeting with Princess Kundavai flashed in his mind. On seeing Vandiyathevan, the astrologer received him with a smile.

'Welcome, young man! Aren't you Vandiyathevan?'

'Yes, sir. Your predictions may go off the mark at times but not your memory.'

The next moment, Vanathi and her maid entered the astrologer's house.

Vandiyathevan said, 'Princess! Had I known you were coming here I would have avoided my visit to the astrologer's house. Princess, you please finish your work with the astrologer. I will wait till then.'

'Actually, I did not come to see the astrologer. I have lost faith in astrology.'

The astrologer was offended.

'One day you will realize the power of my astrology.'

'Let us see,' said Vanathi and then she turned to Vandiyathevan, 'I saw you on your horse and thought you would stop to have a word with me.'

'Princess! I thought it would be disrespectful for your stature if I were to talk to you on the way. Is there anything I can do for you now?'

'I have decided to embrace Buddhism and become a monk. Now I'm going to the Buddhist Monastery at Nagapattinam. Please come with me to Nagapattinam.'

Vandiyathevan was shocked,

'I am sorry Princess, what you ask is beyond my means at this time. The prime minister and the princess have asked me to go to Kanchi with an important message.'

'Sir, if you can't help me, it's fine, god is with me. Astrologer, let me take leave of you.'

Vanathi got into the palanquin and left the place.

She was timid till recently but now this girl has become bold enough to travel alone and that too in the night!

'What is the reason for this change?'

Vandiyathevan started to think.

Is it about Ponniyin Selvan drowning in the sea? Or the news about his presence in the Nagapattinam monastery? Or the news about Poonkulali which I shared with Kundavai? What could it be? Why should she choose the Nagapattinam monastery of all the places?

He took leave of the astrologer and resumed his journey.

Vandiyathevan saw Vanathi's palanquin at a distance on the road. Suddenly he heard the loud scream of a woman. He was shocked to find that the palanquin suddenly disappeared. He spurred his horse on. He found Vanathi's maid bound to a tree and her mouth had been stuffed with a cloth. Vandiyathevan jumped off his horse and ran up to her to release her from the ropes.

'What happened to the princess?'

The maid was not coherent and Vandiyathevan inferred something from her words:

'Some Kalamukha ascetics hit and gagged me and ran away with the palanquin along with the princess.'

Vandiyathevan mounted his horse. The horse galloped down the rough road unmindful of the bumps and bushes on the way.

It was a new moon day. The whole area was in total darkness. Not a single star was to be seen in the sky. Only the fireflies provided some light. Kundavai's friend was in danger. It was his duty to save her. Vandiyathevan decided to try his best. Even after traveling a long distance, he could not see the palanquin. He heard some sounds at a distance. He rode slowly, examining the path. He looked around. There was no sign of the palanquin.

Maybe I am wasting my time.

Suddenly he heard the hoofbeats of a horse. He saw a lone horseman riding ahead of him. Vandiyathevan did not want to expose himself; he looked around and saw a dilapidated building. He reached the place and hid himself behind a blank wall and peered hard to see that horse. He was startled when he heard a voice.

'Who is that?' said a royal tone.

'Your Excellency! It is I, your slave.' Somebody responded to the royal voice from behind a tree with a torch in hand. In the light of the torch, Vandiyathevan identified the rider on the horse as Prince Madurandakan! The bright light of the torch frightened the horse which lifted its forelegs and toppled the prince into a canal adjacent to the forest path before galloping away wildly.

The torch bearer ran behind the horse shouting, 'Oh! My God! Our king! Our king!'

The torchbearer tripped and fell into the canal. The torch in his hand went out. It started drizzling. Vandiyathevan heard a cacophony of sounds—the swaying of trees, drizzling of rain, croaking of frogs, the call for help from some men and the sound of horses.

Vandiyathevan was worried about the safety of the future king and was lost in deep thought.

What should I do? Should I go after Vanathi or help the prince in distress. Why should I be caught in this hopeless situation? Why can't I find the highway to Kanchi?

However, he decided to return to the dilapidated building and stay there till the rain stopped instead of getting drenched. He was able to see a horse standing alone in the flash of lightning.

Madurandakan must be somewhere here. Why can't I help him?

'Is anybody there?' thundered Vandiyathevan, more thunderous than the sound of thunder. The downpour continued; he reached the dilapidated building by sheer intuition. He jumped off the horse and went inside the building.

He heard the sound of, 'Ma! Ma!' It was the voice of a child. Perhaps a child without a mother. Vandiyathevan walked towards the voice.

'Who is there?' he asked

'Who is there?' the child's voice replied

'It's me, what are you doing in the dark? Come out, the rain has stopped.'

A small child walked out. In the starlight Vandiyathevan saw that the small child was well dressed with a necklace made of gems around his neck.

The child must be from a royal household. Who is his mother? Why did the mother leave the child here?

Meanwhile the child also saw Vandiyathevan.

'You are not a horse. You are a man.'

The child noticed the horse.

'Is this for me? But I was told a palanquin would come for me.'

The child's words ignited Vandiyathevan's mind.

Who is this child? Who had promised to send a palanquin for this child?

'Why did your mother leave you here?'

'No, my mother did not leave me. Mother advised me but I ignored her and went running behind a horse. Meanwhile it started to rain and I went inside this building.'

'Are you not afraid to be alone in the dark?'

'No, I am used to darkness.'

'Are you afraid of the tiger?'

'I am not afraid. I am a fish. Fish will swallow the tiger.'

'Can a fish swallow the tiger?'

'I am no small fish. I am a shark. I can swallow tigers and lions.'

Vandiyathevan was astonished.

Who could have tutored the child like this?

Suddenly a crowd of men was coming towards them with burning torches. He also saw a palanquin in their midst. They were running towards the dilapidated building.

'They have all come along with the palanquin. I hate to go in a palanquin. Will you let me ride on your horse?'

Vanditathevan liked the child, his fearlessness and his commanding words. He felt like kissing the child.

'I have to go on urgent work to Kanchi.'

'Kanchi? That's where my enemy lives.'

Vandiyathevan was shocked. He wanted to leave immediately but the crowd came very close. He moved aside and stood near the wall under the cover of darkness. The child ran towards his mother and hugged her.

'Child, what you have done! Pandiya!'

Then came sorcerer Ravidasa and he spoke, 'Emperor! You frightened us all.'

The child laughed, 'Yes, I will frighten you. I asked for a horse but you have brought a palanquin.'

Soon the child was surrounded by Soman Sambavan, Idumban Kari and Thevaralan.

'Emperor! Why one horse? We will bring you a thousand horses. But please get into the palanquin now,' Soman Sambavan said with reverence.

'No! I will ride on that horse only,' the child pointed out to Vandiyathevan's horse. Only then did they notice the horse and its rider. Ravidasa was outraged and walked towards Vandiyathevan.

'Rogue! How did you come here?'

'Hi! Ghost, how did you manage to come here from Kodikkarai?'

Ravidasa laughed louder. The child intervened, 'I like this new man very much. He gave company when I was alone. Let him come with us.'

Ravidasa went back to the child.

'Emperor! Fine, we will take him with us. Please get into the palanquin just for today. Tomorrow, we will get a horse for you.'

Ravidasa went back to Vandiyathevan.

'Join us. You know all our secrets. We can't leave you here, come with us. If you refuse...you can't escape from us. Here are twenty of us.'

'Ok! Where are you going?' asked Vandiyathevan.

'Good! We are going to see the young queen of Paluvoor at the enemy's war memorial. Are you coming with us?'

Vandiyathevan agreed to join them to find more of their secrets. The child too got into the palanquin. Everyone began to proceed.

But he was troubled by the thoughts of Vanathi and Madurandakan. The strange procession continued and entered a dense forest near the enemy's war memorial.

34

Opportune Time

The war memorial built a hundred years ago was now in utter ruins in the midst of a dense forest. Vandiyathevan and the others reached the war memorial. They left Vandiyathevan and his horse near the side wall of the ruined memorial with instructions not to move an inch. Nobody could venture in or out of this place without help.

The others assembled in a circle a little way away near a bush. A man brought a throne from inside the memorial. The small boy—the little emperor—was asked to sit on the throne.

After some time, the young queen of Paluvoor arrived in her palanquin. But now she looked different and appeared like the fierce goddess, Durga Devi. Vandiyathevan had never seen her like that. When she came near, the boy ran into her arms and embraced her calling her 'mother' and asked,

'You are my mother, right? Not this lady.'

'Yes, dear!'

'Then why does she keep saying she is my mother?'

'She is the mother who brought you up.'

'Why are you not with me? Why should I be in a godforsaken place with her?'

'Only to fulfil your father's wishes dear! And avenge the death of the killers of your father.'

'I know…'

Nandini hugged and kissed him and parted the child from her. She pulled out the decorated sword and placed it on the throne.

'Can I take this sword in my hand?' asked the child.

Asking him to wait, Nandini addressed Ravidasa as army chief and continued her conversation.

'All along we have been patiently waiting for an opportune time. The time has come now. We are few in numbers but the Chola army is mighty. If you are rash, all our efforts will be wasted. It is only because of your patience; we are near our goal now. All of you can voice your opinion.'

Only Ravidasa spoke, 'Queen! It is your turn. We will simply abide by your words.'

'I have come here only for that. I have brought our little emperor along also for the same reason. The officials and chieftains of the Chola Empire are divided now. A war may break out anytime.'

'Queen! We understand you have arranged peace talks at Sambuvarayar's palace in Kadamboor to avoid that conflict.'

'Yes, you are right. Can you guess the reason?'

'Queen! I can't. Who can guess what's on a woman's mind?'

'I know you can't. Sundara Chola and his prime minister won't keep quiet. They will pacify the warring factions and achieve peace. Our mission will fail. That is the reason I have initiated the peace talk; our mission should be completed before the war.'

Nandini's words enthused all her men and they looked upon her in awe.

Ravidasa remarked, 'Splendid. Who is going to do that? When and how?'

'I have invited our first enemy for peace talks at Kadamboor Sambuvarayar's palace. When he arrives, let us fulfil our vow.'

All her men jumped with joy. Some played the drums. Vandiyathevan was startled as was his horse.

Ravidasa spoke, 'We are excited as the time has come to kill our first enemy. Please tell us who amongst us will have the honour of doing the great deed.'

Nandini addressed the little emperor, 'Darling, this noble sword belongs to your father. Hand it over to the person you like the most.'

The eyes of all, keenly watched the boy. The child looked at everyone twice or thrice and finally handed over the sword to Nandini.

35

Cunning Foxes

Nandini took the sword from the little emperor and held it closely to her chest. She then hugged her son. Everyone was shocked to see Nandini becoming so emotional. Shedding tears of joy, Nandini spoke, 'I am very happy the sword has come to me to avenge the death of our beloved king Veerapandiya.

Half of you come with me to Kadamboor, the others may leave the little emperor in our hiding place. Some of you wait in the vicinity of the Kadamboor Palace with horses. All of us should come out of the palace alive once our mission is over.'

Ravidasa spoke, 'Queen! Princess Kundavai and the prime minister have sent message…so our first enemy Aditya Karikalan may not come to the Kadamboor Palace.'

'I know that. That serpent Kundavai and that demon prime minister don't know Karikalan. If someone tells Karikalan not to do something, he will surely do it. He won't listen to others. It is his nature.'

'But, Queen, the message will never reach Karikalan.'

'What…?' asked Nandini with excitement.

'We have captured their messenger while he tried to kidnap our little emperor.'

'Bring him here,' ordered Nandini.

Two men went to Vandiyathevan who was fast asleep. He did not resist when they bound his hands with a long rope and dragged him to the queen.

On seeing Vandiyathevan, Nandini sported a seductive smile on her beautiful face.

'Oh! You again…' said Nandini.

'Yes Queen, it's me again. But this time I did not come on my own.'

The little emperor spoke, 'Ma! I like him. This man saved me from the ghosts in the dark. He has a fine horse. I want it. Why is he bound with ropes?'

Vandiyathevan teasingly said, 'Boy, don't interrupt while elders speak. Or else, the tiger will swallow you.'

'I'll swallow the tiger,' said the little emperor.

'But a fish cannot swallow a tiger,' said Vandiyathevan mischievously.

'See this fellow! How he reacts. We should never leave him alive,' roared Ravidasa.

'All of you move away. I want to get some news from him.'

She then whispered in the child's ear,

'Darling! Go with these men. I'll get the horse for you.'

Ravidasa and the others moved away with the boy.

Nandini looked at Vandiyathevan in the dim light of the torches.

'There is a bond between us. You cross my path often.'

'Yes, it is a very strong bond,' said Vandiyathevan indicating the ropes binding his hands.

'Stop joking. Did you come here intentionally or by chance?' asked Nandini.

'Neither, your men dragged me here.'

'Are you not happy to see me? You always want to get away from me.'

'No! I always feel sad to leave you. I know you are caught between that old man Paluvettarayar and these scary sorcerers. Order me. I will free you from the clutches of these people and take you away. I will take you to your mother in Lanka, roaming in the forests like an orphan.'

Nandini sighed in disappointment.

'To become an orphan like her? Soon I will let you know. But for now, please help me in my mission.'

'Depends on your mission. These crooks will use you and discard you.'

'You are wrong. Rather, I am going to use them for my purpose. I will make the little emperor or someone of my choice as the emperor of the mighty Chola Empire.'

'With the help of these cunning foxes? You can never win over the mighty Chola army with these foxes who hide during the day and come out only at night. Ridiculous!'

Nandini held her sword close to her heart and said,

'I have faith in my sword.'

'Queen! You will never use that sword.'

'Why? I may use it right now!'

Bending his head, Vandiyathevan said, 'I will consider myself lucky to be slain by your beautiful hands!'

'Be serious. What did that devil Kundavai do on hearing the death of Ponniyin Selvan?'

'She was sad. How can it be otherwise? All the women in this world are not heartless.'

'I understand that the Kodumbalur Princess tried to kill herself by jumping into the lake. Is that true?'

Suddenly remembering Vanathi, Vandiyathevan mumbled. *Oh my God! What would have happened to her?*'

But he remained silent.

Nandini spoke harshly, 'All right. I know you won't reveal anything. Are you going to prevent Prince Aditya Karikalan from coming to Kadamboor Palace?'

'I'll try my best to do that.'

'You will never succeed.'

'I never said I will. I only said I will try. Besides, it is very difficult to change his mind if he decides to do something.'

'You know him very well. I also know very well that you will never come to my side. You will always be with my enemies.'

'Who is your enemy?'

'That princess at Palayarai. Who else?'

'She is not your enemy. Let me reveal the truth…'

Nandini cut him short. 'Your truth is always a blatant lie. Keep it to yourself. My husband has gone to the banks of river Kollidam to attend the Kalamukha ascetics annual meeting. He will be back any moment. I have to return before that.' Then she clapped her hands.

Ravidasa came running, 'Queen! We will sacrifice this man in the sacred place and then leave.'

'Don't touch this man!' Nandini roared.

'I want to use him for many other things. Free him.'

'Queen! He has a horse. It is not wise to free him immediately.'

'Then bind him to the pillar. Let him take time to free himself.' So saying Nandini left the place.

Ravidasa and his men bound him to a pillar and left.

For Vandiyathevan, all that he had witnessed appeared like a wild dream. Owls hooted, wolves and foxes howled. It was pitch dark. He could only hear strange movements and could see nothing in the dense jungle. Among the various sounds suddenly Vandiyathevan heard the footsteps of someone approaching. His horse neighed in fright. He tried to loosen the knots around his wrists but in vain. He could clearly see a dark form approaching him. He gathered all his strength and kicked it when it came within his reach. It banged against the wall and fell. Then he heard two stones being rubbed against each other. Soon there was light. The form appeared holding a burning shrub in its hands. It was the form of a gory looking Kalamukha ascetic with long beard and hair.

36

Canvassing for Madurandakan

Vandiyathevan was shocked for a moment to see that ghastly looking ascetic at this time of the night in this godforsaken jungle. Soon his natural courage took over. The ascetic looked very familiar.

He came close to Vandiyathevan.

'I guess you are a spy.'

'How did you guess?'

'I saw some people leaving the forest. I know who they are. They must have suspected you to be a spy. That's why they have bound you.'

'I will tell you about that but first set me free,' said Vandiyathevan

'I will do so if you promise not to interfere in others' matters and do a hundred and eight push ups…'

Even before he could finish, Vandiyathevan freed his hands and knocked down the ascetic and sat on his chest. He pulled at his beard which came off in his hand!

In this fistfight, the torch had fallen down from the Kalamukha ascetic's hand but was still burning. Vandiyathevan picked it up and held near his face. It was not a Kalamukha ascetic, it was Alvarkkadiyan! Both started laughing.

'My dear fellow, what are you doing here?' asked Vandiyathevan.

'I came to help you. You can never get out of this jungle by yourself. You'll become a feast to the wolves.'

'Tell me why you were disguised like the Kalamukha ascetic and where were you earlier this evening.'

'Nothing much. I wanted to know what was happening at the Kalamukha's meeting. So, I disguised myself as one of them and went to the banks of river Kollidam. Their leader was there but one other important person expected did not come,' said Alvarkkadiyan.

'Were they expecting Prince Madurandakan?'

'How did you know?'

'We will have wonderful governance if Madurandakan ascends the throne,' said Vandiyathevan sarcastically.

'Why do you say that?'

'He could not even control the horse he was riding. How is he going to govern the empire?'

Alvarkkadiyan laughed and asked, 'Did you see him on the way?'

Vandiyathevan told him about the events he had witnessed earlier.

'Poor man! He had a very bad fall from the horse and must be badly wounded. Shall we look for him and help him?' finished Vandiyathevan.

'Why should we bother? Let us attend to our work.'

'What if Madurandakan is dead or battling for his life?'

'The prime minister will take care of it.'

'Is he aware of all this?'

'What a stupid question! Nothing happens in this empire without his knowledge.'

'Oh, so the prime minister knows about the conspiracy at Kadamboor Palace and about Prince Madurandakan taking part in the Kalamukha meeting!'

'Yes, otherwise he would not have sent me. And he also ensured Madurandakan did not attend that meeting. By now some of the prime minister's men would have found Madurandakan and sent him safely to Tanjore. Come let us go,' said Alvarkkadiyan.

'I am not coming with you. I have to find Princess Vanathi. She was kidnapped by someone.'

'Why are you so concerned about her?'

'She is the best friend of Princess Kundavai and prospective bride of Prince Arulmoli. I am afraid the Kalamukha ascetics may harm her,' replied Vandiyathevan

'Don't worry about that. The Kodumbalur clan belongs to the Kalamukha sect. When they come to know that she is a Kodumbalur Princess they will not harm her. They will escort her safely to her palace,' said Alvarkkadiyan.

'Oh my God! How come I did not know all this?'

'Almost all the big names in this empire belong to the Kalamukha sect. Chieftains, army chiefs and so on. That's why Paluvettarayar wanted to gather their support for Madurandakan in today's meeting. Unfortunately, he could not be there. Are you coming with me or not?'

Vandiyathevan got up reluctantly. The distant howl of a dog was heard.

37

Vanathi's Shock

Princess Vanathi was on her way to the Buddhist Monastery at Nagapattinam to see the ailing Prince Arulmoli. The sun was setting, kissing the darkness. Her mind was in a confused state.

Will the Buddhist monks allow a young girl into their monastery? Even if permitted, will they allow me to serve him? Once I express my love to the prince, I'll be happy to die. Or I will renounce this world and become a Buddhist nun.

When she parted the screens of her palanquin, she noticed Kalamukha ascetics hiding behind the tall trees. Suddenly they came running towards the palanquin, tied her maid to the tree and ordered the bearers to carry the palanquin to a deserted place. When she screamed one of the men said,

'Don't shout, girl. If you answer us, we will drop you at your destination.'

Vanathi's fears were confirmed. A big change happened in her. So far, she had been a doe. Suddenly she turned into a lioness.

'It's none of your business. I won't answer.'

'No need to answer us. We know. You are traveling all alone to see Prince Arulmoli. Tell us where he is hiding. We won't hurt you.'

'Do whatever you want. You can't get any information from me.'

These crooks must be the henchmen of the conspirators. I won't mind their torture for the sake of the prince.

It was this thought that gave her that unusual courage.

Vanathi's attention was diverted by a long procession of elephants, horses and palanquins. Vanathi thought it was a divine intervention and said, 'Beware! Look up, there comes our prime minister. If I scream, he will hear me. Run away! Otherwise…'

'Yes! It is our prime minister. It is on his orders only we have captured you here.'

Vanathi was shocked.

An eerie silence followed punctuated only by the croaking frogs. Vanathi could play a trick and escape those ascetics but definitely not the prime minister. His intelligence and his political astuteness were famous throughout the empire. None could dare to defy him. Even the softest whispers in the Empire would reach his ears. Even the emperor won't forgive any slandering against the prime minister. Princess Kundavai too adored him. But she was perplexed by his action.

Why should the powerful prime minister order my capture? Perhaps those ascetics are lying. Whatever may be. I won't open my mouth.

The prime minster's palanquin came nearer. He got down and started talking to Vanathi.

'Oh! It's you Princess of Kodumbalur, daughter of my good friend. My intention is not to trouble you. I will ask you one or two questions. I will be happy if you answer them honestly and you may go.'

'Most revered Prime Minister of this empire. I am happy to see you here at this hour. These men say you ordered them to capture me. I don't believe it.'

'My dear child! What they say is true.'

'The greatest prime minister the world has ever known. You are responsible for law and order in this great empire. Even when the emperor errs, you have the right to admonish him. Is it a right deed to abduct an innocent girl going on her way and threaten her with torture? I thought the Chola roads were safe for young women. But this is quite shocking…'

The normally eloquent prime minister was nonplussed. However, he spoke in a tough voice, 'Don't display your eloquence. I have my own reasons. It all depends on your answer to my questions. I had information that a lady was traveling to Nagapattinam to meet a proclaimed offender. I had ordered my men to capture her. My men might have made a mistake.'

Vanathi was furious. However, she controlled her emotions. Instead of directly answering the question Vanathi asked, 'Most respected, Sir! Are you accusing Prince Arulmoli, the darling son of the Chola Empire of sedition? Is it not a crime to talk like that? Most respected Sir, even if I am tortured to death I won't part with any information.'

'I admire your determination, Princess of Kodumbalur. You said you won't answer my questions but you have already unwittingly parted with some crucial information. So no harm in telling something more.'

Vanathi was shocked.

Did I unknowingly say anything? No, I said nothing. This old man is trying to elicit some information from me.

She felt more courageous now.

The prime minster continued speaking, 'I only said a lady was traveling to Nagapattinam to meet an offender. I never mentioned anything about the prince. Since you spoke about him, I am obliged to explain. The prince abused his position and tried to grab the Lankan throne for himself. Is that not sedition? He spread rumours that he was drowned. If you try to help the prince, you will be charged as a party to the crime. Please tell where is the prince?'

Now Vanathi's pent up anger burst out as she could not bear the slandering on Ponniyin Selvan.

'Sir! Whatever you said is not true. You are maligning the prince. He did not jump into the sea to escape, that was a noble act to save his dying friend. He never conspired against the state.'

'Look girl, if people hear your passionate words in support of the prince, they will say that you two are lovers,' said the prime minister with a smile.

'Respected Sir, only half of that is true. Yes, I have given my heart to him, but I don't know if I am in his heart.'

'You know so many things, tell me where is Ponniyin Selvan?'

'Sir, the whole world knows whatever I said about the prince. No more information from me and no point in holding me any longer.'

Suddenly there was a roll of thunder and lightning.

'Yes! You won't answer me. You have to face the punishment for it. You see that elephant over there?'

Vanathi looked in the direction indicated. There was a huge elephant looking like a dark hillock. She was taken near the elephant and she closed her eyes.

The elephant will throw me down and trample me. It is a good end for this orphan...

The elephant lifted her up swirling its trunk; luckily, she fell unconscious.

The elephant lifted unconscious Vanathi and placed her on the lap of Princess Kundavai who was on the elephant.

The prime minister spoke to Princess Kundavai,

'It is already late evening. It's time for both of you to leave. Princess, you called Vanathi a coward but I have never seen a more courageous girl than her,' laughed the prime minister.

'She traveled alone, unmindful of the dangers. I tried to stop her but in vain. That's why I sought your help. Today's experience will make her bolder.'

'It is all your training. God be with you!' said the prime minister as he got into his palanquin.

The elephant with the pincesses also started moving, well guarded by soldiers.

Vanathi felt the cool air on her face.

The way to heaven is so cool and pleasant! My face is resting on a very soft cushion. I feel secure in my mother's lap! My only regret is I couldn't see my beloved Prince Arulmoli.

Seeing Vanathi stir in her sleep, Kundavai caressed her cheek and called, 'Vanathi, Vanathi.'

'Sister are you also coming to heaven with me?' asked Vanathi.

'What is the hurry to go to heaven?'

'Oh! But I had very bad nightmare. A few fanatics attacked me on the orders of the prime minister and an elephant was about to trample me.'

'The elephant did not harm you. You are safe on my lap and we are on our way to Anaimangalam to search for the prince.'

They reached the coastal town of Anaimangalam near Nagapattinam early in the morning.

38

Madurandakan's Gratitude

A few minutes after the depature of the prime minister, it started to rain heavily. Suddenly he heard a moaning sound coming from the bushes. He got down from his palanquin and went near the bush. He was shocked to see Prince Madurandakan moaning in pain. When he was about to lift him, he screamed.

'Oh! I'm gone. My legs are gone.'

'What happened to you prince?'

'My legs are broken. I can't walk. I can't even stand,' wailed Prince Madurandakan.

'How did this accident happen? Why are you lying here in this wilderness in the heavy downpour? What happened to your retinue?'

'Prime Minister, I brought no one with me. I came alone on a horse. There was lightning and thunder followed by heavy rain. The horse was frightened and ran amock. I was caught in the branches of this tree and fell down. I don't know whether my bones are broken. Thank God, you have come here at the right time.'

'It is all because of the good deeds of your father I happened to pass this way. Let us go to my home nearby.'

The palanquin was brought near the prince. The prince was lifted into the palanquin which gently moved on. They reached the prime minister's mansion.

On examination they found no fracture. After having some food the prime minister asked him to go to sleep.

'Prime Minister! You have wronged me in several ways but all that has been compensated today. I will be grateful to you and I will make you my prime minister when I ascend the Chola throne.'

'Thank you, Prince, my duty is to provide advice and help anyone who belongs to the great Chola clan. Hence no need for thanks. You said that I have wronged you but to my knowledge I have done nothing against you. I will make amends if you explain.'

'Prime Minister, you are very smart. The whole world knows your smartness in the game of politics but don't exhibit your smartness.'

The prime minister smiled, 'Yes, my dear Prince, I request you not to go horse riding alone. The best way is to travel by a palanquin. Times are bad now. You saw it today with your own eyes at Palayarai. Better to travel in a closed palanquin; even better if it is the palanquin of the junior queen of Paluvoor. None will suspect.'

Madurandakan was stunned with fear. He struggled to compose himself. He then blurted out:

'How dare you suggest that I should travel in junior queen's palanquin. Prime Minister, why insult me?'

'Prince, I never intended to insult you. I said that you used to travel in that mode frequently. From when did you start thinking like this? Perhaps after the trip to Sambuvarayar's palace…?'

Madurandakan was even more stunned, 'Prime Minister, I… Kadamboor Palace…I…' he blabbered.

'Prince, didn't you visit Kadamboor Palace along with our finance minister, Senior Paluvettarayar? I vividly remember your travels in junior queen's palanquin. Honestly, I don't like that. Young men like you should always travel on horse or elephant. But you need proper training. Soon I will make arrangements for that.'

'Don't think that I don't know how to ride a horse. In view of your age and the help I got from you today, I forgive you.'

'Oh! Prince I am pleased by your patience. Like the earth that bears its offenders, those who want to rule should have this quality of the earth.'

'What are you talking about? Are you accusing me of a desire to rule this empire?' his lips quivered. His fear manifested as anger.

The prime minister was unruffled. 'Oh! Prince, why take it as an accusation? If you want to rule this Empire how can that be an offence? You are born in the clan of great warriors. You have every right to ascend the throne. Nothing wrong in your aspirations. If somebody tells you that you can get the crown only by conspiracies please don't believe it. Prince, please listen. Your parents had planned something else for you. For a while you accepted their plan. But now your mind has changed. You can express your desire to the emperor. Instead of doing that, you came alone in the dark on a new moon night to seek the support of the Kalamukha ascetics. It doesn't look nice. Likewise, there is no need to congregate at the palace of Sambuvarayar like a band of thieves and conspire against the emperor. Those who advise you on these lines are your real foes. Beware of them.'

Madurandakan was surprised and confused, 'Prime Minister, how do you know all these things? Tell me which betrayer acted like my friend and gave information to you?'

'No point to trying to know about my sources. I have eyes and ears everywhere. Nothing happens in this empire without my knowledge.'

'Does the emperor know all these things?'

'No, my eyes and ears inform me of many things but unless the occasion warrants, they will not come out.'

'Yes. Your heart holds many dangerous secrets. If only they come out, the empire will be shaken.'

The prime minister did not mind the malice in his voice.

'The emperor is my best friend, but he himself does not know all the secrets of my heart. Prince, I will never say anything about your activities to the emperor.'

'Prime Minister, what is the reason for the sudden love towards this innocent prince?'

'Prince, my love for you is not sudden. So far I had no opportunity to show my love to you.'

'You got that golden opportunity today? Please don't think that I don't know anything. I am not that gullible. You worked against me even when I was in my mother's womb. Don't think you are the only one with eyes and ears everywhere.'

Prime minster though astonished talked gently, 'Yes, prince, I am proud of you.'

'My stars are on the ascent. You are suddenly fond of me. You hate Crown Prince Aditya Karikalan. You were planning to make Prince Arulmoli the king. Since Arulmoli is dead now, you are leaning towards me. I will forget all your wrongs and I will make you my prime minister as soon as I become the king.'

'Prince, your words make me happy.'

39

Where Am I?

Ponniyin Selvan remained unconscious for three days with delirious fever. The monks in the monastery at Nagapattinam took excellent care of him giving him medicines regularly and frequently giving him water to avoid dehydration. On the fourth day he felt better and was fully conscious and his mind was fresh and active. He started recollecting the chain of events starting from the time he left Lanka till he and Vandiyathevan were struggling for their lives on the turbulent ocean.

A monk came to his room and offered him milk mixed with some herbs.

'Master, where am I now? How long have I been here?'

The monk looked at the prince and smiled, 'Prince! You are now at our monastery in Nagapattinam. You came here three days ago with delirious fever. We are blessed to serve you.'

'Master, I'm also very fortunate. I have always been longing to visit this monastery. Once while passing this way in the boat, we saw this monastery from outside. Now by divine grace I am here.'

The chief monk replied, 'Prince! No need to thank us. Lord Buddha has ordained to take care of the sick. We are indeed indebted to the Chola clan, especially your father, your sister and yourself for all the patronage given to us. We are immensely pleased by your efforts to renovate the Buddhist Monasteries in Lanka.'

'Master, left to myself I would prefer heaven to this treacherous world.'

'Prince! When the time comes, angels will take you to heaven.

You have a lot to do on this earth now.'

'Yes Master! I want to do a lot on this earth. I have seen the monasteries in Anuradapura. How great they are! I want to rebuild this monastery also on those lines. I will also build a huge temple in Tanjore, so high that it kisses the sky. People born in this divine Tamil land after a thousand years will be amazed by its architecture and magnificence.'

After this passionate speech, the prince fell down in his bed and the monk gently touched his forehead and spoke softly, 'Prince, you will do great deeds to the utter astonishment of this world. But for that you need to have complete rest now.'

'Master, your medicines have worked wonders. I feel perfectly fine now.'

'Prince, currently the people in this kingdom are restless. Everyone from infants to the elderly are praying for your safety. You need some rest. If you are careless the fever may relapse. If only you had heard the screams and wails of the people, when they heard that you had drowned in the sea while traveling from Lanka to Kodikkarai...'

'Master, why should people grieve? Was there news that I was dead? Who brought that news? Why?'

'I don't know who brought the news. One morning it spread like wild-fire throughout the kingdom that you had drowned in the sea when you traveled from Lanka to Kodikkarai. Senior Paluvettarayar started a massive hunt to find you. You were not found. That made the people infer that you really had drowned in the sea. When I was plunged in grief, you were brought here by a young man and woman.'

'Do you know who they are?'

'One Amudan and a Poonkulali.'

'Did they tell why I was brought here? Did you tell anybody that I was here?'

'Those who brought you here told me I should not reveal anything about you. I too thought that it was prudent to keep your stay here a secret.'

'Master! I smell something foul. My father, the emperor ordered for my arrest. Obeying his orders, I left Lanka, so many things happened subsequently. Now it appears that somebody wants to accuse me of violating the orders of the emperor. They also spread rumours that I had drowned. Even you keeping me here will be construed a serious offence. Please send me back to Tanjore.'

'Prince, we are not bothered by the royal consequences. Your safety is more important for us.'

'Master, I'm touched by your love but I wonder how you accepted me blindly without enquiry.'

'What is to be enquired? Our foremost task was to save you. Your sister Kundavai had also said that you might come here one day for a short stay.'

'Oh! Really? Did the princess say that?'

'Yes, she informed me. Amudan brought you here as per your sister's wishes.'

'Master, I want to meet those people who brought me here.'

'Prince! They are here in this city and they come here everyday to enquire about you. They will come anytime now.'

'Master, I won't stay on here even for a second. I don't want this ancient monastery to be harmed on my account.'

The chief monk smiled.

'I won't hold you here against your wishes you may leave any time... A boat is waiting for you at the canal.'

'Where will the boat take me?'

'That is something you have to decide.'

'Have they both come back? Did they say anything?'

'Yes, they did.'

'If you sail for thirty minutes, you will reach a place called Nandi resthouse. They also told me that two ladies are waiting there to see you.'

The monk took the prince to the boat. Amudan and Poonkulali were delighted to see the prince walking majestically. As soon as the prince boarded the boat, the chief monk said, 'Please come again and complete your treatment. We will be happy to serve you again.'

'Master, I will definitely come back to thank all the monks in the monastery.'

As soon as the boat started moving, the prince keenly watched the faces of Amudan and Poonkulali alternately.

'Please tell me who is waiting for me at Nandi resthouse?'

Poonkulali remained silent. Amudan replied that Princess Kundavai and the Kodumbalur Princess were waiting there. The boat reached Nandi Pavilion.

40

Let Us Save Our Country

The boat came near the beautiful Nandi resthouse located at a picturesque setting. Amudan and Poonkulali parked the boat and hid it.

'Brother, you have lost a lot of weight,' spoke Kundavai with eyes full of tears.

'Sister, let us discuss about me later. Why are you crying? I think you are hurt by the recent developments. Otherwise, you would not have sent that kind of a message to me.'

'Yes, brother. I want to share many things with you.'

Ponniyin Selvan touched his sister's feet reverentially and Kundavai blessed him.

'Brother, I should not have dragged you here. The delirious fever has played havoc on your health.'

'Sister, don't feel upset. Even at the height of my fever, you were ruling my mind. I have to say something about the messenger you had sent. What a brave and valiant man! He came out with flying colours in all my tests. Sister, where is he?'

Kundavai was cheered by his words.

'He has completed his mission and gone back to see Aditya Karkalan.'

'Sister, he has gone back on his word. He told me that he would not go back to Kanchi and that he would stay with us here.'

'How is that possible? What he can do here? If you love him so much, why don't you ask the emperor to give him back the country ruled by his ancestors?'

'Sister, that is a small fiefdom for him. What will that great warrior do with that small territory?'

'Brother, you refused the Lankan throne. Do you think he would also refuse his kingdom?'

The prince smiled, 'Sister, I refused the Lankan throne in the presence of witnesses. Yet I have been charged with sedition.'

'Brother, you should have accepted the Lankan throne. Then nobody could arrest you.'

'Sister, how can I go against our father's wishes?'

'Our father would have been happy had you accepted the Lankan crown. He would have easily divided the remaining Chola Empire between our brother and Madurandakan. Our father expects your help in this process. He sent for you earlier. Since you didn't come, he ordered your arrest to ensure your coming. The emperor knows very well that you refused the throne.'

Sister, I won't tolerate the division of our empire. Nothing more shameful than that. Rather we can give the whole empire to our uncle Madurandakan.

Sister, I'm least interested in my marriage but you are building dream castles about my son. If your Vanathi has any such funny idea of marrying me, tell her it won't happen at all. I don't want a kingdom. Rather I would prefer to be an officer in charge of temple renovation and temple building.'

'Brother, that's crazy thinking! Let that be for now, our empire is surrounded by great danger right now, from both external and internal enemies posing as friends. Let us join our hands to save our country from that danger.'

Brother and sister were deeply immersed in their conversation. Vanathi decided to go for a walk and look around the garden.

'Sister, do you remember me almost drowning in the river Cauvery when I was a child? You remember Mother Cauvery rescued me and suddenly vanished?'

'How could I forget it, brother? It is only because of that that you are fondly called as Ponniyin Selvan.'

'I saw Mother Cauvery, the one who saved me from death. She saved my life several times in Lanka. The love she has for me...Oh! My God...even if I give all the fourteen worlds to her, it won't be equal to her love.'

'You are right. Her heart is full of love for our father, now she has transferred all that love to you.'

'Do you know that she is our stepmother?'

'Brother, I guessed it from what our father and Vandiyathevan said after returning from Lanka. The throne lawfully belongs to the mute woman. Her love is something very selfless and unique.'

'Sister, do you think it is possible for one to look exactly like another person?'

'Why not brother?'

'Sister, Vandiyathevan told me that our stepmother looks exactly like the junior queen of Paluvoor, Nandini. What do you think, sister?'

'Yes, I have seen Nandini but I have not seen our stepmother. I guessed from what our father said.'

'Our father himself has talked about it with you? What did he say?'

'A few days ago Vanathi and I had been to Tanjore. He narrated all the happenings in Lanka during his younger days. The feeling of guilt is killing our father. We should produce our stepmother before him otherwise he will never find peace in this life.'

'I am extremely grieved to see her roaming like a mad woman in the forests of Lanka. I want to bring her to our father.'

'Our father often screams at night imagining that the dead girl is coming as a ghost to haunt him.'

'How do you know that?'

'Vanathi told me.'

Princess Kundavai narrated all that Vanathi had witnessed.

'What is the nature of the form that appeared before our father? Is it a hallucination?'

'Brother, it was not hallucination. What Vanathi saw was real. A midnight drama was enacted by Nandini before our father. I guessed the truth even at that time. My views were confirmed by what you and Vandiyathevan said about that mute woman.'

'Sister, what is the motive of the junior queen?'

'Nandini has her doubts about her birth and her parents. Once the emperor fainted after seeing her. Our father has not seen Nandini as Senior Paluvettarayar's wife because he was very unhappy when Senior married at this age. He forbade him to bring his young wife in his presence. Nandini knows that and avoids appearing before the emperor. Perhaps she is enacting this drama for reasons unknown.'

'Do you think she does not know the truth?'

'Brother, I don't know. Even the creator cannot assess her mind. All men who see her fall for her instantly. The only one gentleman who does not fall for her beauty is Vandiyathevan. That is why I have sent Vandiyathevan to our brother with a message to avoid that meeting with Nandini. Karikalan does not know that Nandini is our elder sister. I don't know whether Nandini knows her true identity.'

'Is she really our sister?'

'No doubt about it. When we were children, I hated Nandini and I insulted her. I was jealous of her beauty. I prevented you and Karikalan from talking to her. I have insulted her several times after she became the wife of the old man of Paluvoor. Now my mind has changed and I would like to atone for my sins. My sister had to marry an old man and my heart bleeds for her. Nandini should have lived in our palace with all royal luxuries like a princess.'

'Sister, why was Nandini brought up in some stranger's house like an orphan? Why did she marry Senior Paluvettarayar at his old age?'

'Brother! There are only two persons who know all the secrets—our grandmother Queen Sembian Madevi and our prime minister—but they won't share their secrets. There is no urgency now to dig out those dark secrets. Our immediate task is to prevent the defamation of the Chola clan at the hands of Nandini. She also keeps a unique sword with the fish symbol and worships it everyday. I am deeply worried that Nandini might harm the Chola clan without even knowing she is a part of it.'

'Why don't we tell all this to Nandini herself?'

'That will make her more furious.'

'Sister, let us inform everything to our father immediately. Can we leave for Tanjore now?'

'No brother we should not. I'm leaving for Tanjore in a few days. You have to stay in the Buddhist Monastery in Nagapattinam for some more time.'

'Why sister? Why should I be like an outlaw violating the orders of the emperor?'

'Yes, your visit to Tanjore will create chaos. The emperor's orders of arrest have angered the people. If they see you now, they will become very emotional and they will raise their voice demanding that you should be made the king immediately.

You stay in Nagapattinam for one more week. I will inform our father that you have come and then I will send a message to you.'

41

Love Has No Reason

While prince Arulmoli and Kundavai were deep in conversation, there was a parallel conversation going on between Poonkulali and Amudan.

'Amuda I will ask you something. Will you give me an honest answer?'

'Poonkulali, nothing but truth will pass through my lips.'

'Why did you fall in love with me Amuda?'

'Does love have any reason, dear?'

'There has to be some reason for your love.'

'Poonkulali, nobody in this world knows how love starts and what makes it happen.'

'People are attracted by beauty?'

'Yes, they are. Beauty fans the desire or lust but that is not true love.'

'But your friend Vandiyathevan often praises my beauty.'

'Maybe, but he never fell in love with you. He also praises the beauty of the Paluvoor Queen quite often but he never fell in love with her either.'

'Yes, I know the reason. The warrior has lost his heart to Princess Kundavai.'

'This shows that there is no connection between beauty and love. You are several times more beautiful than Princess Kundavai. Even Nandini is no match for you in beauty. You have such divine beauty.'

Poonkulali remained silent for a while. Soft words flowed from her, 'Amuda, suppose I don't love you. What will you do?'

'I will be patient. I will wait for your mind to change.'
'Ok, but what if my mind does not change?'
'I will try to forget you. I will divert my mind to God.'
'Amuda, your love for me is not genuine.'
'How do you say that?'
'If your love is real, you should kill me when I refuse.'
'Poonkulali, mine is divine love of sattvik nature. The love you refer to is that of a demon. Taking revenge is not human nature. Rejection of love will be painful initially but we should suffer it. I would never subscribe to your views.'
'Amuda, you are an angel like our elder aunt.'
'Who is that? You have never talked about her till now.'
'Our aunt is in Lanka roaming around like a mad woman because of the betrayal of a Chola Prince. When I came to know of my aunt's story, my blood was boiling. I almost decided to join the Pandiya group and avenge the royal clan that cheated my aunt. But I gave up that idea when I came to know my aunt's heart. She not only forgave her betrayer but also saved his son, not just once but several times.'

Poonkulali picked up a stone. Almost at the same time a huge bull was coming out of the dense coconut grove. Poonkulali transferred all her anger to the majestic bull and threw the stone on the beast. The bull became furious and turned around and started running fast towards Vanathi who was walking alone towards the palanquin. When she saw the raging bull Vanathi was frightened. The bull came very close to her. She had no other option than to move backward and fell into the canal screaming for help.

The prince and princess looked in the direction of the scream. The prince sprang to the canal like a flash of lightning and held the falling Vanathi in his arms.

For a second Kundavai's heart almost stopped but when she saw Prince Arulmoli holding Vanathi in his arms, she was delighted.

'Sister, take your friend from me.'
'Brother how could you touch a young girl?'

'Sister, is it a crime to save her? Thank God she does not know that I am holding her. She fainted even before I caught her.'

Vanathi opened her eyes laughing loudly and jumped from the arms of the prince.

'Sister, please ask her why she pretended to be unconscious?' asked the prince.

'Sister, I didn't pretend. When he touched me, I felt very shy and closed my eyes. That's all. I won't faint in future. But let him not forget the help he received from me today.'

'What? She helped me? It was the other way round!'

Kundavai was also perplexed.

'Sister has your friend lost her mind?'

'My mind is perfectly alright. Only your brother is confused. When he was a child, he was rescued by a woman when he fell into the river. Recently a boatgirl rescued him when he fell into the stormy sea. It has become habitual for him to get into danger and then be rescued by some woman or the other. Now I helped him get rid of that bad name. I gave him the credit of boldly rescuing a woman from danger. I made him more chivalrous and courageous. He should be grateful to me.' Vanathi laughed. Kundavai laughed too. The prince also burst out laughing. The sound of their laughter echoed in all directions, even Poonkulali and Amudan in the boat heard their laughter.

'Amuda, do you hear those three crazy people laughing?'

Poonkulali burst out laughing at these words. Amudan also started laughing. The birds in the coconut grove also laughed in their own way. The bull also left, laughing in its own way. The waves in the ocean and the cool breeze coming from the ocean also joined their laughter with its soft voice.

42

Aditya Karikalan at Kedilam River

Many rivers and tributaries run through the Chola Empire making it very fertile. River Kedilam was one of them. That part of the region where the highway crosses the river Kedilam was always buzzing with activity throughout the year. All the travellers would stop there for rest and food.

On one such day there was noise followed by a cloud of dust, startling the travelers. They saw the royal paraphernalia—elephants, horses, palanquins, chariots—and heard a soldier heralding the arrival of Crown Prince Aditya Karikalan.

People ran to catch a glimpse of the crown prince. They stood on both sides of the road to give him a royal reception. They were delighted to see Prince Aditya Karikalan with the golden crown on his head shining like a million suns.

The crown prince was followed by Prince Parthiban and Kandamaran and Thirukkovalur Malayaman, the emperor's father-in-law and Karikalan's grandfather followed the prince in a chariot along with their retinue.

The grandfather and the grandson dismounted from their chariots and walked towards the platform under a huge pipal tree.

Thirukkovalur Malayaman started giving a sermon to his grandson: 'Aditya, you were born twenty-four years ago at Thirukkovalur. We had a grand celebration to mark your birth, attended by a royal gathering from your clan, my clan and all the chieftains of the Chola and neighbouring kings and thirty thousand soldiers. I hosted a grand feast for all of them. No words to describe the grandeur of the feast—grander than even the coronation ceremony of your father. What my ancestors had accumulated in the treasury for a hundred years, I spent on the three-day-long celebrations to mark your birth.

Your great-grandfather Emperor Paranthaka, your grandfather's brother Kandaraditya and your father Sundara Chola had come. Your father was the only son to your grandfather Arinjaya Chola.

I insisted that you should be named after your grandfather's brother, Rajaditya, the greatest warrior. Some suggested to name you after your illustrious ancestor Karikala Vallavan. Finally, we arrived at a compromise by having the best of both the worlds—you were named Aditya Karikalan a combination of the two greatest warriors.

Look there, you can see the temple tower of Thirunavalur. Twenty-five years ago, Prince Rajaditya Chola had camped here to gather a large army and invade the provinces in the north. He chose this area between the two rivers Kedilam and Thenpennai to recruit men for the army and train them.

My child, you were not fortunate enough to witness the scene that unfolded. And those who saw it could never forget it. Several thousands of soldiers were recruited and trained for the war. Several other chieftains along with their armies, huge battalions of cavalry, armies of elephants and the three great infantry regiments of Kaikolas also camped along with us.

We had plenty of mock battles amongst ourselves for training. When elephants clashed against elephants, the sound resembled that of an earthquake. When the soldiers wielding shining spears rode on the horses, the resultant sound resembled the roar of the stormy oceans. When the soldiers shot a barrage of arrows in the air, the skies were covered by a screen of arrows. Scores of civilians would come there to witness the feat.

The people of this region were very good and known for their valour. As the army was stationed here, their agricultural activities suffered. But they did not mind. As a measure of gratitude to these people, Rajaditya ordered his soldiers to create a lot of lakes in these regions. The one person who derived the maximum benefit from that project was Kadamboor Sambuvarayar. In those days he used to be very humble and subservient. When I see his pride and vanity now, I am greatly surprised.'

Aditya Karikalan intervened.

'Grandpa, why worry about Sambuvarayar? Tell me about the great war at Thakkolam. How did our great army face defeat in spite of the vast arrangements and meticulous planning? You also took part in the war. You must have seen what happened at the great battlefield. Uncle Rajaditya, the greatest warriors of our times was heading such a mighty army. How come the enemies defeated him at Thakkolam?'

'My dear grandson, due to some reason, he could not leave the place as planned. Meanwhile, a war broke out in Lanka. A part of our army had to go there. So, the emperor decided to send the army to the north after the Lankan war was over. Rajaditya did not want to go against the words of his father, the then Chola Emperor. He waited patiently for the Lankan war to end. But the enemies were not patient. The King of the North, Kannara Thevan came with a huge army to invade the Chola Kingdom. His ally Boothukan, the Kanga King joined forces with him. Their huge armies appeared like a vast ocean eager to drown the Chola Kingdom. Our spies brought the devastating news of invasion.'

'Even that happened for good,' said Emperor Paranthaka. 'If our armies had travelled up to the north to fight the enemy, they would have been exhausted by the long journey reducing their enthusiasm to fight. Better to face the enemy on home ground and corner them on all the four sides.

Rajaditya was heading a huge army up North. After three days of travel, the armies clashed against each other at Thakkolam, two miles north from Kanchi.

We were outnumbered; their army was twice the size of ours. But there was none in the enemy side who was half as valiant as your elder uncle Rajaditya. The goddess of valour and the goddess of victory were on our side.

The war lasted for ten days. The enemy's side became weak quite soon. The enemies soon found out the reason. Wherever Rajaditya's elephant went proudly displaying the tiger-flag, our soldiers became excited and attacked the enemy with greater ferocity.

The enemies, knowing our strength, hatched a mean conspiracy which we came to know about only later. Suddenly the treacherous enemy, Kanga King Boothukan hoisted the white flag of peace on his elephant, lifting both his hands above his head repeating the words, "surrender". Rajaditya's heart melted when he saw the enemy king surrendering to him. He wanted to know whether the king of the northern provinces wanted to stop the war or was the Kanga King Boothukan surrendering alone.

He blew his conch and ordered his bodyguards to stand away. He allowed the enemy king, Boothukan, to come very close to him. He did so with folded hands and tearful eyes. Rajaditya's heart melted more and he asked, "What's the news?"

The treacherous king said that he had parted ways with Kannara Deva of the Twin Provinces because he refused to surrender. Rajaditya was furious and told him that he would never entertain a traitor on his side and advised him to go back to his ally Kannara Devan. As Rajaditya was talking, Boothukan committed the meanest treachery ever recorded in the history of wars. He took out this bow and shot a poisoned arrow into the chest of Rajaditya and flew away on his elephant. Nobody expected that sudden act of meaness and betrayal from Boothukan. Everything happened in a flash.

Rajaditya died while remaining seated on the elephant. It was the most devastating news for our army. Chieftains, generals and soldiers stopped fighting and started wailing. The enemy gained an upper hand. Soon our army was forced to retreat from the war. I am ashamed to say that I was one of those who fled the battle at that time. The enemy's army reached up to the bank of river Kedilam.

I started gathering an army on the slopes of the mountains. I came back here every now and then to drive away the enemy forces who had set up their base here. Even then the enemy did not leave this place for a long time. Kanchi was under their control. Three years ago, you reclaimed the city of Kanchi.'

'Grandpa, though I already know all about uncle Rajaditya's heroic deeds I love to hear them any number of times. Tell me, why did you remind me now about him?'

'My child, Rajaditya wanted to extend the Chola Empire up to the banks of river Ganges but he died of treachery without realizing his dream. Now the whole empire says that my grandson is as great as his illustrious ancestor Rajaditya. They say that you will fulfil Rajaditya's dreams. I don't want you to fall prey to treachery like he did. That's why I reminded you of his story.'

'Grandpa! My elder uncle lost his life because of mean treachery. But I am not going to war. I am just going to see my father's friends. I don't think they'll betray me.'

'My child, listen to me, as sage Thiruvalluvar says, internal enmity is more dangerous than the external one. You are now going in the midst of internal enemies feigning friendship. I tried my best to stop you. But you won't listen. They have called you to mediate on a dispute concerning the Chola Kingdom. I also learned that they are planning to get Sambuvarayar's daughter married to you. I also heard that they have a plan to divide the Chola Empire into two and give one half to you, while the other half goes to your uncle Madurandakan. I don't know what kind of conspiracy will be there in their partition plan. I will be here with my army and wait for you at the bank of the river. If you suspect anybody or anything at Sambuvarayar's palace, send word to me.'

The old king, Malayaman, knew that Aditya Karikalan was not keenly listening to him. His attention was elsewhere.

'Grandpa! Look there.' Aditya Karikalan spoke with trepidation. The valiant old man looked in the direction pointed out by him.

43

The Falcon and the Dove

There was an old wayside resthouse made of stone meant for the convenience of the travelers. There were some sculpted images at the entrance of the rest house and Aditya Karikalan was pointing to one of the sculptures.

'Grandfather, see the huge falcon with broad wings holding a small dove in its claws. What a surprise! There is another dove hovering near the falcon. Maybe it could be the beloved of the captured bird. She's pleading for her lover's life. Oh God, she is now trying to fight with the falcon for her beloved's life. Grandpa, do you think that the falcon will have mercy on the dove? No, it won't.'

Aditya Karikalan took a pebble and threw it at the falcon. The pebble hit the falcon and fell down.

'Devil. You deserve this.'

Aditya Karikalan laughed in a devilish manner.

His grandfather Malayaman's doubts about his grandson's sanity grew stronger now.

'Grandpa, go closer and have a look. The sculpture looked very real.'

Malayaman appreciated the good work of art.

'Grandson, the miracle is not just in the stone. It's in your eyes as well as in your mind.'

'I'm furious. I want to destroy the sculpture right now.'

'What is this Karikala? Your heart used to be as strong as a diamond. The falcon devouring the dove is its nature. If a lion were to show compassion to sheep, it won't be a lion. It too would become a sheep. Those who want to sit on the throne, have to destroy their enemies and traitors and kill them.'

'Ok, Grandpa. When you are about to kill your enemy, if his lover were to fall at your feet begging for your mercy what will you do? Will you show mercy on your enemy?'

'Never Karikala, never! If a woman comes in between, I'll just push her away and kill my enemy. A woman's tears are more dangerous than a man's, because a woman's tears have the power to melt our heart. And a person who lets his heart melt can't do anything great in life.'

'Grandpa, why are you degrading women? Remember my mother is also your daughter.'

'The love that I have for my daughter is beyond comparison. I had six sons, who were all great warriors like the legendary Bheema and Arjuna. But I lost them all in the battlefield. But I have no regrets. But when your mother got married and went away from me to adorn the Chola throne, I was devastated. Do you know what I told her when she got married?

"Don't be proud you are marrying a great emperor. It will only add to your woes. If you bear sons, bring them up as warriors. If they die on the battlefield, don't cry. If your husband is sad, make him happy. If he falls sick, attend to him".'

'Grandpa, my heart swells with pride. But let me ask you one thing. Suppose my father is captured and is about to be killed by his worst enemy. What will my mother do? Will she beg the enemy for her husband's life?'

'Never, she'll live to avenge her husband's death.'

Aditya Karikalan let out a long sigh.

'Shall we now leave, Grandpa?'

'Yes…initially I had asked you not to go. After hearing about your brother, I think it's better that you go. But I don't think Arulmoli is dead.'

'Nor do I.'

'Arulmoli is sure to come back soon. The whole nation is grieving like your parents. Had I been invited I would have surely come along with you. They have deliberately avoided me.'

'Do you fear for my safety?'

'Karikala! I know your valour. But I tremble in fear to send you before a cunning woman.'

'I don't think Sambuvarayar's daughter is that cunning. I am not that rash to marry a girl without getting my parents' blessings.'

'I'll be happy if you marry Sambuvarayar's daughter. You see, I have become old. I can't help you any longer. You need some new friends.'

'Grandpa, I am visiting Sambuvarayar's palace as a guest, not to seek his friendship nor for marriage alliance. You can be at peace.'

'Then why should you go, my child? I heard that you are going there on the invitation of that devil whom Senior Paluvettarayar has married.'

'You are right.'

'You hail from a clan with blemishless character. They never indulge in anything scandalous. Never look at that devilish woman who is married to Senior Paluvettarayar.'

'Let me tell the truth. Once I did her a grievous wrong. I am going to seek her pardon.'

'How can you beg the pardon of a cunning woman?'

For a while Karikalan remained silent. Then he told his grandfather everything. He narrated how he caught hold of Veerapandiyan and how Nandini begged for his life and how he mercilessly killed him and how he had been suffering since that day.

'That memory is haunting me, Grandpa. I won't be at peace unless I meet her once and seek her forgiveness. She is also interested in avoiding succession problems in the Chola Empire. I'll finish my work and return to Kanchi very soon. And once I come back, I'll take a ship to search for my brother.'

The old man sighed.

'Many things are becoming clear to me. One thing is very sure, my child. Nobody can win over destiny.'

44

The Ayyanar Temple

Alvarkkadiyan and Vandiyathevan were crossing river Kollidam on a boat and they were heading towards Kadamboor.

River Kollidam was in floods. The overcrowded boat capsized. Vandiyathevan and Alvarkkadiyan reached the bank by swimming to it. Vandiyathevan's waistband with some signet rings and the message given by Princess Kundavai along with his spear and some gold coins were washed away in the flood waters.

They reached Kadamboor at sunset. Kadamboor, as expected, was buzzing with activity. The palace was colourfully decorated and security had been tightened to receive the crown prince of the Chola Kingdom. Moreover, the finance minister of the Chola Empire, Senior Paluvettarayar and his wife the junior queen of Paluvoor were also paying a visit.

They came to know that none of the dignitaries had arrived so far. Kandamaran, son of Sambuvarayar, had gone to Kanchi to escort the crown prince to Kadamboor.

Vandiyathevan and Alvarkkadiyan did not want to spend the night in the town to avoid being seen by anyone. They were searching for a resting place on the outskirts.

As they crossed the city limits, they saw an Ayyanar temple inside a dense bamboo forest and reached it with great difficulty.

It was a small Ayyanar temple with an altar, images of elephants and horses made of mud surrounded it.

Suddenly Vandiyathevan noticed some movement between the images and soon something like a man's head appeared near the altar, in between the mud horse and elephant.

The head turned in all four directions. It was a ghastly sight to see a human head very near the altar turning in all the directions. As they were watching, the head moved up a little more. Then they saw the whole man.

They recognized him in a few seconds. He was a part of Ravidasan's conspiracy gang working in the Kadamboor Palace. It was Idumban Kari.

Idumban Kari did not make any attempt to cover the hole through which he had emerged. He looked around a few more times and then started walking towards the temple. He opened the door and walked into the temple. A few seconds later they could see a dim flickering light inside the temple.

'Brother, what do you think of this?' Alvarkkadiyan whispered.

'While Idumban Kari is busy serving God, let me find out where he appeared from all of a sudden.'

'How will you do that?'

'Can't I look into the hole from which he came out?'

'Possible. But risky...'

'Nothing worthwhile is without risk. Nambi, you stay here and find out what's happening.'

They heard some voices at a distance.

Vandiyathevan reached the hole. It was a dark tunnel. The next second he vanished.

Idumban Kari came out of the temple. He saw the open hole. He then went near the altar and rotated the trident on the temple floor.

The dark hole closed. Idumban Kari then moved to the entrance of the temple. At the same time Ravidasan, Sambavan and others arrived there from different directions. Alvarkkadiyan hid himself behind the bamboo bushes. Ravidasan and his men started discussing their plans.

'The D-day has come very close. It's just a matter of a few days now. We have got news that Aditya Karikalan has left Kanchi already. The old man from Thirukkovalur, King Malayaman tried his best to stop him but all his efforts have failed.'

45

Hunters' Hall

Vandiyathevan entered the dark tunnel and walked down a few steps. Then he heard the sound of some wheels moving and realized that the door had been closed behind him. He could not find his way in the darkness.

He decided to abandon the venture. He turned around to go back and walked a few steps. But he could not locate the opening in spite of his earnest efforts. He heard the voices of Idumban Kari and other conspirators. So, he decided to go further down the tunnel to find out where it led to.

Vandiyathevan marched forward. Generally, in times of danger such tunnels were used to save the women of the palace and also carry the treasures out of the palace in times of crises.

Is Idumban Kari using this tunnel to smuggle out the treasures of the palace? Why are they indulging in such acts when the crown prince and other important dignitaries are visiting the palace? Do they have any other motives?

Suddenly he could feel a gush of cool refreshing air. He looked up to see a light at a distance and heard some voices. The thought that he had entered the Kadamboor Palace filled his mind with some hope.

His heart stopped beating when he saw hundreds of fiery eyes of wild beasts staring at him. He decided to go back.

There were tigers, leopards, lions, bears, bison, wolves, foxes and even rhinoceroses. And there were two elephants too. The animals were ready to pounce on him. But why had they not done that yet? There was also a crocodile with its mouth open wide displaying its lethal teeth. But crocodiles would normally be in water. This was on dry ground in the midst of the wild animals.

Soon he realised that the beasts around him were not alive. It was the Hunters' Hall in the Kadamboor palace with stuffed animals.

He touched every animal and tried to move them. He also searched the walls for possible exit points, but in vain.

He saw the face of an elephant embedded in the wall. Holding on to the tusks, he turned them around. Immediately, the elephant's ear moved showing a gaping hole in the wall. He put his face into the hole and looked around.

He saw a young lady's beautiful face with large eyes wide open. Surprise of surprises! He saw his own face next to the woman's face, close enough to kiss her.

The woman's wide eyes opened wider still expressing a feeling of shock and she screamed.

Vandiyathevan instinctively took his hands off the elephant's tusks. The next moment, the small gaping hole became the wall.

46

Princess Manimekalai

Princess Manimekalai, the darling daughter of King Sambuvarayar was a darling child for all in the palace. Even her slightest whims became the unwritten law. Life was all song and dance for her.

Whenever her brother Kandamaran returned from war, he would tell her about his friend Vandiyathevan, particularly about his valour, handsomeness and intelligence.

Manimekalai fell in love with him even before seeing him. She saw him through the eyes of her imagination. She would talk to him, laugh with him, play with him, fight with him in her dream castle. She was living with him in the hassle-free imaginary world. Four months ago, her dream-world was destroyed by the turn of events. Kandamaran's tone changed.

'Sister, Vandiyathevan has no country and no status. Forget him.'

He told her that his mission was to see her as the Chola Empress by marrying her to Prince Madurandakan. Although he was already married to the daughter of Junior Paluvettarayar, Manimekalai's parents endorsed Kandamaran's words. But Manimekalai was furious as she had lost her heart to Vandiyathevan.

Moreover, Madurandakan was a coward who had never been to a war field in his life. Until very recently he was seen smearing holy ash all over his body, wearing holy beads around his neck and leading a pious life. She was determined not to marry him.

She also came to know that Madurandakan was always traveling in the ivory palanquin in the guise of the junior queen of Paluvoor. So Manimekalai's aversion for the prince turned manifold.

She could never forget Vandiyathevan's smiling face and cheerful voice. She told her brother clearly that even if the almighty God commands her to marry Madurandakan, she would not yield. She hinted to her brother that her heart was lost to Vandiyathevan but Kandamaran was furious.

'Vandhiyathevan is not my friend. He is my foe. He tried to kill me by stabbing me in my back. And if you try to marry him, I'll kill you both. But for the Junior Queen Nandini's kindness, I wouldn't be alive.'

He showed the stab scar to his sister.

Manimekalai's heart slowly changed upon knowing Vandiyathevan's attempt to murder her beloved brother.

At the same time forgetting Vandiyathevan was not easy for her. His face was always haunting her.

She was happy to know that her parents and her brother had abandoned the idea of marrying her to Madurandakan.

Manimekalai was overawed to know that Aditya Karikalan, Senior Paluvettarayar and Nandini the junior queen of Paluvoor were visiting the palace. She had heard a lot about Nandini's beauty and intelligence. So Manimekalai was very excited when she was given the assignment of taking care of Nandini. She took meticulous care in making arrangements for the royal guests. She was very busy. Yet she could not completely forget Vandiyathevan.

When she was checking the chambers reserved for Nandini, she stood before the mirror to look at herself and when she was about to move away, she saw another face in the mirror close enough to kiss her cheeks. That was the face of the valiant Vandiyathevan. In shock and surprise, she screamed. The other face vanished.

47

A Tailless Monkey

Manimekalai was vividly aware of having seen Vandiyathevan in the mirror. She pinched herself to see if she was awake or not. She now remembered the secret passage on the wall opposite to the marble-mirror. The doors to the passage could be opened either from this chamber or from the other end. Manimekalai placed her ears close to the wall and listened. She could hear some sound in the Hunters' Hall on the other side of the wooden door. She gently opened the door to the passage and peeped out. It was totally dark.

Clapping her hands Manimekalai asked, 'Who's there?' She heared somebody clearing his throat. And then she heard a very light coughing sound. A bat was flying from one end to the other end of the hall. She immediately called out to her maid to come with a lamp. The maid came with a lamp.

'Princess, the room is already well lit. Why do you need a lamp here?'

'I want to visit the Hunters' Hall.'

'There will be nothing there but a few bats.'

'No. A few minutes ago, I saw a face near mine in the mirror.'

'What did the face look like?'

'Hey girl, are you teasing me?'

'No, Princess. You always talk about a face. Perhaps the same person appeared in the mirror.'

'Yes, you are right.'

'Girls of your age lose their minds. When you see the crown prince, the old face will vanish.'

'Let's have a look at the Hunters' Hall now.'

'Princess, the hall will be full of dust.'

'I don't mind. Let us check the Hunters' Hall right now. Hold the lamp.'

Manimekalai and her maid entered the Hunters' Hall. They were looking around the large hall. Manimekalai observed the fresh footprints on the floor.

'Princess! Look there. That monkey without a tail has moved a little.'

'What? Why are you shouting? Perhaps it is happy to see you, dear.'

'Why are you teasing me, Princess? The monkey is moving again.'

'No, it's the shadow cast by your lamp. Come let's go. I don't see anybody here,' said Manimekalai.

The two girls returned to the personal chambers reserved for the junior queen of Paluvoor.

Vandiyathevan came out from behind the tailless monkey. He sneezed because of the dust. He decided to leave the chamber. He was searching for the lever to open the secret door from inside but he found nothing.

There was no way out except the ladies' chambers. He thought he could deal with Manimekalai easily as she had a soft corner for him.

Vandhiyathevan looked around. He saw the stuffed crocodile on the floor. In disgust, he kicked the crocodile pretty hard. The crocodile moved a little and at the same moment a small gap opened up on the floor near the wall.

Vandiyathevan bent down and moved the crocodile further. The hole near the wall became larger and larger and a staircase became visible.

48

Horror in the Hunters' Hall

Vandiyathevan was awestruck by the crafty design of the passages in Sambuvarayar's palace. Any stranger venturing into these secret passages was as good as dead.

Oh God! I hear the sound of footsteps. It could be Idumban Kari and his gang.

In a trice, he hid himself behind the tailless monkey.

He saw Idumban Kari entering the Hunters' Hall from the hole in the direction of Ayyanar temple. The door to the ladies' chambers was also open. Manimekalai entered the Hunters' Hall with a lamp.

When Idumban Kari noticed Manimekalai coming in, he acted as though he was dusting. He stopped and looked at her.

'Is that you, Idumba? What are you doing here?'

'Princess, the royal guests may visit the Hunters' Hall. I'm cleaning it as ordered by Prince Kandamaran.'

'Yes, Idumba. The prince trusts only you in this whole palace. I was just checking the rooms a while ago. I heard some noises from here. How long have you been here?'

'About thirty minutes. But Princess, why did you come alone? What happened to that chatterbox Chandramathi?'

'I was worried about the noises coming from here. So, I have sent her to inform my father. Now that I know that you are here, I'll stop her.'

Manimekalai observed the change of expression in Idumban Kari's face. Then she looked at the tailless monkey. It moved a little again.

'Princess, you may please retire for the day. I'll continue my work.'

Manimekalai left the Hunters' Hall. The secret door closed.

Idumban Kari went near the face of the elephant and listened for any noise. Then he moved the crocodile and the hole opened. He went down the steps. An owl hooted. Idumban Kari returned the signal in response. And human footsteps were heard near the hole.

A bat swiftly flew across the hall making much noise. Suddenly, the tailless monkey fell on him like thunder. Idumban Kari lost his balance. He did not know what hit him. Finally, he found that the tailless monkey had fallen on him accidentally. He restored the monkey to its original place.

Meanwhile a pair of human hands from above the monkey-figure pushed him further down. Idumban Kari was horrified and looked up and down. The tailless monkey had fallen in the hole, head down, closing the hole. He was now sure all that had happened had been a hallucination.

By that time, Ravidasa and the others arrived. 'Hey, why did you scream like a devil? Any danger? Do you want us to leave now?'

'Nothing, no dangers. As I was opening the door to the hole, this giant-size stuffed monkey suddenly fell on me. I was terrified. Now this monkey is blocking our way. Give me a few seconds. Let me clear the way.'

Vandiyathevan ran back to the elephant and turned its tusk. A narrow opening appeared on the wall. He entered through that small opening before the conspirators came inside the Hunters' Hall. Thanks to the goddess of fortune, he escaped.

He tried to squeeze himself into the circular hole. He could not squeeze his full body. There was nothing to hold on to. At that time, the lamp in the room was put off and darkness surrounded him.

Vandiyathevan called for help:

'Chandramathi! Chandramathi! Please save me!'

He heard a woman laughing aloud.

'Oh my God, Chandramathi are you here? What are you looking at instead of helping me?'

'Your entering the ladies' chambers secretly is neither fair nor good.'
He recognized the voice of Manimekalai. But he feigned ignorance.
'Chandramathi, I came in here because you wanted me to come. People are chasing me. Please pull me in and save me.'
'Is Chandramathi so smart? Ok. Let her come. I'll teach her a lesson.'
'Oh, are you Princess Manimekalai? Please forgive me and save me from danger.'
Two slender hands reached for Vandiyathevan's mighty shoulders. The hands held the shoulders and then gently pulled him down to the floor of the ladies' chamber. The opening in the wall closed on its own making the room even more dark.
'A million thanks to you, Princess.'
'Your thanks can wait till you know what I am going to do to you.'
'Whatever you do is okay with me, Princess. You have rescued me. That's more than enough for me. Dying at your graceful hands is a far greater blessing.'
'Oh! You talk like a warrior. Who are those killers? But before that, let me uncover the lamp and see your face.'
'Why Princess? Some time back when you were standing in front of the marble mirror, a monkey's face appeared from behind. It was mine.'
The princess laughed. Manimekalai removed the cover on the lamp. The lamp glowed. She forgot herself when she saw Vandiyathevan's face.
Now a group of people were entering the Hunters' Hall at the same time.

49

A Ferocious Dog

Manimekalai's heart beat fast as her eyes fixed on Vandiyathevan's charming face. Vandiyathevan smiled.

How can I get away from her?

Manimekalai locked the door signaling Vandiyathevan to follow her to the other end of the room. She asked him:

'Did Chandramathi ask you to come here? When and where did she see you?'

'I was standing behind the tailless monkey. After you left, she asked, "Monkey, can you come to my chambers to frighten away the unwanted guests?"'

Manimekalai smiled at his sense of humour.

'You are not like a monkey. But you are as naughty as a monkey.'

'Did you stick your neck near the mirror a few minutes ago?'

'Yes, Princess. I did.'

'Then why did you retreat?'

'I saw the beautiful face of an angel and thought that she might be scared to see my face.'

'Who is that angel?'

'The darling daughter of King Sambuvarayar, the only sister of my dearest friend, Kandamaran and the one and only Princess Manimekalai.'

Manimekalai smiled.

'Oh, is that so? Is my brother your dearest friend?'

'Why doubt it, Princess? I came here four months ago and even visited the ladies' chambers to pay my respects to your mother.'

'Oh, you are that great Vandiyathevan, the famed prince of the Vaanar clan.'

'Yes, Princess.'

'Young man, why did you secretly enter this palace now?'

'Some killers were chasing me in the forest behind the palace. As I was running away from them, I saw a hole in the ground and entered it without knowing that it was a secret passage which landed me here.'

'You are one of the bravest warriors I have ever met and you say you were running for your life!'

Vandiyathevan enjoyed her sense of humour.

'My enemies were armed to their necks. I lost my spear in the floods at the Kollidam River.'

'In a way it's good it was washed away in the floods. That was a treacherous spear. It could stab a dear friend in the back. Were you running away from your killers? Or have you come here to kill me or somebody?'

'Oh god! Will I dare to kill my dear friend's darling sister?'

'Who knows? Didn't you stab that dear friend in the back?'

'Oh my God! Did I stab Kandamaran? I could never do that meanest act of betrayal. I would rather cut off my hands. Princess, who uttered these lies?'

'Who else but my own brother? If somebody else had said so, I would not have believed it.'

'Very unfortunate. Somebody stabbed him in his back in Tanjore Fort. I found him bleeding and unconscious. I carried him to Amudan's hut for treatment. And now I have been amply rewarded for my help. Why should I try to kill my dear friend? Did he offer any reason?'

'Yes, he did. You called me ugly. You had told him that the women in the Tanjore Fort are real beauties. Kandamaran was furious and he slapped you. You did not have the courage to fight him face to face. So, you hid behind him and stabbed him in his back?'

'Lies! Absolute lies! I would rather pluck my tongue out of my mouth than call you ugly. It was only your brother who insisted that I should forget you.'

'But why?'

'He said that a number of princes are in line to marry you. So, he insisted that I should forget you.'

'And you listened to him?'

'Honestly, I couldn't forget you altogether but from then on I've been considering you as my sister. Please take me to Kandamaran. If he thinks it is the truth, I'll change his mind.'

'Kandamaran is not in town.'

'Where is he?'

'He has gone to Kanchi to bring Crown Prince Karikalan. They will all be here tomorrow night. Till then... you...'

'Till then you want me to stay here?'

'No. I never said that. The junior queen of Paluvoor is coming here shortly. Then even air can't enter this place. Oh my God, how the old man loves his wife!'

Manimekalai and Vandiyathevan started laughing

'Oh, is that so? Does Paluvettarayar love his young wife so much? Then where should I stay till your brother returns?'

'My brother has a dedicated room. I'll take you there.'

'No, Princess. Staying here is risky.'

'Why?'

'If Kandamaran were to ask how I got here...'

'Tell him the truth.'

'When I spoke the truth and told you that killers are waiting for me in the next room, even you didn't believe my words.'

'Ok, let me verify it myself.'

'Princess, what are you going to verify?'

'I'll visit the Hunters' Hall to find out if they have come to kill you or you brought them with you to kill somebody.'

'Oh God! They are ruthless killers. Why take the risk of visiting them?'

'No need to worry. Our servant in the Hunters' Hall is cleaning the place. He could have brought his men to assist him. Anyhow, let me find out what is happening. You wait for me in the grain repository.'

Manimekalai entered the Hunters' Hall. Vandiyathevan hid himself inside the huge grain repository. It did not look like a grain repository. There were several steps and, on each step, a musical instrument was kept—the veena, the yazh, etc.

Vandiyathevan was wondering about Manimekalai's courage. Then Chandramathi entered the hall to inform Manimekalai about the arrival of the guests from Tanjore.

Vandiyathevan climbed up a few steps to avoid being seen by her. His knees hit a veena and there was a loud sound. Vandiyathevan was shocked and climbed a few more steps. His head hit the ceiling. The wooden ceiling plank moved up further to his surprise. Vandiyathevan moved the wooden plank and climbed up. He could see the light of an open terrace and hear some sounds at a distance. He also saw stars at a distance. He walked on to the terrace, carefully, looking in all directions.

The terrace was virtually deserted. Vandiyathevan thanked his luck and started walking fast.

The palace gate was buzzing with activities; drums and other musical instruments were being played at a high pitch. People's hailing sounds pierced the sky. Paluvettarayar's retinue reached the gates and the whole palace was there to receive the visitors. No better opportunity for Vandiyathevan to escape. Suddenly he saw Alvarkkadiyan between the branches of a tree and then he disappeared.

Vandiyathevan looked around. The place was still deserted. He started to climb down the other side of the wall using the branches of a nearby tree. Suddenly he saw a girl on the terrace above him. Even at this hour of crisis, he waved his hand mischievously at the girl. He was just a few steps away from the ground and wanted to jump. His blood froze to see a ferocious dog on the ground ready to pounce on him.

He had no time to think. He could not climb up the wall again. But if he jumped down the dog would surely have its pound of flesh. He heard somebody laughing. His legs were dangling in the air trying to escape the dog's mouth which was jumping higher and higher to bite his legs.

50

Manhunt

Vandiyathevan was in a dilemma whether to jump down or climb up the wall again. He was holding a shrub on the palace wall and his foot was resting on a protruding brick on the same wall. He heard somebody laughing. He looked around to see if anybody was hidden behind the trees. Even if he managed to escape the dog's mouth, he was sure to be caught by some men.

He remembered seeing Alvarkkadiyan's face over the wall when he was on the terrace.

Perhaps that Vaishnavite has been bored of waiting at the Ayyanar temple and has come here. Why don't I call him?

'Oh Nambi! Please help me!'

A figure with a spear emerged from behind a tree. It was not Alvarkkadiyan but Thevaralan of the conspiracy gang. He came near Vandiyathevan.

'Your stars are favourable, young man. You always escape death at the last minute.'

'I know that. But tell me, why have you come to me again?'

'Only to show you that you can't escape this time.'

Thevaralan aimed the spear at Vandiyathevan.

'Thevarala, beware! Remember the orders of your boss, the junior queen of Paluvoor—not to harm me.'

Thevaralan laughed like a devil.

'The Queen of Paluvuoor is not my boss. My only boss is Goddess Durga. I will let you go if you help me.'

'What do you want? Send this mad dog away.'

'I saw that Vaishnava fellow somewhere around here. If you help me to capture him, I'll set you free.'

'Why do you want him?'

'I have vowed to sacrifice a Vaishnava fanatic to Goddess Durga.'

Precisely at that moment the shrub that Vandiyathevan was holding on to, started to give way. Vandiyathevan was now exploring the possibilities of directly falling on Thevaralan in order to escape his spear.

'That Vaishnavite is my friend. I'll never betray him. Why don't you sacrifice me in his place?'

'Then be a victim to my spear.' Thevaralan aimed the spear at Vandiyathevan.

Vandiyathevan jumped down. Thevaralan was shocked. Before he could come out of the shock and lift the spear, a figure armed with a heavy stick ran out from behind the trees and hit his head with great force. Thevaralan now fell on Vandiyathevan.

The dog pounced on the person who tried to attack its master. Immediately Alvarkkadiyan pulled off the cloth above his waist and covered the dog's face. For a few seconds the dog went blind. Alvarkkadiyan pulled out a creeper and bound the dog to a tree.

They bound the unconscious Thevaralan with creepers and left the place with his spear.

Except for the gates all the other sides of Sambuvarayar's palace were surrounded by thick forest. The two men knew this and kept walking on. Alvarkkadiyan said to Vandiyathevan,

'I thought you were smart. When that crook Thevaralan asked you to help him capture me you should have said a big yes. Why did you refuse and get caught?'

'I knew pretty very well you were hiding somewhere nearby. If I had told Thevaralan that I would help him capture you, you would have overheard and 1 don't think you would have helped me then,' joked Vandiyathevan.

They had come out of the forest by then. They could see the front entrance of the Kadamboor palace. The Place was bustling with activities. Senior Paluvettarayar's retinue consisting of elephants, horses and infantry had just reached the palace gates. Sambuvarayar and his retinue were waiting at the heavily decorated entrance to receive the visitors.

Senior Paluvettarayar and his junior queen got down from the elephant. This time the junior queen did not come in a closed palanquin.

Vandiyathevan moved back. Alvarkkadiyan stood where he was. He was looking at Nandini. Nandini also noticed him and her face turned pale. Paluvettarayar noticed the sudden change on his wife's face. He also looked in the same direction. He saw two figures — Vandiyathevan and Alvarkkadiyan hiding behind the dark shadows cast by the trees.

He whispered something into Sambuvarayar's ears. Sambuvarayar whispered orders to his men to capture Vandiyathevan and Alvarkkadiyan.

Paluvettarayar and Nandini entered the palace amidst great fanfare.

Sambuvarayar's men entered the forest on horseback searching for the two men.

They were riding below the tall trees when they heard a devilish laughter from above. They looked up. There were two ghosts sitting on the tree which suddenly jumped on them, pushing them off their horses. Then those naughty ghosts mounted the horses and rode away fast.

51
A Friend or Foe?

The Crown Prince Aditya Karikalan, his friends and his retinue were crossing the beautiful place where two rivers Manimuthar and Vellaru merged. They were discussing the renowned Saint Sundaramurthy and his divine songs.

Parthiban was all praise for the saint.

The crown prince was curious.

'What did he do?'

'The saint refused to sing in praise of the presiding deity of the temple in Thirumudukundram, Viruthagereeswarar which literally means the old lord and his consort denoting an old goddess. So, the people of the town installed another statue of the Goddess Balambikai, which means a young maiden.'

Aditya Karikalan laughted after hearing the story.

'I think a poet must have told Senior Paluvettarayar something similar to what the saint said. He must have refused to sing in praise of the old man and his old wife. Perhaps that was the spark for the old man to marry a young Nandini.'

Parthiban and Kandamaran burst into laughter.

Parthiban was philosophising.

'Why did God create old age? He should have let us always be young.'

'To attain old age or not is in our hands only,' the crown prince retorted.

'I don't understand, Prince.'

'Do we think of the legendary Abhimanyu of the Mahabharata as an old man?'

The other two were silent. They knew that Abhimanyu had died young.

'If you visit the Tanjore art gallery we have paintings of our ancestors. My grandfather's brother, Rajaditya always appears as a young man. Do you know the reason? He died young. He was blessed with immortal youth. And people know him only as a young prince. I don't know how many of us will have that blessing.'

Parthiban and Kandamaran were silent.

'Why are you silent? Afraid of death? Why do we fear death? If only my friend Vandiyathevan were here, he will happily endorse my opinion. Very rare to find a man as enthusiastic as Vandiyathevan. Even if you put him at the door of death, he will still be laughing.'

Meanwhile Vandiyathevan and Alvarkkadiyan were coming on their horses from the opposite direction. The crown prince was thrilled to see Vandiyathevan. Throwing aside all protocols, he jumped from his horse and went towards Vandiyathevan to hug him.

'Brother, you'll live for a hundred years. Just a second ago, I was talking about you.'

Kandamaran and Parthiban were burning with jealousy at this abundant show of affection.

Kandamaran then complained to the crown prince about Vandiyathevan.

'Prince, this Vandiyathevan is your friend. He was my friend too. But I have to level grave charges against him. He stabbed me in the back. Please be careful with this man.'

52

The Broken Spear

The crown prince laughed out loud after hearing the charges leveled against his friend Vandiyathevan.

'Kandamara! Vandiyathevan stabbed you on your back? But why did you show your back to him?'

Again, the crown prince laughed.

The dark face of Kandamaran went red with anger.

'Prince, is it a laughing matter?'

'Kandamara! Are you saying that I should not laugh? Laughter is a boon; gifted by God only to humans. The cow can't laugh nor can the sheep. Even monkeys who play mischief all the time can't laugh. Why do you want me to stop my laughter?'

'Prince, your happiness only makes me happier. I didn't show my back to this all-time great warrior. He stabbed me at the most unexpected moment. By the grace of God and Queen Nandini I'm alive today. Please enquire into this blatant act of betrayal and render justice.'

'Dear friend, let me enquire.'

'Vandiyatheva, why don't you answer the charges leveled against you. Did you really stab him in the back?'

'Prince, I didn't stab Kandamaran. I found him stabbed in the back. He was bleeding and unconscious. I carried him to Amudan's house for treatment. Now I regret helping him. He accused me of having betrayed a friend. But this man has not only betrayed his friend but his boss as well. Ask him where that back-stabbing incident happened and under what circumstances. Ask him whom he secretly brought to the Tanjore Palace through the secret tunnel. Ask him whom he saw in the Senior Paluvettarayar's treasury. Ask him what happened at the Kadamboor Palace on the eighteenth day of the Tamil month of Adi? Ask him who came in the closed palanquin to Kadamboor Palace on that day.'

Kandamaran trembled and could not speak clearly. 'Stop speaking rubbish. Otherwise, you'll become a prey to my spear!'

Kandamaran took out his spear.

Aditya Karikalan grabbed the spear from Kandamaran and broke it into two pieces.

'I can't tolerate my friends fighting in my presence. Kandamara, Vandiyathevan has answered your charges. I'll take my time to verify the truth in his statements and pronounce my judgment. Meanwhile will you answer his questions now?'

Kandamaran was in a fix. 'Prince, I am under an oath not to disclose those matters.'

Parthiban intervened.

'Prince, judging from the way these people trade charges, I am afraid that the problem centres around a woman. Better if you enquire them individually.'

'You are right, Parthiba. All three of you have fallen in the net of seduction cast by the Paluvoor Queen. That explains your urgency to destroy each other.'

Parthiban's face fell and he fired his salvos against Vandiyathevan.

'Prince! Please give me a chance to explain my side. I have my own reservations against Vandiyathevan. Your dear brother jumped into the sea only to save him from a burning ship. And we never saw Ponniyin Selvan after that. But this man is here hale and healthy. This man is fully responsible for the drowning of your brother.'

Karikalan turned to Vandiyathevan: 'What's your answer to this?'

'Before I answer his charges let him answer my question. It was this man who took Ponniyin Selvan on his ship. Our prime minister and the Lankan Commander had advised Ponniyin Selvan not to leave

Lanka. But he got into this man's ship. And it was the responsibility of this man to deliver Ponniyin Selvan safely into your hands. Did he do that? When Ponniyin Selvan jumped into the middle of the sea, why was this man a silent spectator? Why didn't he or his men jump into the sea to save Ponniyin Selvan?'

Parthiban was furious. His hands and lips quivered.

'Prince, this fool is now accusing me. He might even say that it was I who killed the prince. I can't bear this nonsense.'

Karikalan looked deeply into his eyes.

'Parthiba, didn't I tell you earlier? You, my dear friends, have turned sworn enemies. I am not blaming you. It's the power of the Paluvoor Queen. I have felt those powers myself. Parthiba and Kandamara, you proceed on your horses before us. I will listen to the details of Vandiyathevan's travels. We'll be following you. But you should not fight. Nothing saddens me more than you three fighting with each other.'

Parthiban and Kandamaran reluctantly started riding forward.

Alvarkkadiyan came near Vandiyathevan and whispered into his ears:

'You are very smart. You did not tell the truth. Nor did you lie. But you escaped from them.'

Aditya Karikalan noticed Alvarkkadiyan only now.

'Who is this funny character? His face looks familiar to me.'

'Yes, Prince. You have seen me a few years ago. You heard my voice three years ago.'

A black shadow spread across the crown prince's face.

'Did I hear this voice when I was searching for King Veerapandiya in an island of the Vaigai River?'

'Yes, Prince. That voice was mine. It was I who told you about the enemy's hiding place. I was hiding behind a tree when I spoke.'

'What a horrible day that was! I was in a state of killing frenzy. Even now, when I think of that day, my body shivers. Nambi, why were you hiding? Why didn't you appear before me?'

'Prince, you were killing everyone who came in your way. And I wanted to live for some more time.'

'Is that the only reason? I shouted several times but you did not come out.'

'Because I did not want to earn the fury of my adopted sister Nandini, who is presently the Queen of Paluvoor.'

'And you wanted me to earn her fury?'

Karikalan unsheathed his sword. Alvarkkadiyan remained unfazed. Vandiyathevan whispered in the crown prince's ear.

'Prince, this man has come from the prime minister. He has got a message for you. Please listen to him before punishing him.'

'What's the use of punishing him? What's the use in punishing anybody for that matter?'

Karikalan put the sword back in its sheath.

Alvarkkadiyan spoke to Karikalan with a smile on his face.

'Prince, I know you'll direct your anger on me. That was why I was avoiding you till now. My sister is also still angry with me. She refuses to see me now. But I know she is no longer angry with you. You are visiting Kadamboor Palace only on her invitation. Am I right, Your Highness?'

'Scoundrel. How do you know that?'

'I work for the prime minister. Nothing happens in the Chola Empire without his knowledge.'

'One day or other I'll banish you and the prime minister from the Chola Kingdom. Now you two, mount your horses and ride on either side of me. Let's chat as we go.'

53

Her Heart's Secret

Nandini was reclining on an exclusive bed made just for her in the special chamber at the Kadamboor Palace. She was in her finest costumes and finest jewels. Her beauty was beyond description. She heard Manimekalai's voice asking for permission to enter her chamber.

'Manimekalai please come in. Why ask permission to enter a room in your palace?'

Manimekalai gently walked in as if dancing her way into the room and took her seat.

'Queen, my brother has told me I should not enter your room without permission.'

'Forget your brother's advice. Hereafter don't call me queen. Call me sister.'

'Sister! It sounds very sweet! Hope you won't mind my disturbing you often.'

'It'll be a disturbance if you come now and then. If you stay here itself it won't be a disturbance at all.'

Nandini smiled. Manimekalai was bowled over by her seductive smile and her stunning beauty.

'Sister, I have never seen anyone half as beautiful as you.'

'Please don't fall in love with me. Already the whole kingdom is calling me a *seductress*. Any man coming near me falls for me. That's the charge against me.'

'Sister, if anybody talks ill of you, I'll cut off their tongue.'

'No point in blaming others, Manimekalai I am married to an old man. That makes their tongues wag.'

Manimekalai became dull.

'My brother and I feel sorry about it. But still, none can talk ill of you.'

'Ok, let's not worry about my problems. Now tell me about you. You told me in the evening that you'd reveal the secret in your heart?'

Nandini gently tapped Manimekalai's cheeks.

'Sister, if women were allowed to marry women, you would be my life partner.'

'I am happy, Manimekalai. I'm longing for a dear friend like you. But you have to marry a man. You have no other option.'

'Sister, I don't like the idea of getting married at all.'

'No, dear. The world won't let you remain unmarried. Tell me whom you want to marry, given a choice. Prince Madurandakan or Crown Prince Aditya Karikalan?'

Manimekalai burst out laughing.

'Marrying Madurandakan would amount to marrying a woman. He travels in your palanquin like a lady.'

Nandini smiled.

'Yes, I know you won't like Madurandakan; I said this to your brother. He is already married to my brother-in-law's daughter. She is also very arrogant. You can't be with her even for a single day. I think the crown prince would be the right match for you.'

'You are right, sister. The crown prince is one of the greatest warriors of our kingdom. Is it true that he cut off King Veerapandiya's head in a single stroke?'

Nandini's face suddenly turned white. But few moments later she turned to Manimekalai.

'Manimekalai, it is an act of valour. But it is a terrible gruesome act.'

'Sister, how can it be gruesome?'

'Suppose an enemy comes to kill your dear brother. Will you praise him for the valour?'

Manimekalai thought for a while.

'Sister, I won't be silent. I will grab the sword and kill the enemy.'

Nandini fondly hugged Manimekalai.

'A very apt reply, my dear. I should ensure the right husband for an intelligent woman like you. I doubt if Aditya Karikalan will be the right match for you.'

'I too think so, sister. After knowing about Karikalan, I am only afraid of him. Sister, shall I now reveal my heart's secret?'

54

Manimekalai's Dream

Manimekalai was bubbling with joy when Nandini lifted her chin.
'Dear, don't open up your heart to a stranger like me.'
'No, sister. I feel like I have known you for ages. My heart is keen on sharing with you.'
'Tell me Manimekalai, who has seduced your heart?'
'Sister, I saw him for the first time about four months ago. Even before that, my brother used to talk about him with much admiration. Ever since I saw him, he has been visiting me in my dreams, both at night and during the day.'
'Can I reveal your handsome lover now?'
'Please, sister,'
Nandini closed her eyes for a while and then opened them again.
'The man who has stolen your heart is from the Vaanar clan. He is Vallavarayan Vandiyathevan.'
'Oh my God! You have divine powers.'
'Manimekalai, why don't you tell this to your brother?'
'Sister, my brother does not like him. It was he who introduced me to Vandiyathevan with the hope of marrying me to him. Now there is a sudden change in him. There is a reason for that also. He stabbed my brother in the back when he was in Tanjore. Thanks to your grace, he is alive today.'
'What are you going to do now? Your lover has become your brother's foe.'
'But Vandiyathevan swears that he never stabbed Kandamaran. On the other hand, it was he who saved my brother.'

'Did you meet Vandiyathevan?'

'Yes sister, but I am confused. I am not sure whether I saw him or his apparition. When I think back on what happened yesterday, everything feels like a dream.'

'Tell me what happened yesterday. I'll clear your doubts.'

'Yesterday I came to your room to oversee the arrangements. I was looking at my face in the mirror. Suddenly another face appeared in the mirror. It was very close to mine. I was shocked!'

'Why? Tell me exactly what happened.'

'It appeared as if his face came close to kiss me on my cheeks. I turned around in shock. There was nobody there. So, I opened the door and went into the Hunters' Hall.'

Nandini became curious now.

'Was the thief hiding in the Hunters' Hall?'

'Sister, why do you call him a thief?'

'Didn't he steal your heart? Tell me, was he in that hall?'

'Sister, surprise of surprises, he was not there. There was only our man, Idumban Kari who was cleaning the hall. When I asked him if there was anybody else in the hall, he insisted there was no one other than him in that hall.'

'Do you think he would have lied?'

'I don't know. I then returned to this room. But I heard the sound of some people speaking in the Hunters' Hall and I also heard something fall. Then I heard the call for help "Danger! Danger! Please save me." Then I saw my dream hero and my heart skipped a beat. When I asked him how he had managed to enter the ladies' chambers, he told me that some men were chasing him to kill him. I accused him of back-stabbing my brother. He totally denied that.'

'You believed him?'

'He appeared credible. As I was talking to him, I was also listening to the sound of several men talking in the Hunters' Hall that confirmed his statement. I decided to save him. I wanted to see the persons chasing him. I even suspected Idumban Kari. Or he could be an accomplice to this man. I wanted to know.

So, I asked him to stay here and went back to the Hunters' Hall to see who else was there. There were five or six men. They were shocked to see me. I wanted to ask about the strangers. By that time, my maid Chandramathi came to this room looking for me. I remembered my lover in the room. I was afraid that Chandramathi might scream after seeing him. Therefore, I rushed back. By that time my lover had vanished.

When I asked my maid if she saw anybody here in this room, she said no. Again, I visited the Hunters' Hall to probe further. All those men whom I had seen earlier were not there. Idumban Kari alone was there, busy with his cleaning work. When I asked him "What happened to those people?" He said there was no one there except him. I didn't believe him.

Then Chandramathi informed me about the arrival of our guests. So, I left for the palace gates. As I was walking on the terrace, I saw my hero jumping down the wall.

Sister, I need your help. My brother is devoted to you. If you tell him, he won't refuse... Please... sister...'

'You smart girl! You are making me work against the very purpose of my visit.'

55

Royal Reception

The gates of Kadamboor Sambuvarayar's palace witnessed a grand royal reception. There was a sea of men, women, children and the aged; people even from the remote villages had come to see their Crown Prince Aditya Karikalan.

The first to arrive was Kandamaran, to inform the arrival of the crown prince to Sambuvarayar and Paluvettarayar.

'The crown prince is not in his usual mood. I came before him to caution all of you.'

He then approached the Paluvoor young queen, Nandini.

'I have brought the prince as ordered by you. But he is like a rogue elephant. Dealing with him will be a tough task.'

'Why worry about it when your sister is here?'

'Sister, what's this?' asked Manimekalai.

Kandamaran responded to his sister.

'Manimekalai, nothing wrong in what the young queen says. One must have done penance to have Aditya Karikalan as one's husband.'

Before Manimekalai could reply, Nandini intervened.

'Is anybody else coming along with the prince?'

'Yes, Parthiban and Vandiyathevan are also coming.'

Nandini threw a pointed glance at Manimekalai and asked Kandamaran:

'Your friend Vandiyathevan?'

'Yes, the friend who stabbed me in my back. He joined the prince half way. I put up with him only for the sake of the prince.'

Manimekalai was upset.

'Brother, if he has stabbed you, why let him inside our palace?'

'Don't poke your nose in men's affair. Today they'll fight, tomorrow they will become friends,' said Nandini.

Kandamaran left.

The three—the crown prince, Vandiyathevan and Parthiban entered the palace gates. The bands started playing. Their retinue was stopped much before the gates. The herald announced the arrival of the crown prince. Flowers were showered on Prince Aditya Karikalan. Vandiyathevan looked up and saw the fully blossomed face of Manimekalai.

Immediately after they crossed the palace gates, the gates were closed.

'Why should they close the doors in such a hurry? Do they want to imprison me like my father in Tanjore?'

The two old warriors, Sambuvarayar and Paluvettarayar were shocked.

Paluvettarayar spoke to him in a sweet voice.

'Prince, your father and you are eternally imprisoned in the loving hearts of millions of people in this kingdom. How can anyone imprison you otherwise?'

Sambuvarayar added, 'Prince, if all those who are assembled were to come to see you enter this palace, can you imagine what would happen?'

By that time, the noise from the crowd outside the fort increased. Karikalan decided to move to the terrace to cheer up the audience.

Kandamaran took the crown prince along with his friends to the terrace to see the royal women and pay his respects.

When he saw Nandini, Karikalan exclaimed, 'Oh, it is my little grandmother from Paluvoor! I am very happy to see her.'

Nandini did not respond. But her eyes pierced Karikalan like sharp daggers. Karikalan felt the intensity of her glance.

Sambuvarayar and Paluvettarayar decided to stay back when the prince went to the terrace.

'How to manage his harsh behaviour? We have invited disaster on ourselves,' commented Sambuvarayar to Paluvettarayar.

They decided to bear it for a few more days.

'There is another young man with him. He looks like a spy.'

'Oh, he is my son's friend. Don't worry about him. Why have they gone to the ladies' side?'

By this time Parthiban returned and heard the last words spoken by Sambuvarayar.

'Sir! The crown prince does not have a weakness for women. You need not worry about it.'

'Then how will our plan work?' Paluvettarayar asked him.

'Well, that depends on Sambuvarayar's luck.'

'Parthiba, why is the prince irritable?'

'Till Vandiyathevan and Alvarkkadiyan joined the prince halfway, he was cheerful. Later, they must have poisoned his mind.'

'We thought so. Tell me what we can do now.'

'Be a little patient. I'll take care of him. I have a score to settle with that young man, Vandiyathevan.'

Now the Crown Prince Karikalan, waved to the people from the terrace. The crowd which was dispersing came back to the gates of the palace in sheer excitement. Karikalan made some announcements to the people through the herald.

'Prince Aditya Karikalan will stay in this palace for a week. He will be visiting the surrounding villages as well, to meet the people and receive petitions from them.'

The crowd hailed him in chorus touching the sky.

Karikalan came back from the terrace and went to Sambuvarayar, Paluvettarayar and Parthiban.

'Parthiba, why are you stuck up here? You too have started to conspire with these old men?' asked the prince sarcastically.

The old men were shocked.

Sambuvarayar managed to speak:

'Prince, a little while ago you said that you were imprisoned here.

Now you are talking about conspiracy. I swear, that during your stay here in my hut you will be absolutely safe.'

'Do you think I am afraid of danger? Even in the midst of thousands of enemies, I never thought about my safety. Why should I fear when I am in the midst of my close friends? Please don't call this mighty palace a hut. What kind of enemies did you have in mind while designing this mighty palace?'

'Prince, we don't have any enemies.'

'Your son sees my friend Vandiyathevan as his enemy. Is it not a blunder? Please advise him.'

Kandamaran was embarrassed.

The crown prince was taken to the palace courtyard to witness the folk dance—Kuravai Koothu. After the folk dance, the prince expressed his desire to go hunting the next morning. He also recalled the words of his grandfather King Malayaman's advice not to sleep at night as enemies may try to kill him. He also recalled his reply that he hadn't slept for the last three years at all and none would dare to kill him. After recounting this, Prince Karikalan laughed loudly.

Paluvettarayar, in his attempt to give a retort, cleared his throat. The noise resembled the roar of a lion.

'See? When my Paluvoor grandfather clears his throat, the whole world shakes. Will you be half as strong as him at his age? You can never bring a young girl to your harem at his age.'

'Grandpa, Paluvoor's junior queen has also come with you. Tell me this, how did she travel? In a closed palanquin? Or in an open chariot?'

'I brought her along on top of the elephant. I wanted the whole world to see,' replied Paluvettarayar restraining his anger.

'Grandpa, let her travel in the same way hereafter. Never bring her in a closed palanquin giving rise to many juicy rumours about my uncle Madurandakan.'

Vandiyathevan bit his tongue.

Oh my God! I have done the greatest blunder of my life by disclosing everything to this crazy prince.

The senior Paluvettarayar's mind was like a volcano. Before he could speak, Parthiban diverted the topic.

'My Lord, why would the grandson of the great emperor Paranthaka, Prince Madurandakan travel in a closed palanquin?' remarked Parthiban.

'You know why? He visits every town in Tamil Nadu in that palanquin gathering support to ascend the great Chola throne. Isn't it funny? A few months ago, he visited this palace in a closed palanquin to attend conspirators' meeting at mid-night. Parthiba, my grandfather King Malayalan told me all these things in your presence. My grandfather is even afraid that in his anxiety, he might even pack off my father to the other world earlier than his time. Don't you remember all that my grandfather said? I didn't believe it. Otherwise, I would not have come here as a guest.'

'My Lord, you know the enmity between our clan and King Malayaman? We try to forget the past but Malayaman always accuses us of something or the other,' said Sambuvarayar in anguish.

'Grandpa Malayaman is old. He is also too worried about my safety here.'

'Prince, do you doubt...' Sambuvarayar was at a loss for words.

'But our relationship with the Paluvettarayars has been for six generations. Am I that crazy to think that he'll do anything against the Chola clan?'

Paluvettarayar spoke in a majestic voice.

'Prince, I won't do anything against the Chola clan. That's a promise. I won't do anything against fairness and justice. My second promise is two times stronger than the first.'

'Yes, there is something called justice and fairness. If we have some time left after hunting tomorrow. We'll discuss Madurandakan's conspiracy in the presence of all the chieftains. There is no place more ideal for that than this palace.'

56

Poonkulali's Desire

Poonkulali and her cousin Amudan traveled together in her boat and reached Kodikkarai. A parrot screeched and flew away from a nearby tree.

'The heartless princesses-devils in palaces cage the parrots.'

'Poonkulali why hate princesses? In a way, they too deserve our sympathy. Their fate is no different from those caged parrots. Oh my God! How many security restrictions! How many protocols! Do you think they can row their boats and roam in the forest as you do?'

'Who asked them to be caged? Let them also roam in the forests.'

'Poonkulali, that depends on their birth. You were born on the seashore and you have so much of freedom. If you were born in a palace, you wouldn't be so free.'

'I'll neither be a parrot nor a princess caged in a palace.'

'Good! Then you should not desire to marry a prince in a palace.'

There were flashes of lightning in Poonkulali's fiery eyes.

'Who told you that I want to marry a prince?'

'I just guessed. If you do not have that kind of a desire, then it's good.'

Amudan gathered his courage and spoke.

'Will you marry me?'

'Why do you ask this question?'

'Because I love you.'

'Should love always end in a marriage?'

'That has been the practice of the world from time immemorial.'

'Can you give me a royal life, if I marry you?'

'I cannot. But I will give you a peaceful life which is more precious than all those royal comforts. Poonkulali, my hut is in a beautiful garden in Tanjore. My mother and I will look after you very well if you stay with us.'

Poonkulali laughed aloud.

'Amuda, my aspirations are different. I want to go to the celestial world and marry the chief of gods. We will ride through the clouds in the celestial world...'

'Poonkulali, stop that nonsense. I am sorry I proposed to you without knowing your mind.'

Poonkulali suddenly looked towards a tree on the bank of the canal. Amudan also looked in the same direction. A woman's face was seen between the branches. Amudan was stunned for a moment to see her resemblance to his mother. He guessed that it must be his aunt—his mother's sister. Poonkulali jumped from the boat and ran towards the woman.

57

The Arrow

Poonkulali saw the mute queen behind a tree on the bank of the canal. She was running away towards the dense forest. Poonkulali ran behind her. Amudan also followed them.

Amudan was curious to meet the mute queen. Then they began running towards the dense forest of Kodikkarai.

'She resembles my mother. Does she come here often?'

'No. She comes very rarely. Perhaps she is here to know the fate of her foster son, Ponniyin Selvan. She might be anxious to know whether he is alive or drowned in the stormy sea.'

'Prince Arulmoli is her foster son? Then who is her own son?'

'That's what I want to find out. I won't give up till I find out.'

'Amuda, you said that she resembles your mother. Tell me whether her face reminds you of anybody else.'

Amudan replied after a pause, 'Yes… She has a striking resemblance to Queen Nandini. Surprising! How is that possible?'

'I saw the Paluvoor Queen here in Kodikkarai a few days ago. The moment I saw her, I noticed the strong resemblance.'

They entered the forest but they could not locate the mute queen.

Suddenly they heard a strange voice from the forest. A few deer ran towards the direction of the voice.

'Amuda, follow me without noise,' said Poonkulali.

They started walking towards the direction of the voice. They saw an interesting scene there.

The mute queen was feeding the deer leaves.

'My aunt does not know the human language. But she knows

the language of these animals,' said Poonkulali proudly.

Poonkulali made a signal. The lady did not run away now. When Poonkulali went near her, the mute queen hugged her and kissed her. Amudan was waiting at a distance.

The aunt and her niece spoke for a while in sign language. Then Poonkulali beckoned Amudan to come near them.

The mute queen looked at Amudan. She then blessed him. Then all of them left the place and reached the bank of the canal.

The mute queen sat on the bank and asked Poonkulali to bring her some food.

Poonkulali and Amudan started walking towards the lighthouse to bring her some food. On the way, they saw a man and a woman hiding behind a bush discussing something serious.

'Oh my God, that's my sister-in-law, Raakammal talking to some spies from the Pandiya Kingdom.'

Raakammal emerged from behind the bushes and was shocked to see Poonkulali. Without revealing her shock, she said,

'Poonkulali, where were you all these days? Your father and brother were worried.'

'Why should they? This is not the first time I have gone out of the house.'

'But this time you took your cousin along. They were worried whether you two had had a secret marriage.'

'Raakammal, I have warned you several times…'

'You can marry your cousin or the prince. Who cares? Your aunt came from Lanka looking for you? Did you see her?'

'No. I didn't.'

Poonkulali spoke privately to Amudan before they reached her house.

'My sister-in-law is a part of the spy gang of Pandiya Kingdom. She'll try to pull out words from your mouth. Don't answer any of her questions.'

'I'll be dumb so long as I am here in your house.'

The same afternoon, Poonkulali was rowing her boat towards Nagapattinam. The mute queen was the only other passenger in the boat. Poonkulali was always blissful while in the company of the mute queen. But this time she was not.

She recalled her journey with the sick Ponniyin Selvan in her boat. The memory of that trip was haunting her. Now she felt bad that she took all the trouble only to unite the prince with another princess.

Poonkulali recollected her father's words of caution.

My dear child, a lot of conspiracies are going around in our kingdom against the crown. I see new faces coming to our place often. Our family is forever indebted to the family of the Chola Kings. I don't want you to be caught in the net of conspirators.

Poonkulali connected her father's words and the clandestine activities of her sister-in-law.

Perhaps those strangers who want to know the whereabouts of Ponniyin Selvan are following me. I should be very careful.

The sudden rustling sound heard near the bank made her tremble.

What causes the rustling sound when there is no wind?

The mute queen could not hear anything but her other senses were abnormally sharper. She was anxiously looking at the banks of the canal to know if anybody was following them.

Poonkulali felt relieved to see a herd of deer on the bank.

Suddenly an arrow landed on one of the deer and the mute queen jumped from the boat and ran towards the injured deer.

As she came near the deer there was a rustling of leaves all around her. In the next few seconds, she was surrounded by seven or eight men armed with spears.

Raakammal, Poonkulali's sister-in-law who had guided them to the place was seen at a distance.

The mute queen tried to run away but she was overpowered. Two men came near her and bound her with ropes. All this happened in a few seconds.

Poonkulali sprang from the boat and ran towards the men but

those men dragged her to her boat and bound her with ropes. The men then went away. The mute queen followed them submissively as she had no other option. Soon they all vanished from the place in a few seconds.

58

Raakammal the Crook

Poonkulali released herself from the ropes after a great struggle. She now heard the sound of footsteps. Then she saw a moving shadow. She decided to throw her sharp knife at the person as soon as he appeared. But she heard Amudan's voice. Soon he came running towards her.

'Poonkulali, are you alive?'

'You don't want to see me alive?'

'Why are you harsh, Poonkulali? Oh! My God, see what those crooks have done to you! I can see the rope marks on your body.'

'You couldn't have come a little earlier? I suffered a lot to free myself from these ropes.'

'I didn't know you were in danger. You drove me away with your words.'

'Then why did you come back? Perhaps to see me dead?'

'Your sister-in-law told me that you might be in danger. So, I came running.'

'Where is that devil? I would like to kill her with this knife.'

'Why are you so angry? Is it an offence to ask me to help you out of danger?'

'No. She is the one who betrayed my aunt, the mute queen. You also saw her talking to somebody hiding behind the bushes.'

'Poonkulali, I don't know who she was talking to. She did not betray your aunt. Those crooks who forcibly abducted your aunt tied your sister-in-law to a tree. They also hit your sister-in-law on her head. She is badly hurt. I saw her when I was on my way to Tanjore and saved her.'

'I saw Raakammal grievously bleeding and bound to a tree. I freed her. As I was freeing her off the ropes, I posed her with questions: "Who did this? And why? Who were those men? Who is that woman in their midst?"

Raakammal informed me that the soldiers were kidnapping your aunt. She tried to prevent it. That's why they beat her up and tied her to a tree. She did not know what happened to you. She thought you might be in danger and asked me to find you. I started running and came in search of you. I felt relieved when I saw you alive and unhurt. Poonkulali, you need not suspect your sister-in-law!'

'Where did you leave her? Let's go there.'

'Will she still be there?' asked Amudan.

'I don't believe it. She might come looking for us. Didn't she ask where my aunt and I were heading to?' replied Poonkulali.

'Yes, she did.'

'I hope you didn't tell her. The crooks might have got the information through my sister-in-law and once their purpose was over, they might have abandoned her after beating her. She always has some evil intentions. So be careful with her.'

Poonkulali and Amudan were walking through the forest and talking.

'Amuda, we must have been together in our previous births also.'

'I am not bothered about our previous births. If you could give a favourable answer regarding this birth, I'll be grateful.'

Poonkulali gave a reply not connected to his question.

'Then do whatever you like. Once we reach the highway, I'll go my way to Tanjore,' said Amudan in disappointment.

'I won't leave you like that, Amuda. After talking to my sister-in-law, I'll come with you to Tanjore to seek justice for my aunt. I will complain at the emperor's court.'

'Poonkulali, it won't be easy to approach the emperor.'

'Why not? If they refuse to open the fort gates, I'll break them open. And if that is not possible, I'll scale the wall and jump in.'

'How will you deal with the security guards at the gates of the fort?'

'I'll frighten them with my screams and they will take me to the emperor.'

'Poonkulali, you can't easily frighten the person in charge of the fort security, I mean Junior Paluvettarayar. Without junior Paluvettarayar's permission, even the lord of death cannot enter the fort. The emperor is still alive because of that.'

'What if I can't see the emperor? I'll see the Paluvettarayars and seek justice for my aunt. And if I don't get justice, I'll meet the prime minister. If I fail to get justice, I'll meet the queens at Palayarai. I won't rest till I know what happened to my aunt. Amuda, you have to support me.'

'Sure, Poonkulali, but your first priority should be to find your aunt and save her from danger.'

'Amuda, my aunt has divine powers. Nobody can harm her. I am not worried about her. I can't bear the gross atrocities happening in broad daylight in the Chola Kingdom. People say that in Sundara Chola's reign, even a young woman can walk alone at midnight without fear. If criminals can abduct an old mute woman in broad day light in such a great country…'

Amudan spoke,

'Yes, ever since our emperor has become bedridden, evil has gained an upper hand. Women are not safe. Therefore, girls should get married to the right man at the earliest.'

Poonkulali laughed.

'Amuda, if a young woman marries you, can you protect her? Do you know how to handle a sword?'

'I only know how to make a garland of flowers and sing in praise of my Lord. I don't know the art of fighting with a sword. So what? Didn't you teach me how to row a boat? In the same way, I'll learn to fight. When Madurandakan can have the ambition of ruling this empire, learning to handle a sword is not at all a difficult task.'

They had reached the place where Poonkulali's sister-in-law was bound to a tree. But they could not find her there. They saw only the blood stains.

'They must have roughed her up. Probably my sister-in-law was not working for the gang who abducted my aunt. We should try to find out whom she is working for.'

'Poonkulali, why should we bother about all these things? There are secrets within secrets involving the emperor and his family.'

'Amuda, it could be a sensitive political issue or a deep mystery. But how can I be a silent spectator? And she's your mother's sister also. You also cannot distance yourself from her.'

'Well, judging by the way it appeared, she was willingly going with the abductors.'

'Possible, Amuda. That's my aunt's nature. She would like to know where she is being taken. She can't be so easily captured. I am not worried about her safety. I want to correct the injustice meted out to her. No, I am not talking about what happened today, but what happened twenty-five years ago. That was the greatest injustice committed against a woman. I won't rest till I seek retribution for that.'

'Oh! My God! It is such a difficult task,' Amudan sighed.

Just then, they heard the voice of Raakammal talking to the doctor's son on the Tanjore High Road. Poonkulali was disgusted on seeing the doctor's son.

Raakammal was shocked to see Poonkulali.

'Oh, you are safe! I thought that they might have killed you. See, what those crooks have done to me! All because I tried to save your aunt! I am asking for some medicine from the doctor's son.'

Poonkulali, restraining her anger, asked her sister-in-law:

'Raakammal, do you know where the abductors are taking my aunt?'

'I don't know. But this doctor's son says that they went towards the Tanjore High Road.'

'Amudan and I are going to find her. Please tell my father.'

Poonkulali and Amudan started to leave.

'Stop, Poonkulali. I have a horse with me. I can chase them easily. In return, I need a small favour from you. Just tell me where your aunt and you were going before the crooks captured her,' said the doctor's son.

Poonkulali spoke to her sister-in-law.

'We don't need his help. We'll find them on our own.'

Poonkulali's eyes became fiery. She then grabbed Amudan's hand and started walking. They started walking towards Tanjore. They asked the people on the way if any of them had seen seven or eight men going on horses along with a woman. Nobody could give them a proper answer.

Amudan enjoyed the company of Poonkulali while traveling. Poonkulali taught him to fight with a sword which they bought on the way. When they saw the Tanjore Fort at a distance, Poonkulali became serious. How were they going to enter the fort to seek justice?

They were happy to see the closed palanquin of the Paluvoor Queen going to the fort.

'If only we could get her signet ring, all our problems would be solved,' said Amudan.

Poonkulali liked the idea.

'But how to draw the attention of the junior queen?'

'Don't worry Amuda. The fort is still a mile away. We'll have enough time,' said Poonkulali

And they got a wonderful opportunity in the most unexpected manner.

59
Golden Opportunity

Amudan and Poonkulali continued walking.
'The kingdom is in a mess.'
'The political affairs are in a state of confusion.'
'No news about the prince.'

Amudan and Poonkulali overheard these bits of conversation throughout their journey.

The Paluvoor palanquin passed by their side. Suddenly they saw dark clouds in the sky. It started with a drizzle and then it turned into a torrential downpour. The sun had set. Amudan and Poonkulali abandoned the idea of entering the Tanjore Fort before nightfall. They started walking towards Amudan's house outside the city limits.

There were strong winds and trees were falling down. They decided to take shelter in any resthouse on the roadside.

'How do we find a resthouse in this darkness?'

There was a flash of lightning and they spotted a resthouse close by. There was another flash of lightning. They were shocked to see a big banyan tree fallen down just opposite to the resthouse. Its branches and aerial roots were everywhere. Two horses and a few people were trapped under the fallen tree. Some others were trying to rescue them.

The Paluvoor palanquin was on the ground near the fallen tree. Two men were guarding the palanquin and the rest were involved in the rescue operations.

'Shall we go to the palanquin and seek the help of the junior queen to enter the fort?' asked Poonkulali.

Meanwhile, there was another flash of lightning and they saw two men lifting the palanquin.

'Oh! My God, they have started. No, no. Looks like the palanquin is coming here.'

In a few seconds the palanquin reached the resthouse. The bearers gently placed it on the floor.

'Who's in there?' asked one of the bearers.

'Brother, we too are travelers like you. We are halting here because of the rains.'

'Ok. But don't come near the palanquin.'

'We won't,' answered Poonkulali.

'How many of you are there?'

'We are only two. But this rest house can hold even two hundred' said Amudan

Poonkulali and Amudan did not see the third person in the resthouse hiding behind one of the pillars. But they saw a woman in the palanquin when the lightning flashed again. That woman recognized them and smiled.

The next moment the place was plunged into darkness.

Poonkulali whispered.

'Amuda, it is not the junior queen of Paluvoor. It's my aunt, the mute queen. Let us rescue her.'

'That's impossible!'

'I want to get her released right now.'

Now something unexpected happened.

The screens of the palanquin moved apart. A figure came out. It walked like a cat without noise. The next second it was near them. As all this happened in total darkness, it escaped the eyes of the bearers and guards. The mute queen grabbed the hands of Amudan and Poonkulali and dragged them to the back of the resthouse.

She then hugged Poonkulali. The aunt and niece talked for a while in sign language. Everything went unnoticed.

Poonkulali then spoke to Amudan.

'She wants me to go in the palanquin. She wants you to take

her to your place. It's a good idea, to find her captors.'

Poonkulali hugged her aunt once again and took leave of her. She too walked like a cat towards the palanquin, got into it and drew the screens.

60

Disappointed Prime Minister

The prime minster was camping in the capital. His palace was buzzing with activities. Government officials, chieftains, generals, foreign ambassadors, representatives of trade leaders, trustees of temple trusts and scholars swarmed in his palace, seeking to have a private audience with him.

The prime minster kept his official retinue and security guards to the barest minimum to avoid friction with the Paluvettarayars.

Junior Paluvettarayar was not happy about the prime minster extending his stay in the capital. He thought that the security arrangements were lax ever since his arrival in the city. All and sundry entered the Fort on the pretext of seeing the prime minister.

A few days ago, the prime minister wanted some soldiers to be sent to Kodikkarai for some important work. Junior Paluvettarayar obliged. Earlier the prime minister wanted the closed palanquin of the Paluvoor Palace along with the bearers to bring a lady of high rank to his palace. Junior Paluvettarayar complied with this request as well. But he started deliberating.

The prime minister is involved in some conspiracy. Who is that high ranked woman to be brought in the closed palanquin? And why is she to be brought here? I should find that out.

Alvarkkadiyan met the prime minister, his mentor, with all reverence and humility.

'Nambi, what happened to your mission?'

'Master. It failed.'

'I expected that. Were you able to meet the crown prince?'

'I did meet him, Master. But I couldn't prevent the crown prince from visiting the Kadamboor Palace.'

'Malayaman and Kodumbalur Chieftain have gathered huge armies to march towards Tanjore. God alone can save this country.'

'I will make one last attempt to save this country from danger.'

'What are you going to do, Master?'

'The first step of my plan has already been executed. Nambi, I have succeeded in a task which you said was impossible.'

'No surprise, Master. But what's the task?'

'Didn't I ask you to bring the mute woman roaming in the Lankan islands? But you said that you couldn't do it. But I brought her to my palace last night.'

'It's a miracle, Master. How did you do it?'

'I expected the mute woman would come to Kodikkarai to know the fate of the younger prince. I had sent men to capture her. Without giving any trouble, she let herself be brought here. I had her brought in the Paluvoor palanquin.

But her journey was delayed on account of the storm. I am yet to see her. You have come at the right time. Let us go meet her together.'

'Master, I am also eager to see her.'

'Then come, let's go to the ladies' chambers. You are already known to her. She also knows that you are dear to the younger prince. She will have a soft corner for you.'

The master and the disciple walked to the ladies' chambers. But he was shocked. There was a sarcastic smile on Alvarkkadiyan's face.

The prime minister was staring at the woman and turned towards Alvarkkadiyan

'Nambi, something has gone wrong!'

'I too think so, Master.'

'This woman is quite young. The woman I expected should be forty. Have you seen Mandakini in Lanka?'

'Yes, Master. Whom did you send to bring this woman? Which idiot has bungled? I would like to see him.'

'Pinakapani, the son of the chief doctor of Palaiyarai. I gave him all the identification marks about that woman. He even sent a message to me about the success of the mission. But he met with an accident last night in the storm while bringing her to Tanjore.'

'Yes, Master. I too took refuge in a roadside resthouse when the storm was in full fury.'

'A huge tree on the roadside fell on those who came behind the palanquin. The doctor's son was caught underneath the fallen tree. The palanquin had a narrow escape.'

Then they heard a high-pitched female voice.

'Only the tree fell on that devil? And not the lightning? And the thunder? Very sad!' screamed Poonkulali.

The prime minister looked at Poonkulali in surprise. All along the prime minister had been under the impression that the lady was mute so he was taken aback when she spoke.

'Who is she? What is her motive? Why did she act like a deaf and dumb woman all along?'

'Why don't we ask her, Master?' When Nambi said this, the prime minister saw the mischievous smile on Nambi's face and suspected he knew everything already. However, he asked the girl, 'Hey girl, aren't you deaf? Can you hear me?'

'It would have been better if I had been deaf. Prime Minister, please tell me if that devil Pinakapani is dead,' Poonkulali asserted.

'Hey girl, why didn't you say anything ever since you came here?'

'Prime Minister, I had the ability to speak till I reached your palace yesterday night. But when I saw your palace, I was too stunned to speak. Your women spoke to me in sign language. I thought all of them were dumb. And I too spoke to them in sign language.'

'You chatterbox, I pity the doctor's son who brought you here.'

'Prime Minister, that fool did not capture me. If he had attempted that, he would be dead by this time.'

'Oh girl, after all he did not capture you. Why are you so furious with him?'

'Yes, but his men tied me to my boat. But that devil of the doctor's son told me that he had no hand in that.'

'To that extent at least, he is smart. He followed my instructions.'

'Oh! My God! Prime Minister, was it you who ordered that my aunt be caught and brought before you?'

'Is Mandakini your aunt? Then tell me, how are you related to the caretaker of the lighthouse?'

'Yes, she is my aunt. The lighthouse caretaker is my father, Prime Minster.'

'I never knew that he has such a talkative daughter. You said that your aunt was captured by some men. Do you know where they are? How did you get into the palanquin meant for your aunt?'

'Prime Minister, first tell me why you had sent your men to capture my aunt, a dumb and innocent woman.'

'I can't reveal that to you.'

'Then I too can't answer your question.'

'I know how to extract the truth from you. I'll put you in the underground dungeons.'

'No prison can hold me.'

'Nobody has ever come back from the Tanjore dungeons.'

'Wrong, again, Prime Minster. Amudan returned from the underground dungeons.'

'Who is Amudan?'

'He is the son of my other aunt. The two of us were travelling from Kodikkarai together.'

'What for, my child?'

'To see the palaces, mansions and other high-rise buildings of Tanjore. I also wanted to meet the emperor.'

'Girl, but you can't meet the emperor. Tell me first how you got into the palanquin that I had sent for somebody else. Did somebody force you into the palanquin?'

'When I was near the Tanjore Fort, I saw a vacant palanquin. It was raining outside. Just to escape from the rain, I got into it.'

The minister now spoke to his disciple.

'I now understand. They must have kept the palanquin down during heavy rain. At that time, this girl must have changed places with her aunt unnoticed. Nambi, is my guess correct?'

'Perfect! Master! I saw that happening with my own eyes.'

'What? You saw that? Then why didn't you say that earlier? Tell me what happened.'

Alvarkkadiyan narrated how this girl got into the palanquin and how the mute escaped along with Amudan.

'What happened to those two people?'

'They left the place a few minutes after the palanquin left. I too left the place.'

'Nambi, why were you a silent spectator? Why didn't you stop this girl's aunt?'

'Master, first of all I never knew that you were behind the abduction drama. Because the palanquin belonged to the Paluvoor Palace, I thought that Junior Paluvettarayar was abducting that lady.'

'She could not have gone far yet. It was raining almost for the whole of last night. She should be somewhere near here. Nambi, we should somehow get her here. Hey girl, what's your name? Do you know where your aunt will be now?'

'Poonkulali is my name, Prime Minister. If you tell me why you sent your men to capture her, I will share her whereabouts with you.'

'Nambi, there is no point in talking to this headstrong girl. She will not reveal anything. Do you know where to find her?'

'Master, she must be in Amudan's garden outside the fort. If you send some men with me, I'll bring her here.'

'If you try to do that I'll complain to the emperor. I'll tom-tom your atrocities to the whole town,' said Poonkulali.

'Nambi, we have to send her to the underground dungeons. There is no other way.'

'Master, there is no need to send this girl to the dungeons. Instead, we can send her to Princess Kundavai's palace. Princess Kundavai is here in the city at this moment. She'd cure this crazy girl and get a few things done through her.'

'Why do you say that? How can this silly girl help Princess Kundavai?'

'You don't know, Master? The storm which we had last night has wreaked havoc in the coastal area of Chola Kingdom. Nagapattinam is in great danger. I hear that the sea has come into the town and the whole town is submerged. Messengers have come to you from all the four directions bearing the bad news.'

'Yes, yes. Thanks for reminding me. I need to see them now. I've lost precious time talking to this silly girl.'

At that moment, Princess Kundavai and Vanathi arrived. When the princess saw Poonkulali, her face brightened.

61

Flood Relief

The prime minister welcomed Princess Kundavai and Princess Vanathi.

'Princess! Anything urgent? Hope the emperor is doing fine.'

'The emperor's health is as usual. He is much disturbed by the storm. He requests you to immediately provide relief measures on a war footing.'

'The storm has affected the whole of the kingdom. My ardent disciple, Alvarkkadiyan has brought terrible news. He claims that the sea has drowned all the coastal towns from Kodikkarai to Nagapattinam. Anyhow let us do whatever is possible from our end.'

Princess Kundavai struggled hard to calm herself.

'Prime Minister, I too heard about the tsunami in Nagapattinam. I am worried about the monks at the monastery there.'

With these words, she threw a pointed glance at Poonkulali.

'Prime Minister, how did this girl come here? Isn't she the daughter of the Kodikkarai lighthouse keeper?'

'She is. But she is tough unlike her father. She has the habit of poking her nose into matters unrelated to her.'

Princess Kundavai grew suspicious. Perhaps, the prime minister had brought Poonkulali only to spy on the whereabouts of Prince Arulmoli. The prime minister was known for such tricks. She decided to take sides with Poonkulali.

'No, sir. I don't agree with you. Poonkulali is a nice girl. Poonkulali, why is our prime minister angry with you? Did you give him any trouble?'

Poonkulali came near Kundavai.

'Princess, did I give him trouble or did he give trouble to me?'

'Ok, dear. You are also angry. Come, sit by my side.'

'Prime Minister, why did you bring this girl here?'

'Your Highness, I did not bring this girl here. It's all her making. She... came...'

Poonkulali spat fire.

'Princess, why is the honourable minister hesitant to reveal the truth?'

The minister responded, 'She came on her own looking for her aunt.'

'Who is her aunt? Oh, Amudan's mother?'

'No, Princess. This girl has another aunt who is also mute. You might have heard of a dumb woman wandering in the Lankan forests. I wanted to bring her here for an important work. I tried my best to do that. I almost succeeded. But you know in the last minute... this girl...'

Kundavai was immensely excited.

'Oh, God! Is that true? Where is that lady? I want to see her right now!' the princess got up.

'Please forgive me, Princess. This girl spoilt everything at the last minute.'

Kundavai sat down disappointed. She then turned to Poonkulali.

'Is that true, Poonkulali?'

'Princess, please ask the prime minister what kind of tactics he employed to bring my aunt. Then you won't blame me.'

The prime minister briefed the events.

Princess Kundavai keenly listened to what he had to say. Finally, she declared.

'Prime Minister, then she should be somewhere near the fort. Why don't you send your men to look for her?'

'Thank God! There is no need to search for her. My disciple here says that she is in Amudan's hut. And that my disciple saw her this morning.'

'Then what are you waiting for, Sir? Let's go and bring her here. If you are busy, I'll go myself. Vanathi, let's go!'

Alvarkkadiyan intervened.

'Let's wait, Princess. If the lady sees strangers coming, she will be frightened.'

The minister endorsed his disciple's views.

'What my disciple says is correct. Ask this girl Poonkulali to bring her here. There are only two people in the whole world whom the mute queen will listen to. One of them is this girl.'

Alvarkkadiyan hesitated for a while.

'The other person is drowned in the sea.'

Kundavai pretended not to have heard Alvarkkadiyan's words. She addressed Poonkulali.

'Poonkulali, please bring your aunt here. I promise you that she won't be hurt. I need to meet her regarding something very important.'

'Yes, Princess.'

'Nambi, you go with this girl.'

Poonkulali and Alvarkkadiyan left for Amudan's garden.

'Sir, after you meet the visitors. I want to discuss some crucial matters with you.'

'Yes Princess, I too need to talk to you.'

The minister went away to meet the visitors.

62

The Prime Minister's Blunder

After meeting the visitors, the prime minister came back to the Princess.

'Princess, our men are assessing the cyclone damages. I have also sent word to Junior Paluvettarayar to open up the royal treasury.'

'Thank you, Prime Minister. Will they be able to bring the mute queen safely? I am worried about it.'

'Princess, why are you so excited about her? How do you know about her?'

'Sir, the emperor mentioned her a few days ago.'

'Oh my God! Did he tell you that she was alive?'

'No, he didn't. The emperor thinks that she is dead. That has troubled him a lot. He told me that it was you who conveyed the death news to him. Then how did you know that the lady was still alive?'

'I was about to ask you the same question!'

'I have no problem in sharing that with you. The warrior of the Vaanar clan who had been to Lanka told me about her. And then my brother Arulmoli...'

Soon Kundavai realized her mistake and bit her lips.

'Princess, if you don't want to discuss about Prince Arulmoli let it be so.'

'No, Prime Minister Sir, I have decided to come clean about everything. That's why I came here. There is no point in hiding things. It gives rise to unnecessary dangers and complications. My brother did not drown in the sea. He was saved by the Ocean King. He is now safe in the Buddhist Monastery at Nagapattinam. I had been to Nagapattinam only to see him. I know that you already knew everything.'

'Your doubts are justified, Princess. But I never showed that I knew. I have a policy not to interfere in any of your matters. Princess, I strongly believe that you'll always be just and right.'

'I am only worried about the prince's safety.'

'Don't worry Princess, the prince will be safe and secure.'

'Sir, I want you to say these words to my father. He is devastated.'

'Alas! Does the emperor know that the prince is in the Buddhist Monastery?'

'Yes sir, I told him yesterday.'

'Oh my God! We could have delayed telling him for a few more days. People have come to know that it was Senior Paluvettarayar who sent ships to arrest the prince. The Paluvettarayars are waiting for some lame excuse to start a war. The Kodumbalur chieftain is coming with a huge army. This great kingdom should not be destroyed by sibling rivalry.'

'I don't want any of my brothers to ascend the throne. I don't have any objection to Madurandakan being crowned as the king.'

'Princess, you may not object but the people will. And there will be mutiny.'

'Yes sir, I am also concerned about it. Yesterday the emperor's condition became serious. I was forced to tell him that Ponniyin Selvan was safe and secure. But he didn't believe my words. He is still under the hallucination that the ghost woman is taking revenge on his sons.'

'Oh my God! Can you tell me what happened last night?'

'Sir, I came here seeking your advice on that. He told me about the mute queen, her death and her ghost that is haunting him. And of late the ghost is haunting him very often.'

'But Princess, do you believe him?'

'Well, I am confused. Initially I thought that the emperor had lost his mind. But when I deeply deliberated those events, I had other doubts. One day, Vanathi heard the emperor screaming. She ran to his room. She saw a figure closely resembling the junior queen of Paluvoor standing before the emperor. The shock was too much for her. She fainted. From then on, I started having doubts about the relationship between the mute queen and the Paluvoor Queen. My doubts were confirmed by what Vandiyathevan and Prince Arulmoli said. Is Nandini Devi the mute woman's daughter?'

'I too had those doubts, Princess. If we go by the appearance our inference is right. There are only three people in the world who know about the relationship.'

'Who are they?'

'The first is the Queen Mother, Sembian Madevi. We can't know what it is unless the Queen Mother herself chooses to share it with us. She revealed it to her husband Emperor Kandarditya on his deathbed. He began to tell me that secret but he hardly spoke two words before he died. The other two can't speak. One is Amudan's mother. And the other is her elder sister, the mute queen. We can't get anything from Amudan's mother. She is fiercely loyal to Sembian Madevi. That's why I took great efforts to bring Mandakini from Lanka.'

'Oh, is her name Mandakini? How did you know that she was alive?'

'Princess, I knew that twenty-five years ago itself.'

'What? You knew that twenty-five years ago? Then why didn't you tell my father? My father believes that she is dead and has been suffering. And you know that very well.'

The prime minister's mind was in a state of turbulence. He started a long narration:

'Devi, I committed an offence twenty-five years ago. I confess it to you for the first time now. Nobody else knows this. Your father sent me to look for that fisherman's daughter. We went to Kodikkarai. We were informed that she had jumped into the turbulent sea from the lighthouse. I came back to Tanjore and conveyed the news to my dear friend.'

'I don't see your fault in this'

'The fisherman's daughter fell into the sea. But she did not die. As we were coming back from Kodikkarai I saw a boat coming in. I saw Mandakini in that boat. I gave loads of money to the boatman and requested him to take her safely to Lanka and keep her there. I came back to Tanjore and told the emperor that the fisherman's daughter was dead. I thought I was helping your father. I never thought that my lie would lead to such disaster.'

The princess intervened.

'Sir, but you did it with all good intentions. But tell me this: did you get any news about her?'

'Even after that I have been closely following her. One day I saw Esana Bhattar's father chatting with her. He revealed another secret to me. He told me that Mandakini stayed in the garden of the Queen Mother's palace for some time. After giving birth to twins she left the palace without telling anyone, leaving her children there. She used to come once in a way to see her children. When I asked him about the children, he refused to say anything about them. He told me that it was a secret known only to the Queen Mother. When Arulmoli fell into the Cauvery River he was saved by the fisherwoman. I knew this even at that time.'

'Very true, Minister Sir. Arulmoli also told me the same thing. Last night when the great storm was raging outside, the storm inside my father's mind was no less. He did not sleep even for a second. He did not let me sleep as well. He told me the old story once again. My father thinks the mute queen is the cause for all the troubles. He thinks she will not rest until Karikalan is dead. I consoled him. He did not listen. Finally, I had no option but to tell him that Arulmoli was safe in the Buddhist Monastery at Nagappattinam.'

'Was the emperor at peace after that?'

'No, sir. He became even more agitated. First, he did not believe the news. But then I told him that I saw the prince in person. He asked me why I had not brought him here. I told him that he was not well and would bring him as soon as possible. I also told him the confusion that would follow if Arulmoli appears on the scene now. But his mind went in a different direction.

He finally announced that he was not in favour of my brothers ascending the throne. Again, he started crying that the mute queen was unable to drown Prince Arulmoli in the sea and that's why she has brought the sea into the land to kill him.

'He was sobbing like a child, Sir!' Saying this Princess Kundavai started crying.

63

Mute Queen Disappeared

The prime minister consoled Princess Kundavai.

'Princess, I'm the one who is responsible for all the sufferings of your father. I have to atone for my sins.'

'Prime Minister, if you tell my father that the mute queen is not dead, he may find peace. I also have another request. Please bring my stepmother here. I know that you are already on the job.'

'Princess, he won't believe my words unless he sees her himself. Till the succession issue is fully resolved, let not the country know about the prince. Let us discuss the issue with the emperor.'

'Does your father worry about Crown Prince Karikalan?'

'Not at all. The emperor knows no one could harm Karikalan. I sent news to stop him from going to Kadamboor and informed him that the junior queen might be our sister. I have also requested the warrior from the Vaanar clan to guard the crown prince and always remain with him.'

'Aha! We can convince your mother but not your mother's father, the Chieftain of Thirukkovalur. Oh My God! I can't even guess how he will react. And if he knows that his grandchildren are not going to be kings, his ire will be boundless.'

'Sir, leave the job of pacifying my grandfather to me.'

Poonkulali walked in just then. All of them were shocked to see her alone.

'Hey, girl! Where is your aunt? And where is Nambi?' asked the Prime Minister anxiously.

'Sorry sir, I could not bring her here as promised.'

'What happened?'

'We brought her into the fort. Then she was caught in the crowd and disappeared.'

Poonkulali narrated.

'When we reached the gates of the fort, the personal guards of the emperor—the Velakkara Army were also entering the fort. The three of us stepped aside to let the army pass.

Suddenly a big crowd barged into the fort along with the army of bodyguards. The soldiers guarding the gates did their best to prevent their entry but they could not. Meanwhile, Mandakini blended in with that crowd and disappeared. We looked for her but she was not found anywhere.

Alvarkkadiyan asked me to inform the prime minister about the developments and said that he will make efforts to find her.'

The prime minister was worried about the crowd gathered inside the palace and a possible mutiny.

Princess Kundavai was very worried and the prime minister comforted her.

'Don't worry about Mandakini. She will be inside the fort only. She will never leave the fort without seeing the emperor. I'll easily trace her.'

64

Mute Queen's Hot Pursuit

The mute queen, Mandakini, saw the conspirator Ravidasan entering the fort along with the crowd. Though she was mute, Mandakini's eyesight was unusually sharp.

Gifted with a strong sense of foreboding, Mandakini felt that Ravidasan had entered the fort with an evil intention. She recalled Ravidasan's earlier attempts to kill Prince Arulmoli in Lanka.

Mandakini saw Ravidasan and Soman Sambavan hurrying into one of the alleys inside the fort. She ran behind them. This was when Alvarkkadiyan and Poonkulali had lost sight of the mute queen.

The two men ran through the alleys. They never suspected that somebody was following them. After reaching the palace of Senior Paluvettarayar, they used an uprooted tree as a ladder to scale the wall. Mandakini also took the same route.

Ravidasan made Soman Sambavan wait in the garden. He then entered the palace of Senior Paluvettarayar. Both Senior Paluvettarayar and his Junior Queen Nandini, were not in the palace at that time.

Ravidasan mimicked the sound of an owl.

Paluvoor junior queen's maid came out to the garden. Ravidasan hiding behind a large tree came out to meet her.

'Oh, sorcerer, when the queen is not here, why have you come?'

'The queen sent me here.'

'Oh my God! Junior Paluvettarayar is suspicious of the maids here in this palace. He has issued strict orders.'

'Let him go to hell. Their period is over. I want the keys of the underground treasury. Please bring them fast.'

'I won't give them to you.'

'If you refuse me, tonight I will send nine ghosts to your bed and carry you to the burial ground and then...'

'Please don't do that! I'll fetch the keys to you when the girls are eating. Be patient until then.'

'Agreed. Bring plenty of food for me.'

The maid left the place.

Ravidasan and Soman Sambavan were chatting. Mandakini was observing them. Her intuition revealed that something bad was going to happen soon.

The maid returned when the other maids had gone for their meal. Ravidasan went inside and got the key-bunch and the food parcel from her.

They reached the entrance to the treasury and opened it with three different keys.

'Oh my God! How can I go in this darkness? Girl, bring a torch.'

'How can I bring it now? If somebody sees me...'

'If you don't...'

'Shut up. I'll bring the torch.'

As soon as the maid left, Ravidasan returned to the garden to give the food to his accomplice.

'You have to stay in the treasury for two or three days. You may have to wait for the right time. Keep this food parcel with you. The girl has gone to fetch a light. You need to go into the treasury before she returns.'

The two men walked towards the treasury. Mandakini followed them closely.

65

Secret Underground Chamber

Ravidasan took Soman Sambavan to the underground secret chamber. He asked him to go in.

'At first you won't be able to see. Go deep inside and stay there till you get used to the darkness.'

Ravidasan went to the garden gazebo to get the torch from the maid. Mandakini silently walked towards the underground chamber. The door was still open and she went in.

Mandakini was used to staying in dense forests during night time. This darkness did not deter her. She saw Ravidasan's companion hit against a pillar in the dark passage. She walked in the opposite direction and stood near a flight of steps leading further down.

The maid was returning with a torch.

Ravidasan approached her and got the torch from her.

'Hey girl, lock the door from outside and take back the keys. Come back with the keys after thirty minutes and knock on the door gently. If I respond to your knocking, then you can open the door. Ensure that nobody is around when you open the door.'

'Ok, sorcerer. But it is my duty to warn you. If you are caught by any chance, don't spill my name.'

'Don't worry, girl.'

The maid went back.

The moment she locked the door from outside, Ravidasan locked the door from inside. He then held the torch aloft and went to Soman Sambavan.

'Sambava, you wanted to ask me something?'

'Did you come here before?'

'I have been here so many times. All the gold we have now came from here.'

'I didn't mean that. You left me here and went out. Did you come in again? It seemed as though a figure walked in. I heard the footsteps.'

'You are hallucinating, Sambava. This underground chamber is like that. At times, there will be shadows in darkness. People who have come here have died of fear. Their skeletons are scattered around here.'

'But is it at all possible to enter in here by stealth?'

'No. Even I have been in here only with the help of the junior queen.

Come, let me show you the secret passages around here. First, I'll show you the way to the King's Palace from here. You go around and familiarize yourself with the places after I leave. It might come handy some day.'

Ravidasan and Soman Sambavan walked along.

In the smoky light of the burning torch, the pillars and their shadows appeared like large black ghosts. The flying bats looked like little spirits. There were many strange creatures that crawled. And now, they could hear many weird sounds.

Soman Sambavan froze.

'Ravidasa, do you hear the sound of footsteps?'

'Why, no. Don't get scared by the sounds and sights. You are shivering in fear even in my presence. How will you remain here all alone for three days?'

'No, I am not afraid. I wanted to clarify certain things with you. Didn't you say that those who entered this chamber died here?'

'Yes, I said their ghosts would also be hovering around here. So what? The ghosts will be scared of us.'

'I'm not worried about the spirits and ghosts. I am worried about the other creatures... snakes, scorpions... Ravidasa. If I get an opportunity a little earlier...'

'No, no. Don't do that blunder. Today is Tuesday. You'll have to wait for Wednesday and Thursday. And during these two days find out the time when Sundara Chola is alone. His queen will go to the Durga temple on Friday. You finish your work at that time. Don't change the plan.'

The men continued to walk fast. The mute queen secretly followed them. They reached the other side of the underground chamber. There were no windows, doors or other entrances through the wall. But at the top of the wall, there was a small ventilator through which dim light entered the chamber.

Ravidasan started climbing the high-rise wall holding on to the crevices. He reached the ventilator and spent some time seeing through it. Then he scaled down the wall.

'If you look through that ventilator, you can see the Chola King's palace and also Sundara Chola's bedroom.'

Ravidasa bent down and firmly placed his foot on a round stone pressing it hard. A passage appeared below.

The two men went down through that secret passage. The light from the torch disappeared.

The mute queen came out of her hiding place and with a giant leap reached the entrance of the secret passage. She then looked at the place where Ravidasa had scaled the high wall. She leapt up and scaled the wall in the same way as Ravidasa had. She reached the latticed window and sat on the place near it. She looked through the window.

She was shocked by what she saw there.

Ravidasan and Soman Sambavan were hiding behind the pillars in the balcony. It was day time; she could see the balcony clearly. Sambavan was armed with a deadly spear. Ravidasan got the spear from him and aimed at a spot inside the mansion. Thank God, he did not throw the spear. He just had a mock drill. Then he returned the spear to Sambavan. The two men disappeared from that place.

Mandakini climbed down the wall. She hid herself without taking her eyes off the entrance to the secret passage. The two men came out and closed the secret passage.

'Do you know how to open the entrance?'

'Yes, I do. Don't worry. Sundara Chola's life will be over by this Friday. You complete your part of the mission.'

'Good Sambava! The junior queen will take care of Karikalan. The little tiger has escaped from the sea. But this time, he can't escape. The two women devils who saved him are right now here in Tanjore. Alvarkkadiyan is also here. So, there is nobody to save that little tiger in Nagapattinam. By this Friday, the entire clan of Sundara Chola will have disappeared.'

'Poor fellow! Let that fool Madurandakan live for some time as the Chola Emperor till our little emperor comes of age.'

Ravidasa and Soman Sambavan retraced their steps to the entrance of the secret underground chamber.

66

Touching Moments

After Ravidasa left, Soman Sambavan sat near the entrance to the secret passage waiting for sunset. Mandakini came very close to him.

He pressed the levers and the door to the passage opened. When he was about to get in, he heard a strange scream which he had never before heard. Gripped by fear, he started running blindly in the dark chamber.

As soon as he disappeared, Mandakini stepped into the secret passage. After a few steps down, she reached level ground. The path was like dark endless hell. Suddenly something hit her head. There were some openings large enough to let her in, near the place where she hit her head. She entered one of them and came out on the other side and reached the Hall of Sculptures in the palace. There were giant-sized statues in the palace including the statue of the ten-headed Ravana uprooting mount Kailasa, the abode of God Siva and Goddess Parvathi.

The Hall of Sculptures ended in a wall. Mandakini placed her hand on the wall and pressed. A small door opened. She came out through the door and into the royal garden from where she could see the palace towers and balconies. Mandakini looked around. There was nobody around as it was late evening.

She carefully scanned all the directions with her x-ray eyes. She sighted the exact place where the villain had stood aiming the spear a little while ago along with his accomplice. There were only a few dim lamps in this area providing her a cover of darkness.

Mandakini reached the palace building. She glanced at all the beautiful objects in the building for a while and climbed a flight of stairs.

She saw light at one place and walked towards it. She hid herself behind a pillar and looked on.

She saw something and could not take her eyes off it. In a large chamber there was a huge artistic cot with a person lying on it. There were four women and two men standing around the cot with full devotion and attention. One of them was her brother's daughter, Poonkulali. But she could not recognize the others. Mandakini slowly moved her eyes to the person lying in the cot. Her heart stopped.

Yes! He was the one who had stolen her heart when she was a little girl several years ago on Ghost Island. Yes, he was the one who had converted that island into a paradise for some time. Yes, he was the one forcibly taken away from her by those people who came in a large ship. Oh my God, how time had changed him!

Of course, she had seen him several times after that, unnoticed by him.

Oh God! He has changed so much in such a short time! With wrinkles on his forehead. Why has he aged so much so fast?

He now sported a moustache and a beard. There was no flesh on his cheeks. The skin had gone dry. His face which used to shine like a golden sun had completely lost its sheen.

Mandakini suddenly remembered the scene that she witnessed a few hours ago. Ravidasan and his accomplice had stood at the place where she was standing now. It was from this place that they had taken aim with a spear.

Oh my God! Did they aim at the person lying in the cot?

These thoughts made her tremble.

67

Grievances Against the Prime Minister

The emperor's health was in a bad state. After Junior Paluvettarayar's visit, he was shattered in mind and body.

Junior Paluvettarayar charged the prime minister with several lapses. Many people had entered the fort on the pretext of seeing the prime minister, thereby posing security threats.

The next charge against the prime minister was graver still. The prime minister who was known throughout the country as a man of high morals had forcibly abducted a woman from Kodikkarai to bring her to the capital having used the Paluvoor palanquin for the shameful act.

Junior Paluvettarayar magnified the final charge that centred on a suspicious occurrence.

'A sorcerer was often visiting my brother's palace at the insistence of the junior queen of Paluvoor. On suspicion, I appointed a spy to keep a watch on the movements near my brother's palace. The spy reported to me today that somebody jumped the wall of my brother's palace. My men caught the offender who is none other than Alvarkkadiyan, the darling disciple of our prime minister.'

The emperor's agony worsened.

'Leave it to me. The prime minister is coming to see me this evening. I'll ask him to explain his actions. Are you sure it's true?' the emperor asked.

'Very true, Your Majesty.'

Junior Paluvettarayar took leave of the emperor.

The emperor was expecting the prime minister since morning.

But he only turned up in the evening.

The prime minister, generally a strong person, appeared shaken that day as his mission had failed in spite of meticulous planning.

He thought he would meet the emperor only after finding out the whereabouts of Mandakini. That's why his meeting with the emperor was delayed. Meanwhile Alvarkkadiyan also brought some bad news.

He reported that the mute queen had scaled Senior Paluvettarayar's palace wall near the alley.

But before he could look for the lady, he had been apprehended by Junior Paluvettarayar's men. He could not tell the real reason to them. He had to use the prime minister's name to free himself.

'There are so many palaces inside the fort. Why should she choose Senior Paluvettarayar's palace? I can't even openly search the place. I hope she won't go back without meeting the emperor. Let us trace her. Let us meet the emperor immediately along with Poonkulali. If the boat-girl who actually rescued Prince Arulmoli told the story herself, the emperor might be convinced.'

Prime Minister Aniruddha Brahmarayar, his disciple Alvarkkadiyan and Poonkulali walked into the palace.

Princess Kundavai and Vanathi were waiting for them at the entrance of the palace. Kundavai was disturbed by the fact that Mandakini could not be found.

She was even more disturbed on knowing that the mute queen had trespassed into Senior Paluvettarayar's garden.

The prime minister then went into the emperor's bed chamber leaving Poonkulali and Alvarkkadiyan with Kundavai.

After paying his respects to the emperor and the empress he explained the reasons for his delay. He was busy in assessing the flood damages and organizing relief measures.

The emperor was pacified on knowing about the relief work.

'It's good you are here in the absence of the finance minister at this hour of crisis. But what is this I hear? Did you abduct a woman from Kodikkarai? Junior Paluvettarayar told me a little while ago. I never expected this kind of conduct from you. Nowadays, you don't share any information with me because I am ill and invalid.

Kundavai says that Arulmoli did not drown and he is safe at the Buddhist Monastery in Nagapattinam. If he is alive, why hasn't he come to see me till now? Why has no one told me till now that he is alive? Prime Minister, why I should continue to live. My own children and my dearest friend are engaged in a conspiracy against me.'

The emperor was choked with tears.

After a pause the prime minister gave vent to his feelings.

'Your Majesty, we have been friends for forty years. And during these forty years I have done nothing against your interests. And I certainly won't do so in the future as well.

Yes, I kept a few things to myself with the good intention of not disturbing you. If you think I have wronged you, please forgive me and now I'll answer all your questions. Please listen to me.

My Majesty, you'll soon come to know who all are really conspiring against you. I am retaining the prime minister's post only in name. I have indicated several times that I would readily hand over the post to Senior Paluvettarayar. I am ready to quit if you have the slightest doubt on my loyalty...'

'You want to desert me at the slightest provocation. The only person who is always by my side is this woman, my wife, Malayaman's daughter.'

Empress Vanama Devi heard these words and broke into a sob and ran out of the room.

'Oh, King of Kings, whatever you said about your wife is true. And your children born of her divine womb are all fully devoted to you.'

'But they don't respect my words, Minister. And you are always on their side. The news has spread throughout the country that the Paluvettarayars sank the prince's ship and drowned him in the sea.'

'It's absolute falsehood. The prince did not come in the ship sent by the Paluvettarayar brothers. He came in Parthiban's ship. And the prince, jumped into the sea to save somebody else on his own accord in spite of Parthiban's strong objection.'

'I know it is a lie they were all fabricated mainly to deceive me. I couldn't bear to think that Princess Kundavai too is a part of this conspiracy...I never expected this from my darling daughter. Even if the whole world goes against me, I thought Kundavai would be on my side. And I even shared with her something which no father would share with his daughter.'

'Oh, King of Kings, even if the whole world accuses Kundavai I won't believe that. You shouldn't believe that either. If the princess holds back something, there must be a strong reason for that.

It's a fact that the prince did jump into the sea to save his friend. The boat-girl who rescued both the prince and his friend is waiting in the ante-room. She is an eye-witness to what happened in Lanka. Shall I call her, Your Majesty?'

'Oh! Call her right now, Prime Minister.'

Alvarkkadiyan and Poonkulali entered the emperor's bed chamber.

68

Emperor in Dream World

The emperor looked at Poonkulali.
'I don't think I have seen this girl before. But her face looks very familiar. Prime Minister, who's she?'

'She is Poonkulali, daughter of the lighthouse keeper at Kodikkarai.'

The king whispered to himself. 'Yes, she resembles her aunt. But there are a lot of differences.'

Poonkulali heard the emperor. It was the first time she was meeting the emperor. She had heard that the emperor was more handsome than even Cupid. But she felt sad to see the emperor struck by sickness and stress. She had planned to argue with the emperor but after knowing his condition she was upset.

The emperor fondly enquired, 'Hey girl, how is your father?'

Poonkulali prostrated before him and stood up with folded hands reverentially.

The emperor asked the prime minister, 'Can this girl talk? Unlike her aunt...'

'Yes, Your Majesty, she can talk as much as nine women can talk at a time.'

'I don't know why everyone becomes silent on seeing me. No one shares anything with me these days.'

The emperor turned his attention to Poonkulali again.

'Girl, the prime minister says that you saved Prince Arulmoli from drowning. Is that true?'

'Yes, my Majesty.'

'The emperor is pleased beyond words for you having saved the prince. He wants to reward you. Now tell the emperor what happened on that fateful day.'

Poonkulali recounted everything from the time she took Vandiyathevan in her boat to Lanka till she dropped the prince at Nagapattinam. The prime minister had already warned her not to reveal anything about the mute queen.

The emperor was pleased.

'Girl, you rescued the prince and brought him to our shores. Why did you take him to Nagapattinam instead of bringing him here?'

'My Majesty, the prince had the delirious fever. We knew that there are good doctors at the Buddhist Monastery in Nagapattinam. Hence we took him there.'

'Paluvettarayar was camping at Kodikkarai at that time? Why didn't you tell him?'

Though Poonkulali hesitated initially, she eventually replied in a fearless voice.

'Your Majesty, the whole country says that Paluvettarayar has been working against the interests of the prince. How can I entrust a sick prince to his avowed enemy?'

'Aha! Is it like that?'

After making this sarcastic comment to Poonkulali the emperor turned to the prime minister.

'Yesterday's storm must have devastated the coastal town of Nagapattinam.'

'My Lord, ours is a blessed country with good governance. Hence...'

'Yes, the Chola Kingdom is blessed. I want to see my sons at least once before I close my eyes.'

'Please don't utter such words, Your Majesty. I'll send my disciple Alvarkkadiyan to Nagapattinam to bring back the prince safely to the capital.'

Only now did the emperor notice Alvarkkadiyan.

'Oh, he is here! Junior Paluvettarayar was blaming him. Did he jump the wall of Senior's palace?'

'Your Majesty, permit me to explain everything tomorrow. You are already exhausted...'

The empress, Princess Kundavai and Vanathi entered the chamber at that moment.

The empress spoke to the prime minister pointing to Poonkulali. 'This girl has a beautiful voice. Ask her to sing.'

'My disciple also sings very well. Let him also sing.'

Poonkulali and Alvarkkadiyan sang. The emperor enjoyed the songs and lapsed into deep sleep.

Everybody left the room.

On seeing Poonkulali the emperor was reminded of old memories which manifested as dreams.

He was on a boat with Poonkulali. Suddenly the sky became dark. There was a storm. The boat rose sky-high along with the waves. Soon the sun rose like a golden ball of fire. There were islands full of green coconut groves at a distance. It was not Poonkulali but evergreen Mandakini rowing the boat.

'Mandakini, is that you? Even if somebody comes here with an offer to make me the king of the Three Worlds, I won't leave you. Let's cross the seven seas and reach the island at the end of the world, free from all disturbances.'

He suddenly woke up from the dream world. He looked in front of him. There was nobody in the room. An oil lamp lit the room.

Now he heard a mild sound coming from the terrace. He turned towards the direction of the sound. He saw a figure coming down from the terrace. Was it also a dream or a hallucination?

69

Why Torment Me?

Sundara Chola was shocked to see a figure coming down from the terrace. He felt the presence of the mysterious figure very close to him.

'Who is that? Come before me!' shouted the emperor. There was no response.

The emperor spoke to himself.

Is it she or her ghost? She used to come only at midnight. Now she has come in the evening in the absence of my queen, my daughter and maids. I am alone. She won't let me be in peace. Did I ask you to jump from the light house and kill yourself? Then why torment me?

He felt the figure move away.

Let me call somebody.

'Anybody there?' shouted the emperor.

Oh my God! Who is standing near my bed? I'll drive you out now.

The emperor angrily picked up an oil lamp near him and threw it aiming it at the mysterious figure.

'Go. Get lost!'

Now he heard a high-pitched voice moaning in unbearable grief. Fortunately, the burning lamp had missed its target. The emperor saw the figure fully for the first time. It was undoubtedly Mandakini still standing there with inexplicable grief on her face. She fondly looked at him for a second before attempting to run away.

It was at this time that a doubt first appeared in the emperor's mind.

Is it the ghost of Mandakini? Or somebody like her? Or her twin sister? Or is she still alive? Why did it not occur to me all these years? Oh my God! What have I done? What a heartless act! Her face reveals some deep anguish. Was she hurt by my cruel act? That's why she is trying to go away.*

Hearing the emperor cry, the empress, Princess Kundavai, Vanathi, Poonkulali, the prime minister and his disciple Alvarkkadiyan rushed into the emperor's chamber.

Everyone was shocked to see the emperor's horror-stricken face. They were even more shocked to see Mandakini standing there.

The prime minister understood the situation and inferred what could have possibly happened. He asked Poonkulali.

'Poonkulali, is this your aunt?'

'Yes, Sir.'

Poonkulali ran to Mandakini and caught hold of her. Pushing her niece's hands away, Mandakini tried to run away.

Alvarkkadiyan bolted the door guarding it.

Mandakini had no other way to escape except the route she had taken while entering. When she looked towards the terrace, everyone understood her plans.

Poonkulali did not try to stop her but spoke to her in sign language. Mandakini pointed out the oil lamp lying on the floor.

'Father, did you throw the oil lamp at her?' asked Princess Kundavai

'Yes dear. I threw the lamp to drive her away.'

'Oh, my father, she is not a ghost, she is my elder mother. She is very much alive. Prime minister will tell you everything.'

Princess Kundavai went near Mandakini and prostrated before her. She slowly took her to the emperor.

Now the empress saw the face of Mandakini who was bleeding from her forehead.

'My Lord, did you throw that lamp at her? What have you done?' screamed the empress.

'No, the lamp I threw did not reach her.'

'Do you know who she is?' screamed the empress at the emperor for the first time in her life.

'My Lord, she is our Goddess—the presiding deity of the Chola clan. She saved my dear son Arulmoli from drowning in the river when he was a child. She also saved you from a bear at Ghost Island in Lanka. That's why I worship her as our Goddess.'

'Oh my God! You know all this? And did you know that she was alive all these years?'

'Yes, my Lord. I told our prime minister to bring her here from Lanka.'

'Prime Minister, is Mandakini still alive? Then why did you lie to me that she was dead?'

'Your Majesty, it is true that she is alive. King of Kings, I beg your pardon,' said the prime minister.

The emperor saw Kundavai and Poonkulali giving first-aid to Mandakini.

'Poonkulali, ask your aunt how she got hurt.'

Poonkulali came forward and spoke reverentially.

'Your Majesty. My aunt says she hit her head against a hill.'

'Prime Minister, there is no hill in Chola Kingdom. And how does this lady claim that she hit herself against a hill in the Chola palace?'

Vanathi who was listening to this conversation spoke now.

'Your Majesty, I know what she means to say. There's a Hall of Sculptures in the palace garden. In that hall, there's a sculpture depicting Demon Ravana holding the Kailash mountain aloft. Perhaps she hit her head against that mountain.'

Vanathi's beautiful insight surprised everyone. The emperor was now staring at Mandakini. The prime minister now responded.

'Your Majesty, I was telling these people that she won't go without seeing you.'

The emperor turned towards the prime minister.

'I don't believe that, Prime Minister. If she had wanted to come, she could have come earlier. She did not turn up for twenty-five years. You lied, you said that this lady fell into the sea and killed herself. You've been repeating that lie for the past twenty-five years. And I believed you.'

'Your Majesty, it is true that she fell into the sea. But she was rescued. She made me promise her that I should never reveal to you that she was alive. I refused to give such a promise. Then she threatened to kill herself. I had no other option.'

'Prime Minister, your lapses have led to many a confusion. It is your duty to clear them now.'

70

Ravana in Danger

The emperor spoke softly to his daughter.

'Kundavai, I would like to discuss some sensitive issues with the prime minister. You may all leave. Let your mother alone be with me.'

The empress whispered to Kundavai. 'Take you Elder mother with you; refresh her and bring her back.'

Kundavai acknowledged the wonderful suggestion of the empress with a smile. She held Mandakini's hand and took her out of the chambers. Vanathi and Poonkulali went along with her.

Sundara Chola looked alternately at the empress and the prime minister.

'Prime Minster, please tell me the truth at least now without hiding anything from me.'

The prime minister responded emotionally.

'Your Majesty, I won't hide anything from you anymore. You hold yourself responsible for the death of that woman. So, the empress and I decided to remove your guilt by producing the lady before you. There is no other way to erase your feelings of guilt. That's why we brought her here.'

These words actually added fuel to the fire.

'Prime Minister, you are wrong. You took enormous trouble to bring her here. How are you going to send her away?'

The prime minister became speechless.

The empress stepped forward to speak.

'My Lord, I want to retain my sister here and I wish to pour all my love on her.'

'Queen, there is no need to prove your love for me by these gestures. And you need not retain her here. It is true that somewhere in the past when I was staying alone in an uninhabited island I fell in love with her. That love has now changed into hatred. Why should I bother about a woman who never cared for me for the past twenty-five years? She has only been haunting and tormenting me. I can't allow her to live in this palace.'

The empress and the prime minister were aghast by the revulsion of the emperor. The empress could not bear it any longer.

'My Lord, I beg of you. She has been sent by my Holy Mother Durga. Let us bring Arulmoli from Nagapattinam to reveal the truth.'

'This woman was not sent by Durga. She is a bad omen. Send her away.'

'My Lord, I beg of you, please grant me this boon. Let her stay in our palace.'

The emperor realized that she had never asked him for any favour till today. So he granted her request. He also asked the prime minister to bring the prince from Nagapattinam immediately.

'I want my sons here. I want to make an important decision. My cousin Madurandakan is the only rightful heir to the Chola throne. I have decided to make him the emperor. I don't care if people object to that. God forbid if my sons object to it.'

The empress intervened.

'That will never happen, My Lord. Your sons will never go against your wishes. They are not enamoured by the throne.'

'If that is so, then why is Karikalan refusing to come here?'

'Your Majesty, the crown prince has built a golden palace in Kanchi and is waiting for you there.'

'I know what he is waiting for. This son of mine will put me in prison and then ascend the Chola throne.'

The empress and the prime minister were shocked.

The prime minister replied in an emotional voice.

'The emperor's mind has been poisoned by some evil elements.'

'Nobody can poison my mind. Somebody has poisoned Karikalan's mind.'

'Your Majesty, if calamity awaits the Chola clan, that can come in two ways. The Paluvettarayars and the Sambuvarayars.'

'Stop it, Prime Minister! The Paluvettarayar clan has been serving our clan for more than a hundred years with absolute loyalty.'

'Your Majesty, I don't mean the Paluvettarayars are working against the Chola clan. I only mean they are desperately keen on crowning Madurandakan.'

'What is wrong in that, Prime Minister? Madurandakan is after all the rightful heir to the throne.'

'I don't deny that but they also do certain things without your permission. They are planning to divide the Chola Kingdom into two and give one to Madurandakan and the other to Karikalan. That is the discussion currently going on in Sambuvarayar's Palace.'

'Prime Minister, I will never allow this nonsense. Perhaps he wants to give at least half the kingdom to my son out of his love for me. But if only he knows my mind, he'll abandon the idea. I will make Madurandakan the king. And I'll see to it that his kingdom is not even an inch lesser than the one I ruled.'

'Your Majesty, even your sons will not oppose you. But the opposition is from a much higher place—a lady whom the people of Chola Empire worship as a Goddess.'

'I know you are referring to Queen Mother, Sembian Madevi. Prime Minister, please make arrangements to bring her here immediately. I'll change her mind.'

'Your Majesty, it is not that easy. The great Emperor Kandaraditya ordered his wife before his death. "Madurandakan should never be crowned. I have a very, strong reason. Only my wife knows it". Kandaraditya ordered me on his deathbed.'

'Prime Minister, is there really such a strong reason against Madurandakan becoming the king?'

'I have no idea. Only the Queen Mother can answer that.'

Now the emperor asked the empress to bring Princess Kundavai.

When the empress rushed to the ladies' chamber, she was alarmed to find Kundavai, Vanathi and Poonkulali in a state of shock. Mandakini was not there.

When the empress asked Kundavai about her, Kundavai burst out.

'Mother, as told by you we beautified elder mother. But, suddenly she was not there. We could not find her in any of the rooms.'

They all went to the garden to find her. They heard a loud noise from the Hall of Sculptures and went in. A strange sight awaited them. They saw Mandakini using a hammer to strike the hands of the demon Ravana holding Mount Kailash.

When Mandakini saw them, she dropped the hammer with a smile. Everyone, except Poonkulali, thought that Mandakini was crazy.

'Girls, let nobody even breathe about this incident in the presence of the emperor,' said the empress.

The Emperor's Anger

When Mandakini was found in the Hall of Sculptures by Princess Kundavai and others, an argument was going on between the emperor and the prime minister.

'Your Majesty, the personal body guards of the slain Pandiya king Veerapandiya are looking for an apt time to fulfil their deadly vow.'

The emperor reacted with a scornful smile.

'Prime Minister, this is old news. That's the reason the Paluvettarayars have tightened the security arrangements for me.'

'Your Majesty, those conspirators are funded from the Chola treasury.'

'What is this new yarn you are spinning now?'

'Yes, Your Majesty. I have much more wonderful yarns to spin. My disciple, Alvarkkadiyan is a direct witness for that.'

'Prime Minister, the Paluvettarayars have done yeoman service for the Chola clan for so many generations. I won't believe your disciple.'

'Your Majesty, I don't blame the Paluvettarayars. Perhaps the gold coins from the Chola treasury are going to the conspirators without their knowledge.'

'Prime Minister, it's impossible. Can anybody die without the knowledge of Yama, the lord of death?'

'Your Majesty, if Yama marries a young woman in his old age even that is possible.'

'I am also unhappy about Senior Paluvettarayar marrying at this age. That's why I refused to see his young wife. But that alone won't suffice to charge him.'

'Your Majesty, I am not accusing Paluvettarayar. I am accusing only his young wife.'

'You are maligning a young innocent woman.'

'Your Majesty, it is my duty to disclose certain details about his young wife to you. Please give me a patient hearing. Nandini walked into the Paluvoor palace three years ago. Since that day some sorcerers have been frequenting the palace. Even Junior Paluvettarayar knows about it. But he could not go against his elder brother.'

'Ideal brothers! True affection!'

'Your Majesty! But their brotherly love should not harm the country's interest.'

'Just because a crazy girl believes in sorcery and invites some sorcerers to the palace, do you think the country's safety is compromised?'

'Your Majesty, her visitors are conspirators in the garb of sorcerers robbing our treasury.'

'Prime Minister, do you have proof?'

'Oh, King of Kings, if we search Senior Paluvettarayar's palace and the underground treasury, we might get some solid proof.'

'Nothing could be more hateful than this. Prime Minister, you are just my friend. But the Paluvettarayars have been the best friends of the Chola dynasty for the last six generations. He is an iron shield to the whole clan. How can I search the palace of a man of such stature? I would rather believe that my wife is trying to poison me than believe that Senior Paluvettarayar is harbouring criminals in his palace.'

'Your Majesty, Paluvettarayar is innocent but infatuated with his young wife. Without his knowledge, his palace has become a sanctuary for the conspirators and the junior queen is part of the gang.'

'What are the further charges against that innocent girl?'

'A few days ago, a coronation ceremony was performed at the enemy's war memorial in the jungle of Thiruppurambiyam. A five-year-old boy was crowned as the Pandiya King. Junior queen and others vowed to destroy the Chola clan without a trace, on this occasion.'

'Prime Minister, which super-intelligent person saw that ceremony? Perhaps this disciple of yours?'

'No, Your Majesty. The one who saw it was the warrior of the Vaanar clan, Vandhiyathevan.'

'You mean the spy who came here once and then ran away?'

'Your Majesty! He is not a spy. He is the best friend of your dear son, Aditya Karikalan.'

'Senior Paluvettarayar and his wife are not in Tanjore. Let us discuss this issue after their return as I was not happy with his marriage. I forbade him to bring his young wife to me. Now I am curious to see her.'

'Your Majesty, a very good idea, I want your permission to let the Lankan Queen stay in our palace till the Paluvoor Queen returns.'

'Let her stay here. But tell me the connection between her and the Paluvoor Queen.'

'Your Majesty! If the two women meet face to face, we will know the connection. That might even soften Nandini's heart and remove the enmity she has for the Chola clan.'

'Prime Minister, why are you so concerned about a woman's enmity?'

The prime minister thought for a while and then spoke.

'Your Majesty, the striking resemblance between Nandini and Mandakini surprises everyone. You are lamenting that Mandakini's spirit has been haunting you at nights. The truth is Nandini guised like Mandakini's ghost has been torturing you.'

The emperor was shocked, 'If what you say is true, I will kill her with my own hands and...'

The prime minister did not let him complete the sentence.

'Your Majesty, never speak like that.'

'Why are you soft towards her? No punishment will be adequate for what she did to me.' The emperor was furious.

'Your Majesty! What if the tormentor happens to be your own daughter...?'

'Prime Minister, are you in your senses?'

'I beg your pardon, Your Majesty. Never think of punishing Nandini. She is not just the young wife of Paluvettarayar. She is the daughter of the great Sundara Chola.'

The emperor was stunned.

72

Mysterious Night

The empress, Princess Kundavai and the others brought Mandakini dressed up well into the emperor's chambers. Mandakini saw the emperor and then looked down. She was shining like a bride thanks to Kundavai's make-up skills. Poonkulali and the empress were delighted. The resemblance between Mandakini and Nandini was unmistakable.

The striking resemblance between the figure that tortured him at nights and the woman standing before him now jolted the emperor. He couldn't believe his own eyes.

Now Kundavai came forward to talk to her father.

'Father! Do you want me to go to Palayarai to bring the Queen Mother?'

The emperor did not respond to his daughter's pleas. Instead, he spoke to the prime minister:

'Prime Minister, I have changed my mind. It looks like they are celebrating the homecoming of a bride. Let all these women stay in the palace. The Queen Mother has very high regard for you. You bring her here and send your disciple to Nagapattinam to bring Prince Arulmoli. Tell Junior Paluvettarayar to bring his brother and his wife to see me when they are back. Please make arrangements to bring Karikalan also. We can resolve all the burning issues. What about relief measures in the flood affected areas?'

'Your Majesty, relief measures are on in full swing; no need to worry about it.'

The prime minister took leave of him.

The emperor had never felt so peaceful in the recent past. The news that Mandakini had not died eased the burden in his heart. He felt rather strange when he ruminated on the words of the prime minister that the junior queen of Paluvoor might probably be his daughter through Mandakini.

The emperor slept well that night. All the women of the palace also had a peaceful sleep, except restless Mandakini. Her thoughts hovered around the conspirators in the underground treasury and the secret passage. She had planned to close the underground passage by breaking the hands of the Ravana statue. Meanwhile, the other women had spoilt her plan. That made her restless. She could not sleep with the emperor being exposed to such a grave risk.

It was almost three in the morning. She saw a scary face peeping through the window. But soon the face disappeared.

She woke up Poonkulali and signaled her to follow her. Poonkulali, knowing her aunt's intuitive abilities, closely followed her.

Mandakini walked towards the Hall of Sculptures with an oil lamp.

She saw the movement of a human head in the middle of the Kailash Mountain. And then the human head vanished.

Mandakini went near the statue. There was a gaping hole between Ravana's heads and the Kailash Mountain. That was the exit to the secret passage. Mandakini had tried to close that exit earlier. But the others, without understanding her actions, had inwardly labeled her a crazy woman. And they did not let her block the passage.

Mandakini entered the secret passage followed by Poonkulali.

The empress, Kundavai and Vanathi woke up early in the morning. They were shocked to see that Mandakini and Poonkulali were missing. They searched for them everywhere, but in vain. How they vanished from the highly guarded palace complex was a mystery to the royal women.

73

Karikalan's Peace Formula

Ever since Aditya Karikalan had arrived at the Kadamboor Palace, the guests felt like they were walking on fire. No one could guess what kind of missiles would burst forth from the prince's mouth.

Paluvettarayar could not bear the insults hurled at him. He even advised Sambuvarayar that they should openly agitate before the crown prince. Sambuvarayar consoled him.

'Please be patient. He is our guest now. Let's bide our time.'

The next day, in the presence of all the chieftains, the crown prince burst out all his feelings:

'I want to seek the advice of all of you. That is the reason I came to Kadamboor. Three years ago, my father made me the crown prince with all your support. Now the emperor has changed his mind. He wants to crown my uncle Madurandakan. He has been inviting me to Tanjore repeatedly. But I am avoiding that.

Why should I meet him to openly disobey him? It is quite unfair on the part of my father to ask me to give up the crown.'

Everyone was stunned to hear the crown prince.

Senior Paluvettarayar responded with hesitation.

'My Majesty, I'm sure you would have discussed this with your grandfather. What is his opinion on this matter?'

'Do you think he will let his grandson give up his throne? He says that he will wage a war to protect his grandson's right to the throne. But I won't listen to him. I'd rather go by your advice,' spoke the crown prince.

Paluvettarayar responded again.

'We are not like your grandfather. We will never instigate the son to rise against his own father. We are bound to obey the command of the emperor. The emperor's request is not completely baseless. We cannot deny Madurandakan's right to the Chola throne.

We think any further discussion on this matter will harm the interests of the country. It is better that we arrive at some sort of consensus to avoid conflicts. In olden days, the Chola Kingdom was small but today it is vast and spreads all over from Kanyakumari to the bank of river Krishna. Let us divide the kingdom in two, giving one half to Madurandakan and the other half to you, my prince. This is our compromise formula. If you agree to this arrangement, we will go ahead with partition. I will convince the emperor in this regard.'

Now Aditya Karikalan laughed.

'You want to divide the Chola Kingdom into two so that the Paluvettarayars can rule the south and the Sambuvarayars the north. It is a good compromise formula. After all your families have been serving the kingdom since the time of my great-grandfather. And this is a fair reward for your services.

But I don't want to divide the kingdom. Dividing the kingdom and sharing it between two claimants is like sharing one's wife with others. You old men may agree for this kind of a sharing arrangement. But I am against it.'

Paluvettarayar's eyes became fiery. He stood up.

The crown prince silenced him, 'Grandpa, why do you want to quit now? Let me tell you, my plan. I am not for dividing this great kingdom. I am ready to give up the entire kingdom in favour of Madurandakan.

But I'll do that on one condition. You should give me an army of three hundred thousand men and the necessary support required for my army to invade the north. I also want three hundred ships. I'll create a Navy with Parthiban as the chief. With the help of my sword and my soldiers, I'll become the emperor of the territory north of river Krishna. And if I die in war, I'll ascend that heaven reserved for the bravest of the brave. Are you ready to support me?'

The two old men were shocked. Paluvettarayar's voice was shaking.

'My Lord, who are we to decide? What right do we have? The emperor alone has to decide.'

Karikalan thundered furiously to the old man.

'Grandpa, how long are you going to deceive us in the name of the emperor? You can deceive anyone but not me. You have imprisoned my father in his own palace. You forced my father to arrest his darling son Arulmoli in Lanka. People are furious with you.'

'Prince, who told you that? Who leveled that gross baseless charge against me? I will cut out their tongues.'

'If it was just one person you could do whatever you like. Thousands of people are accusing you. But don't ever say I'll have to consult the emperor again. The emperor cannot do anything without consulting you.

I request you not to shift the burden to my father, the emperor. If you agree, he too will agree to my plan. After all, the country's treasury is under your control. And if I announce that I am going to invade the north, not just three hundred thousand, but three million soldiers will volunteer to join my army. Getting me three hundred ships is not a big deal for you. But first, you should agree to my plan and then make Madurandakan agree. That is all. What do you say?'

Paluvettarayar spoke in a trembling voice.

'My Lord, I may agree to your strange request. But, how can you go on your great expedition without the emperor's consent? So, I suggest that we go to Tanjore.'

'I can't do that. What if my father orders me to do something else? Then I can't go against him. I suggest that you go to Tanjore and bring Madurandakan here. I will convince him. We will then inform my father. You start making arrangements for my expedition. Once the army, the ships and other things are ready, I'll come to Tanjore to take leave of my parents. Let Madurandakan be crowned now itself. And then let my parents come to Kanchipuram to stay in the golden palace before I leave for the north.'

'How can I go against your orders, my Prince?' responded Paluvettarayar.

'Don't say orders. How can a small boy like me order you around?'

'Okay, let it be so.' Paluvettarayar cleared his throat.

'Thank you very much, grandpa.'

Karikalan laughed.

He then turned to Kandamaran and others.

'Come, let us go hunting. Once I was an expert archer. But I have not touched my bow for the last three years.'

Sambuvarayar who hadn't taken part in the conversation so far ventured to speak.

'There is a dense forest near the Veeranarayana Lake. If you leave early in the morning, you can come home by night.'

'Send word to the hunters right now. Vandiyatheva, come let's go to our room.'

The crown prince held Vandiyathevan's hand and walked out of the hall. Kandamaran and Parthiban were burning in jealousy.

Sambuvarayar went away to issue orders to the hunters. Senior Paluvettarayar went in search of Nandini.

74

Nandini's Anger

Paluvettarayar was excited over the latest political developments. He almost ran towards Nandini's chambers to share his excitement with her as it was Nandini who had given him the compromise formula.

Karikalan virtually humiliated him and Sambuvarayar. Though initially Paluvettarayar was upset with the humiliating remarks of Prince Aditya Karikalan, he was happy with the prince's compromise formula. And he regained his lost enthusiasm. But he also doubted the extent to which he could rely on Karikalan's words. Perhaps the prince had laid a bait for them.

Paluvettarayar reached the chambers of Nandini.

'Has the discussion ended?'

But Paluvettarayar did not respond to her question.

'We shall leave for Tanjore in the morning.'

'My Lord, why so early? Is our work here over?'

Paluvettarayar faithfully relayed to her all that happened in the Court Hall.

Nandini patiently heard him out.

'My Lord, you go to Tanjore. Let me be here to teach that arrogant Karikalan a lesson. Either he should fall at your feet or he should fall a prey to your sword.'

'What are you saying, Nandini?'

'I want to avenge him for insulting my husband.'

'No, Nandini. Our clan has been serving the Chola clan for the past six generations. Simply because a flippant youth behaved whimsically, should I kill the emperor's son?'

'My Lord, I understand you can't take up your sword against the crown prince. But I owe nothing to the Chola clan.'

Nandini's eyes turned red. Paluvettarayar had never seen so much rage on her beautiful face.

Paluvettarayar's heart burst with pride to hear that his young wife was ready to wield the sword against the one who had humiliated him. He had a strange sense of euphoria that Nandini was keen on guarding his honour. At the same time, he pretended as if he did not like that kind of talk.

'Dear, don't you like my idea? You don't trust me dear,' said Nandini

'No, Nandini. I trust you fully. I was just wondering how you will wield a heavy sword with your flowery hands. What is the need while I am alive...?'

'Dear, I know the strength of your arms which can kill thousands of enemies. You silently suffer all the insults because of your loyalty to the Chola clan. I know my hands are very soft but it will do anything to defend your honour.'

'Look here!' saying this Nandini bent down and pulled out a box from under the cot. She opened it and took out a long, shining sword from it and gracefully lifted it up above her head.

Paluvettarayar was surprised as he had thought that the box held nothing but her dresses.

Nandini kept the sword back inside the box.

'I keep this precious sword along with my dresses and jewels in this box to save the honour of my husband and mine.'

'Nandini, you are never alone and you will never have an occasion to use this sword as long as I am alive.'

'That's what I hope. But leave me here and you may go to Tanjore to fetch Madurandakan.'

'Are you not coming to Tanjore?' Paluvettarayar raised his voice.

Nandini remained unruffled.

'My Lord, did you notice a change in Sambuvarayar's behaviour ever since the prince's arrival?'

'Yes dear, I wonder what changed him.'

'Dearest! Sambuvarayar is too ambitious. Karikalan is attracted to Sambuvarayar's daughter, Manimekalai. A new desire has entered Sambuvarayar's mind. He has started dreaming of seeing his only daughter as the empress of Chola Kingdom.'

'You are right, Nandini. Two months ago, we all joined hands to take a vow to make Madurandakan the next Chola Emperor. But Sambuvarayar, blinded by ambition, has gone back on his word.'

'That is precisely why I want to remain here to observe the actions of these people during your absence. And if they plot against you, I'll give my life and soul to thwart their attempt.'

'But Nandini, why get involved in all these dirty affairs?'

'Whatever affairs you are involved in, your wife will be there.'

'Nandini, still I have no mind to leave you here, my dearest.'

'Dear, I am not alone here. Manimekalai adores me and she will even die for me.'

'That's true. Your beauty has enslaved her. But how long will that last? If Aditya Karikalan becomes the king and makes her his empress...'

'Dearest, you needn't have any doubts on that front. Manimekalai will never go against my wishes. If I ask her to kill Karikalan, she will do it for me.'

Now Paluvettarayar spoke in a choked voice.

'Dearest, I know your powers. But don't test them on Karikalan. He is after all a kid. Let us not take his words to heart. If he wants to marry Manimekalai, let us not block it.'

'Yes, my Lord. Let us not oppose the marriage. But there is something called destiny. Who can be against destiny? Tell me. I love Manimekalai like my own sister. How can I let her marry a person facing an untimely death?'

Paluvettarayar was totally unnerved.

'Oh my God! What are you saying, Nandini? I was once the head of the Velakkara Army, the emperor's personal bodyguards. I have sworn to give my life to protect the lives of the emperor and his family.'

'I never asked you to go against your promise.'

'But, if anything happens to Karikalan, the blame will fall on me and the whole world will accuse me. Our clan will lose the honour earned during the last six generations.'

'Then it is all the more important that you should leave this place immediately.'

'What makes you say that?'

'I have been longing to share something with you for quite some time. Now the time has come.

I have some divine powers. I visualize the end of Aditya Karikalan. It won't happen because of you or me. Death God is near him. He may die while hunting. Or while sleeping in this palace. Or he may face death from the hands of a woman. But my dear, his death will not be caused by my hands. If something happens to the prince when you are here, then the whole country will say that you killed him. But take it from me, you cannot prevent his death.

So, leave this place immediately. If you take me with you, people will say that Paluvettarayar knew this already. So, he ran away from the scene along with his wife.'

Paluvettarayar was shaken by Nandini's pointed glances. And surrendered to her alluring charms.

75

Water Sports

Ever since Karikalan came to Kadamboor, Sambuvarayar's mind was totally changed because of his darling daughter Manimekalai. There were some unmistakable signs that Manimekalai had stolen the heart of the crown prince.

Prince Karikalan was always praising Manimekalai's enthusiasm and intelligence. Sambuvarayar also believed that his daughter had fallen in love with the Prince. If his daughter married Karikalan, she would become the empress of the vast Chola Kingdom. And the child born to her would succeed Karikalan to the Chola throne.

Earlier, Sambuvarayar had wanted to marry his daughter to Madurandakan, the heir apparent to the Chola throne. But Madurandakan already had two wives. And one of his wives was the daughter of Junior Paluvettarayar. He also had a son through her. So, if Madurandakan was crowned the king, Paluvettarayar's clan would come in the direct line of succession. Sambuvarayar's daughter Manimekalai would be one of the hundreds of maids in Tanjore palace.

But if Manimekalai married Aditya Karikalan, she would be the empress of the Chola Kingdom. Her son would be crowned the next king. Moreover, it was almost impossible to make Madurandakan the king. People were against him. Even Madurandakan's own mother opposed that move.

On the other hand, Aditya Karikalan's coronation was a decided issue.

Sambuvarayar's mind started thinking along these lines. No wonder he was happy about Paluvettarayar's absence. That would give him the opportunity for a 'heart to heart' talk with the crown prince to assess his mind and plan his strategy.

Paluvettarayar left for Tanjore. Karikalan and his friends went hunting. Nandini and Manimekalai set sail in a boat for some water sports in the gigantic Veeranarayana lake, near a dense forest.

Nandini and Manimekalai were gossiping about the members of the royal household. Manimekalai was indulging in mimicry entertaining Nandini. She mimicked the voice of Paluvettarayar, Karikalan, Kandamaran, Parthiban and Vandiyathevan. Nandini could not control her laughter. At the same time her mind was elsewhere, cooking up something crucial.

Suddenly Manimekalai screamed.

'Sister, we have not come to hunt but a hunt is coming towards us.'

On the low branch of a large tree there was a leopard staring at the two women as if it was trying to decide whether to spring on them or not.

They also heard the sound of horses galloping through water.

Karikalan was in a state of murderous frenzy. Bears and leopards fell dead in quick succession unable to bear the onslaught of his arrows. When Kandamaran shot an arrow at a bear that just managed to miss Karikalan, he exclaimed.

'Kandamara, are you trying to kill the bear or me?'

Kandamaran was disappointed. Thereafter he laid off his bow. He complained to Parthiban about the harsh words of the prince.

When everyone was exhausted, Karikalan alone was nudging his horse with a murderous frenzy.

Vandiyathevan and Karikalan were riding very close to each other. Vandiyathevan never interfered with the prince's hunting but was carefully guarding him.

Meanwhile Kandamaran was grumbling.

'Is it not enough for the day? Let us ask him to return?'

'Brother, something is troubling the prince. It is not easy to give up a large empire. The crown prince perhaps is showering all his pent-up fury on the animals. In a way that's good. If there had been no hunting, he would have vented his feelings on us. Let's keep quiet till he gets tired.'

At that time, the whole forest was shaken by the frightening sound of a wild animal. Kandamaran's face turned pale.

'Oh my God! It's a wild boar. Please ask the prince not to aim at it.'

'Kandamaran! It's just a boar after all. Didn't you see how the tigers, leopards and bears suffered at his hands?' spoke Parthiban.

'You don't know about wildlife in this area. The boars in this forest can kill a tiger or a bear. They even attack an elephant. Horses can't stand their ferocity even for a few seconds. The boar's skin is so thick that arrows and spears will bounce off from its body.'

Two huge wild boars, the size of elephant calves came out of the bushes. They saw the horses and the men riding on them.

'Careful. They are dangerous!' screamed Kandamaran.

Meanwhile the professional hunters ran up to the place and started beating on their drums making a thunderous noise.

Kandamaran saw the boars running.

'My Lord, let them go. Let's not follow them without the help of hunting dogs.'

Without heeding Kandamaran, Karikalan shot an arrow at one of the boars. The arrow did not miss its mark. It stuck to the body of the boar. Karikalan roared in joy. The next second the boar shook its body. The arrow fell off. The boar started running.

Kandamaran laughed as if insulting the crown prince. Karikalan did not miss the insinuation. 'Kandamara! Vandiyathevan and I will go behind that boar. We'll kill it and come back. You and Parthiban go after the other boar. We won't return without killing it.'

He and Vandiyathevan took off on their horses. But they could not sight the boar.

They could see the huge Veeranarayana lake through the canal. They could see a boat on the lake with some women. After some time, the boat disappeared from their view.

'Vandiyatheva, perhaps the women are from Sambuvarayar's household.'

'Quite possible. But why should they come this far?'

'Of course, but are you sure that Paluvettarayar has left Kadamboor?'

'I am sure, Prince. He has gone, leaving behind his junior queen.'

'It is very difficult to find another warrior like him. Even my grandfather Malayaman comes next after him.'

'I have witnessed your valour in the battlefield as well as in the Kadamboor Palace. You made them all shake in fear.'

'That's true. I made that kind of a fuss for a specific reason. I wanted to drive that old man away so that I could do something which I have been wanting to do for ages. The time has come now.'

'You made all those wild animals tremble in fear.'

'Hunting is not an act of valour. At times even a hunting dog can kill a leopard. Paluvettarayar has left Nandini alone. But I am very scared of meeting her.'

'Prince, I understand. You have had a soft corner for her all these years. But now you know she is your own sister, working with the conspirators of Pandiya Kingdom to destroy the entire Chola clan. It is very important to discuss these things with her.'

'My dear friend, I was shocked by this new development. I can't believe even now that she could be my sister. In those days, there was a screen between me and Nandini. Queen Mother was particular that I should not have anything to do with Nandini. But she never disclosed the truth. Had we known that, we could have avoided many complications.'

'Prince! Even the Queen Mother might not know that.'

76

She Is Not a Woman

Childhood memories flooded the crown prince's mind. He then spoke to Vandiythevan in a calm voice.

'Let bygones be bygones. Let's just talk about the future. I shudder to think how I'm going to talk to Nandini about my blood relationship with her. Whenever I see her face, she retains the expression she had when she pleaded for the life of King Veerapandiya. My heart bleeds when I think that my own sister, out of love for Veerapandiya pleaded for his life. Do you think she does not know the truth yet?'

'Prince, had she known she would not have joined hands with the conspirators of Pandiya Kingdom.'

'Vandiyatheva, you are so innocent. You don't know the deceit and treachery that lies in a woman's heart. But I know why she invited me to Kadamboor.'

'Why?'

'She wants to avenge the death of Veerapandiya.'

'Prince! Princess Kundavai and the prime minister sent me here precisely to avert that kind of a catastrophe. I told you several times not to come to Kadamboor. But you never listened to me.'

'Vandiyatheva, Kundavai and the prime minister are very intelligent people. But even then, they cannot change destiny. Who knows what will happen to me here? Vandiyatheva, did you see Kandamaran shooting the arrow from behind? Did he want to hit the bear or me?'

'I didn't see, my Lord. I don't think Kandamaran will kill his guest and that too the emperor's son. He is not smart but he is also not treacherous.'

'My dear friend, you don't know the seductive powers of a beautiful woman. It can make even the best of men betray their friends.'

'Prince, I too know something about the seductive powers of a woman. But never in my life will I betray anyone.'

'Oh! But Manimekalai is a good girl. She will never induce you to do an act of betrayal.'

'Prince! I am not talking about Manimekalai. Fireflies won't be attractive to a man who has seen the full moon.'

'Who is the full moon?'

'Prince! I am referring to the princess at Palayarai.'

'Even the greatest kings on earth are longing for Kundavai's hand. You shouldn't think of my sister even in your dreams.'

'Prince, the full moon gives its rays equally to the princes and beggars of the world. Who can prevent them?'

'You are right. In fact, I intentionally sent you to my sister with a message. I think she was pleased with you. Otherwise, you wouldn't be talking like this. But don't share this with Parthiban. His long-term dream is to become the son-in-law of the Chola Emperor.'

'Right now, Parthiban and Kandamaran are at the feet of Nandini. Even her slightest whim is a divine command to them. They are ready to give up their lives for her.'

'My friend, I am a little afraid of those two people now.'

'Prince! It is high time you meet Nandini and tell her the truth.'

'Why don't you speak to her on my behalf?'

'Prince! She won't believe me. I can help you meet Nandini through Manimekalai. Leave it to me.'

'Manimekalai will dance to your tunes. I'll be happy to get you married to her.'

'No, My Lord. Manimekalai is like my own sister. She has to marry somebody far higher in stature.'

'I don't get it.'

'Prince, Manimerkalai will be a good match for you. If you marry Manimekalai all our problems will be solved. Sambuvarayar and Kandamaran will come to our side. The Paluvettarayars will be isolated. Nandini too will become weak. Madurandakan cannot ascend the throne. We can crush the conspiracy of the chieftains; we can destroy the diabolic plans of the bodyguards of King Veerapandiya.'

'Brother, you are right. But I have not come to Kadamboor to get married.'

'Let us send word to your grandfather, Malayaman, to come with an army.'

'You go and bring him here.'

'Prince, I am sorry, I have strict orders from your sister not to leave you alone, not even for a second.'

'Then let us send Parthiban to Malayaman.'

'Vandiyatheva, it is all right to kill a person to save a kingdom. What if the person killed happens to be a woman? What if the woman happens to be my own sister? In fact, Nandini is not a woman. She is the devil in the form of a woman. And if we let her live, the great Chola clan will go to the dogs. Oh my God! What is that?'

Aditya Karikalan's attention was diverted by a sudden noise. There was a rustling sound coming from the bushes nearby. It appeared that somebody was fighting there. They rode to that place. A wild boar was fighting with a leopard.

After an intense fight, the long teeth of the boar tore the skin of the leopard and finally knocked it down. The leopard lay on the ground dead.

'Brother, the leopard is dead. The boar will now turn towards us. Let us be prepared.'

Karikalan aimed his arrow at the boar.

The arrow hit the neck of the boar. The boar shook its body. The arrow fell off. It now sprang on Karikalan's horse with ferocity. Before Karikalan could load his bow with an arrow, the boar attacked his horse. The horse fell down. Karikalan was trapped under the horse. The boar retreated a few steps and pounced on the fallen horse with even greater ferocity.